ON THE EDGE

Canada Council for the Arts **Conseil des Arts du Canada**  ONTARIO ARTS COUNCIL CONSEIL DES ARTS DE L'ONTARIO an Ontario government agency un organisme du gouvernement de l'Ontario **Canadä**

We gratefully acknowledge the support of the Canada Council for the Arts and the Ontario Arts Council for our publishing program. We also acknowledge the financial support of the Government of Canada.

Cover artwork: Gordon J. Weber, "On the Edge," 2015, watercolour, 11 x 17 inches.
Illustrations in text by Lesley Strutt

Cover design: Val Fullard

On the Edge is a work of fiction. All the characters portrayed in this book are fictitious and any resemblance to persons living or dead is purely coincidental.

Library and Archives Canada Cataloguing in Publication

Title: On the edge : a novel / Lesley Strutt.
Names: Strutt, Lesley, author.
Series: Young feminist series.
Description: Series statement: Inanna young feminist series
Identifiers: Canadiana (print) 20190094168 | Canadiana (ebook) 20190094222 | ISBN 9781771335973 (softcover) | ISBN 9781771335980 (epub) | ISBN 9781771335997 (Kindle) | ISBN 9781771336000 (pdf)
Classification: LCC PS8637.T8523 O5 2019 | DDC jC813/.6—dc23

Printed and bound in Canada

Inanna Publications and Education Inc.
210 Founders College, York University
4700 Keele Street, Toronto, Ontario, Canada M3J 1P3
Telephone: (416) 736-5356 Fax: (416) 736-5765
Email: inanna.publications@inanna.ca   Website: www.inanna.ca

 **MIX** Paper from responsible sources FSC® C004071

ON THE EDGE

A NOVEL

Lesley Strutt

INANNA
Young Feminist Series

To my daughters Shannon and DeeDee—
two intrepid women on this life voyage with me.

I. THE LAST SONG

1. THE STORM

EMMA LEANS WAY OUT over the deck of the sailboat and stares straight down into the water. She's transfixed by the rise and fall of the bow, the swishing spray. The hull seems to take great gulps as it slashes through the waves. Every once and a while the little boat shudders and rolls in the gusty wind, but Emma doesn't care. Her fingers are wrapped tight around the starboard shroud and there's a big grin on her face. It's a sunny afternoon and she's out on the *Edge* with old Jess, her favourite person in the world.

Except she's not supposed to be out sailing. And she's going to get in huge trouble if her aunt finds out she's with Jess again. But she puts all that out of her mind as the *Edge* slices through the waves, and the wind whips at her hair.

When the little boat heels over steeply, she looks up. Her eyes narrow as she takes in the coming wall of blackness. "Jess! Look at that!" She points in the direction of the looming dark clouds.

"Gale!" Jess calls back over the growing wind. "Nasty one!"

Emma scrambles back to the cockpit. "We should come about, right? Head back in?" She takes her position, jib sheets in her hands. Excitement shivers through her. She's never been out in stormy weather with Jess. Not that they planned it that way. It's just that her time with Jess is always so short, only whenever she can sneak away from the farm.

Luck has given them good weather until now.

"You got it, kiddo!" Jess nods. "Ready to come about?"

"Ready," she calls back.

"Coming about!"

The sails flap wildly for a minute or two and then Emma and Jess, working in tandem, trim and tighten the sails till the little 26-footer surges forward again. Emma's hands know exactly what to do now, which lines to reach for, how long to wait to maximize the wind as they tack.

They're an unlikely team—Jess, the seventy-something woman with the long grey braid flying in the wind under the floppy hat, and Emma, a skinny fourteen-year-old orphan who, until she met Jess, was lost in a fog of herself, unreachable, a puppet her aunt could easily control. Too easily.

Now what is she? "You're a rebel," her aunt would tell her, furiously. "Just like your mother. And no good comes to rebels."

"Storm's coming fast. You ready for this?" Jess asks. Emma looks over her shoulder toward the blackened horizon, then back at Jess.

"I'm ready."

"Close up the hatch, put away anything that will fly overboard. Got that?" Jess tightens the mainsheet.

Emma nods, starts collecting cushions, cups, and other loose gear. Her heart's begun to race. She feels the tickle of a memory prick at the back of her neck. Something shocking. Scary, but familiar. Like she's been here before. She shrugs off the weird sensation. Why would she feel like this? She's never been on a sailboat before she met Jess.

"I'll get our life jackets," Emma shouts on her way below decks. She glances in Jess's direction for confirmation.

"Oh!"

"You okay, Jess?"

Jess is slumped against the wheel and puts a hand on her chest, rubbing hard. Her face is pale.

"Probably just ... don't know." Her voice is faint.

Emma starts toward her.

"No." Jess shakes her head. "No time." She straightens, manages a smile. "I'm okay."

Emma hesitates, then goes below to stow the gear. When she comes back on deck to hand Jess her life jacket, Jess seems normal again.

"We've been out too long today and you'll be late," Jess shouts above the wind. "We should head straight back. We'll put her on a run, but it won't be nice."

"I want to take the helm." Emma tells Jess firmly. "I can do it."

Jess shoots her a quick look, assessing, then steps away from the wheel.

"Okay. Fall off to a run." Emma grips the wheel hard. With the wind coming from behind them, the boat rocks from side to side with the steepening waves. She can't steady it. The boom swings too close to the water with each dip, dangerously close. Emma knows if it catches in the water, the *Edge* will flip over.

"I'm going to put her on a reach," she calls to Jess. Jess nods and pulls the floppy hat off her head and stuffs it in her back pocket.

"It'll put us off our course some but our speed will make up for the extra distance." She grins at Emma. "Tighten up! You ready to sail like a banshee?"

Emma grins her agreement, braces her feet wide to steady herself at the helm. The wind is driving the rain down the back of her neck, but she could care less. Jess looks happy again and the paleness has left her face.

They tighten up sail and cross the lake on a screaming reach. The *Edge* lifts out of the water like she's sprouted wings. They approach the shore at incredible speed, but as Jess has predicted they overshoot the harbour mouth by quite a bit.

Jess hollers at her, "You okay to gybe?"

Emma shouts back. "Okay." All her senses are on alert.

"It's going to feel like we're out of control. You have to be on your toes!"

Emma nods. "Gybe ho!"

Emma turns the stern across the wind. The *Edge* sways deeply for a moment. Emma and Jess duck as the boom snaps over. Emma eases out the main sheet, but she sees Jess stumble onto her knees. She recovers quickly and scrambles over to the port side and hauling on the other sheet, but something's wrong.

"You okay?" Emma shouts over the din.

Jess smiles but one arm is hanging limply at her side. Before Emma can say something else the *Edge* heels over hard. The gunwales are almost in the water. They're careening toward the harbour mouth. The breakwater comes into clear view through the rain. The storm's a roar. The wind and the rain lash at them. The waves pound the hull like fists. Emma's heart pumps hard as she feels the boat pick up speed again and slice the water toward the harbour. She glances over at the wind meter—forty knots of wind. She's only ever been out in fifteen knots of wind or less.

"We have to take down the sails," Jess yells.

Emma makes a snap decision. "Can you hold the helm? I'll get the sails." It'll be the first time she's done this by herself. But she knows Jess can't climb up on deck in this storm. She flicks on the motor and turns the nose of the *Edge* straight into the wind. The sails flap insanely. The noise is cacophonous, but the *Edge* slows to a stop, like magic.

Jess holds the helm with her one hand and Emma scrambles up on deck. While the *Edge* bucks under her like a raging bull, she wrestles everything under control. She furls the jib and drops the main, tying it off so it doesn't get swept overboard. Then she comes back to the cockpit to grab the fenders. Up on deck again, she ties them to the life lines and flips them over the side to get ready to dock. When she comes back to the cockpit, she readies the lines for tying up.

She's done it all herself! She's so proud of herself she could burst. She looks at Jess to see if she's proud of her too, but Jess is focused on getting them through the opening of the breakwater to where the water is dead calm. Behind the sturdy wall of rocks, the wind drops to a dull roar. Emma heaves a sigh of relief.

"That was so amazing…" She turns but Jess isn't smiling. She's looking straight ahead at the dock.

Standing in the slashing rain on the dock is Aunt Petra, drenched, rigid, furious. Emma sets her jaw. She knows that what's coming will be worse than the storm.

Emma jumps off the boat and ties up to the dock in few swift movements.

"Where are your proper clothes?" her aunt spits out. "Go and change at once!"

Emma hunches her shoulders at the tone. She steps back up onto the deck of the *Edge* and then goes below to change out of the shorts and T-shirt she's borrowed from Jess into the shapeless long grey skirt, white blouse, and blue cardigan her aunt insists she must wear at all times. It's the *proper* way for a girl to dress, she says.

"In the car!" Aunt Petra says as soon as Emma steps off the boat. Her voice is tight with concern and she reaches into the car and wraps a blanket roughly around Emma's shoulders, then shuts the door with a loud clack.

Emma darts a quick look back at Jess though the rear window. For a moment, time stands still. She sees the ghost of the happy confident girl who just sailed through a storm. And then the vision is gone and she shrinks back inside the body of the girl she is now, dressed identical to her aunt, dowdy and grey, with all the life sucked out of her. When she slides down into the back seat, there's defeat in the curve of her shoulders.

"For Pete's sake, Petra. Stop this nonsense! She's a child, not a criminal!" Jess says moving towards the car.

But Aunt Petra blocks her. "You put her at risk!" she says coldly. "And you know it. It's our job to keep her safe!" Petra glares at Jess for a full moment, then frowns and shakes her head. "You've never understood, Jess. Ever! You don't know what damage you've done."

Uncle Derek sits immobile in the driver's seat.

Aunt Petra's words hit Emma like a splash of cold water, reviving her for a moment. "What's going on?" She forgets she's supposed to remain silent until spoken to, and she leans forward. "What's she talking about?"

Uncle Derek doesn't answer but his hands clench the wheel. For one nanosecond he meets Emma's eyes in the rear-view mirror. But before he can say anything, Aunt Petra gets in the front seat and they drive away.

Emma, looking out the back window, sees Jess standing motionless beside the boat. She sinks deeper in the back seat.

This is the worst thing she's done. She tries to obey her aunt, she really does. Anything to avoid the smacks across the face, the banishment to her room, the bitter reprimands that are part of her aunt's arsenal of punishment for keeping Emma in line. But since sailing season began this year, she's been sneaking out whenever she can.

She always felt so clever about her small escapes. In fact, her aunt never seemed to notice her absences. How naïve she was. Of course, her aunt knew all along about her meetings with Jess. Tolerated them, as long as Emma followed the rules, was home when she was supposed to be, did her chores, and kept her school marks up.

But that's all over now. There'll be no more outings with Jess. Emma's heart plummets. She knows that she won't see her friend, her dearest Jess ever again. Aunt Petra's next words confirm it.

The car crunches over the gravel of the driveway. Aunt Petra turns around and points a finger at Emma. "This is the last time you're going to disobey me. There'll be no more sailing for you. You could've drowned!"

"But…"

"No!" Aunt Petra cries. "There will be no more sailing. That's final!" She jerks her head as if to confirm her words and turns back toward the front of the car.

Emma scrunches down even further in her seat, her anger buried deep inside of her.

2. PUNISHMENT

INSIDE OF EMMA IS A BOILING, raging, inferno. The anger's like molten lava. She's a volcano and the pressure's building. For the last three days she's been confined to her room. The lack of freedom is horrible. She paces the floor, door to window and back again. She's only allowed out at mealtimes, to use the bathroom, and to go to school. Even her chores have been taken away from her.

On one of her passes by the window, she spots Adam, the neighbour boy who helps Uncle Derek with the big farm chores. He's watering the garden. That's one of her chores. She realizes he must be doing the rest.

Strong as an ox, said Aunt Petra when they hired him. And cute, thinks Emma, though it makes her uncomfortable to think of him that way.

As if he feels her watching him, he lifts his head and catches her eye. He looks at her, studying her face as if he's trying to figure something out. They're in the same home-room class but they never talk. But then, she hardly talks to anyone at school. She lets the curtain fall. Begins pacing again. She's like a caged animal.

Instead of taking the bus to school Uncle Derek drives her. On the first morning she tries asking him about what's going on, but he just looks pained. Troubled.

"Your aunt has her reasons."

"What reasons? What are they?" But he just shrugs and focuses on the road.

"It's not fair!" Emma says under her breath, when she figures he's not going to answer.

"I know," he says, surprising her. It gives her a moment of hope. But when she presses him further, he simply stares stonily ahead, as if he knows he's already said too much.

She eats lunch in an empty classroom with a teacher guarding. She's kept in detention during the breaks, too, but no one gives her a reason why. She worries about Jess and how she had stumbled on the boat, and how her arm didn't seem to work.

Then her thoughts turn to the storm. And she can't shake the feeling the storm had brought on—the certainty that she'd been through such a storm before. A familiarity and a dread. She wonders if the feeling has something to do with when she was a baby. She knows nothing about her parents, and she hates it. Were they sailors? Did she live with them on a sailboat?

She's discovered she loves sailing. It feels like it's in her blood. In the end, everything circles around to the biggest mystery of all: what happened to her parents, so she had to come live with her aunt and uncle on a farm?

Emma can never shake the haunted feeling of being lost, of not knowing who she is. It stops her from making friends, as if there's something wrong with her that no one is telling her. As if she's an outcast.

One girl had wanted to be her friend, but Aunt Petra forbade Emma from going to her house after school and wouldn't invite her to the farm, either. Not that Emma wanted to subject anyone to her aunt's rules and strictness. In the end, it was just easier to stay apart from the other girls. If they whispered behind her back, at least they left her alone.

In class she keeps her eyes down. Everyone knows she's in detention. In the school washroom she studies herself in the mirror. Pure rage stares back at her. That's how she knows she can't let anyone look her in the eyes. For sure they'll see the volcano bubbling, roiling, about to erupt.

On the fourth day, she comes downstairs to the kitchen for breakfast, but the door is closed. She reaches for the handle then pauses when she hears her uncle's voice.

"You go too far, Petra."

"I'm doing what we have to do to keep her safe."

"But you go too far."

"You know what her great grandfather wants as well as I do."

"Is this how you see it?"

Silence falls again. Then Emma feels a shimmer of shock as she hears muffled sobs. Her hand is on the door knob when her aunt's next words stop her.

"Flinders will take her from us. You know he will."

Emma sucks in a breath. Old Mr. Flinders? What's he got to do with this?

"And he dared bring that boy here, your brother's boy? It's a sure sign." Aunt Petra says. "He doesn't trust us."

Emma's head's throbbing. What boy? My father had a son? What's going on? But before she has time to think about it, her uncle's next words make her heart skip a beat. Her hands clench at her side.

"What do we tell Jess about the…"

Aunt Petra cuts him off. "I should never have consented. I knew the risk was too high."

"But …"

"Enough!" There's a bang on the table as if Aunt Petra's brought her fist down on it. "She knew the rules. She broke them."

"You can't protect her forever, Petra."

"That was our job!" Emma hears a chair scraping over the floor.

"You did your best."

"Not good enough, though." A cupboard bangs.

Emma springs back from the door, her heart pounding.

There's a metallic taste in her mouth. She turns and scurries back down the hallway to the stairs. She's putting her foot on the bottom stair when the kitchen door opens. She spins around in mid-step, pretending she's just coming down from her bedroom.

Uncle Derek spots her and stops. Slowly, she makes her way past him to the kitchen, eyes down, not daring to look to see if he realizes she's overheard what they were saying.

"Good morning, Aunt Petra," she says as she always does. She must act her obedient self.

Aunt Petra's busy kneading dough for bread. Her hard slaps and thumps fill the room. With each slap and thump, Emma feels the wrongness of everything, the hidden mysteries, the way nothing makes sense. Something's growing inside of her.

"I have a half-brother?" The words burst out of Emma's mouth before she can stop them. She sucks in her breath.

Aunt Petra's hands freeze. "What did you say?"

"And what does Mr. Flinders have to do with us?" Emma stands up, her hands fisted at her side. "What did I do wrong?" Her voice is rising. "Why am I supposed to be protected?"

Aunt Petra starts kneading the dough again, but her hands are unsteady. "You have no idea what's going on. And it's better that way. You've caused us all enough trouble and most of it started when you met Jess."

"I love Jess." Emma's beyond stopping now. "Why can't I see her?"

"You don't understand!" Aunt Petra's voice cuts like a knife.

"Which is why I'm asking." Emma is trembling. "But you never answer any of my questions. You never tell me anything. Nothing about my mother or my father. Or now about Mr. Flinders who wants something from you. Or about Jess?"

She plunges on. "Why do you care so much if I go sailing with Jess?" Her face crumples. "You hate me" She dashes from the room before her aunt can stop her.

Uncle Derek's standing at the kitchen door when Emma

rushes past him up the stairs. She slams the door behind her and curls up in the corner of her room on the floor. She wraps her arms around her knees and rocks herself back and forth.

I can't stand this any longer. I can't. I have to get away from here. Away from the farm. Away from them. Her thoughts are like a chant. She rocks and rocks. She wants to go to Jess. Jess who loves her and understands her.

"Jess will help me," she whispers to herself. "She knows what my life is like. If she hasn't seen me in a few days, she'll know something's wrong." Emma rocks back and forth, back and forth. "Maybe she'll come and get me. Take me away to live with her. Adopt me."

The image of Jess on the boat looking so pale floats into Emma's mind. Jess holding her useless arm. Jess in pain. There was something so wrong about that.

What if she needs me? Emma gets to her knees on rising panic. *What if she needs me and I'm stuck here, prisoner in my own home?*

Her heart's beating hard. She has no idea what to do. All she knows is she has to find a way to get to Jess. She has to get away, to escape.

There's a sound outside her bedroom door. She lifts her head, gets to her feet thinking someone has come for her. She's about to be rescued. She waits, but the door doesn't open. Instead she hears the sound of a wood drill. At first, she doesn't understand. What are they building? It takes a while to compute and when it does she rushes across the room to open the door. But it's locked! Locked from the outside. She's been locked in her room. She hammers on the door, rattles the handle.

"You can't do this. You can't." There's no answer. She pounds harder. "Let me out. You have to let me out. I need to go to the bathroom. I need food and water!"

Through the door hardly discernable, "I'm sorry, Emma." Adam's voice. Then she hears the creak of the floorboards as he walks away.

3. ESCAPE

THE DAYS AND NIGHTS of her confinement are sheer torture now. Her aunt comes at regular intervals to let her go to the bathroom and pass her a tray of food. She stays with her when she takes a shower. At night they leave her a bucket to pee in and make sure the lock is secure on the door.

Emma's rage builds. She paces her floor, thinking of how she can escape. And then she sees it. Right outside her window—the chattering squirrel in the tree clues her into it. They haven't thought of her window, which she slides open easily, quietly, then closes it again. They must think she'd never try to escape this way.

She packs a backpack and hides it under her bed. She lies down, waits until it's dark.

She makes her move after midnight. The moon's only a sliver. Not enough to illuminate her. One leg over the window ledge. The other. She shimmies across the roof, reaches for the branch that's hanging too close to the house. It's sure to be trimmed this summer, but right now it's perfect.

Her backpack's awkward; her skirt makes her clumsy. Still, the minute her feet hit the ground she's running to the line of poplars, the windbreak between the house and the road.

The dogs start barking. Why are the dogs out? They're supposed to be tied up out back. Emma panics and freezes. And that's when someone grabs her shoulders.

She turns and sees it's Adam! *What's he doing here in the night-time?* The words are a scream in her head. He's never stayed on the farm overnight before.

That's when the vulcano that is Emma boils over and erupts. Her arms swing hard. She beats at him, flails her way right out of his grip. Then she runs fast toward the road. Hears his footsteps behind her.

Lights come on in the house. Flood the yard. She makes a dive for the ditch. Adam's panting above her.

"Stay down," Adam says. She freezes where she is. "Stay right here." He drops down beside her, breathing hard. "I'm on your side, okay?" Above them the dogs circle and bark.

"What's going on?" Uncle Derek's silhouette appears in the porch light. One of the dogs lifts its head, whines.

Adam jumps up and runs back toward the house calling the dogs. They hang back for a moment then follow him. "Fox I think, Mr. Visser," he calls out louder than he needs to." Didn't exactly see. I'll check the hen house."

Emma's heart is pounding in her ears. She should make a run for it now. Run! But she's frozen in place. Can't move a muscle. The scream in her head drowns out her thinking. The minutes tick by. She hears her uncle and Adam take the dogs round the back of the house to check on the hens.

A hare darts out of some bushes. As if a start gun has gone off, Emma scrambles to her feet and speeds down the road. Through the field. Going to Jess. Going to Jess, and then going away. Anywhere. It doesn't matter. Jess will help. Jess will know what to do. Jess. The one person in the world she knows she can trust.

Emma arrives at Jess's house by the water in less than twenty minutes. She knocks gently and turns the handle on the door that's never locked.

"Jess?" There's no answer. Where is she? She goes to the bedroom. Knocks again. "Jess?" she calls as she enters.

On the bed. Jess. But not Jess. Too still. Stone cold. Dead.

EMMA HEARS THE SIRENS from a long way off. She has no idea how long she's been sitting beside Jess's bed after dialling 911. She's numb with cold and heartbroken.

Jess! Her best friend. The best thing to come along in Emma's life. Jess, who taught her to speak up, to trust herself, to laugh. To sail! Jess, who is supposed to be there now to answer Emma's questions about what's going on and tell her what to do next.

There's a crunch of boots on the ground outside the window and then two police officers are standing in the room. Her aunt and uncle follow. The stony look on her aunt's face makes her catch her breath. Her uncle's grip on Emma's shoulder is firm, as if she'll run away again if he doesn't keep his hand on her. Then the ambulance arrives and they take Jess away.

After they leave, Emma closes her eyes and sinks under the weight of the layers of numbness. When the tears come she puts her hand over her mouth to stop the sobs. Not here, not here, she thinks. When she gets back to the farm she goes to her room and buries herself under the covers, pulls the pillow over her head to hide the sound of her weeping.

THE OLD MAN RISES from his chair when he hears the news. He lifts his hand with the cane and thumps it down, once. And once more. Then he slowly lowers himself to his chair again.

"Raymond." His voice is stronger than one would expect from such an old man. "Call Drake."

A tall man steps forward and reaches to wrap a blanket around the old man's knees. "It's time, isn't it?"

"Yes," the old man says. "It's time to see what our little queen's made of." He picks up a fine porcelain tea cup from the small table beside him and sips. "Do you think I'm wrong to do this, Raymond?"

"Sir, you have done what you set out to do, and you will continue to pursue this course until you find its end." Raymond gives a small bow and leaves the room.

The old man's face twitches, as if he's struggling with some inner battle. Alone now, he drops his head onto his chest and lets the tears come, silently. No more than a whisper, the words "my girl, my girl" float into the room and are gone. He reaches into his pocket and pulls out a velvet pouch. He tips the pouch over a crystal bowl on the table and empties the contents. The bowl fills with perfectly round small black pebbles. He runs his fingers through them. They make a soft clacking. He sighs.

4. NIGHTMARE

*I*N THE NIGHTMARE, *Emma is four years old. She's huddled in the V-berth of the sailboat that is her home. When Mommy tucked her into bed the ocean was calm and rocking her so softly, the moon was like a big flashlight shining through the hatch over her head. Now the whole night is a black monster that wants to swallow her.*

Like it swallows Daddy. She sees it and its four heads. She sees her daddy struggle and then he stops and then the heads take him over the side. The heads have big eyes and one head looks right at her, just for a minute, where she's crouching on her knees on her bunk. The noise has woken her, so she's looking through the hatch and sees what she shouldn't see.

She scurries back down under the covers ... pretends to be asleep. She hears scraping over her head and she knows the eyes are looking through the hatch at her. She squeezes her eyes shut and keeps them shut long after the scraping stops. She doesn't know when she falls back asleep.

When she wakes again her home is going up and down like a wild thing. She thinks she had a bad dream. She wants to tell her mommy about the dream monster that took Daddy. The sails crack. The wind shrieks. Her body bumps and thumps against the walls of the berth as if she's a ragdoll. Her stomach feels sick. The boat rises and falls, then rolls over one side and then snaps back and rolls again. She throws up in her bed. She can't help it. She cries out but the sound is swallowed by the wailing wind. The smell of her own vomit makes her sick and she throws up again.

She hears her mommy rush up on deck, screaming for her daddy. "Ivan. Where are you? Ivan?"

Emma's heart pounds hard. It wasn't a dream. He's gone, Mommy. The monster took him, she wants to tell her.

She wants her mommy. She wants her mommy to come back inside now and cuddle her. She wants her daddy!

The waves crash over the boat making it shudder violently. Hold on tight, Mommy.

The boat is leaning so far over Emma is crushed up against the hull. She holds tight to her bear, so tight, and closes her eyes as the boat goes down, and down, and down and…

Emma shoots right up in bed. She's had nightmares since she was a child but never remembered them before. This time it was so real, she could see the whole thing like it was a movie. She felt the insane rocking of the boat, the tipping, as if she'd been there. Had it been real, and not a dream? If it was real, what happened to her father? Emma lies back down in bed shivering.

"GET UP!" Emma's aunt is shaking her shoulder. "Wash and dress," she says. "We're going to town in forty minutes. I don't want to be late."

How long has she slept? Emma remembers the dream. The nightmare. Waking up trembling and sweaty. Then sleep again finally. She's so tired.

She showers and gets dressed. But it's as if her body doesn't belong to her. Like she's been drugged.

The silence in the car is heavy. Emma slumps down in her seat, closes her eyes. Then opens them! It's just sunk in that her aunt and her uncle are wearing their Sunday best clothes.

"Where are you taking me?" Emma asks. Maybe they're taking her away? Giving her away like an unwanted puppy.

"Where are you taking me?" she asks again, more sharply this time. "Tell me!"

"There's a will," Uncle Derek answers before Aunt Petra can stop him.

"A will? Who's...?" Emma stops. She sucks in a breath. "Why do you need me?"

Aunt Petra's raises her hand toward Uncle Derek and puts a stop to the conversation. She never even looks at Emma.

A will. Jess's? But why does she need to be there? Clearly Aunt Petra would have kept her locked in her room unless she was forced to let her out. Who knows about her being held hostage in her room? Now that Jess is dead, who else knows or cares what happens to her? The thought is an arrow, painful and sharp. Adam. He knows.

Emma's hopes rise momentarily. She sits up straighter. Adam was there to guard her but he also tried to help. And then the sickening thought that maybe her aunt and uncle figured it out, that he'd tried to help. Her only ally on the farm, gone. She didn't see him when they left.

"What day is it?" No one answers.

"What day is it?" she asks again louder. Why won't they speak to her?

Uncle Derek meets her eyes in the rear-view mirror, shakes his head imperceptibly. Aunt Petra stares out the window, frowning.

Emma lets the silence muffle her from them. From her aunt, who doesn't want her, who wishes she wasn't alive. From her uncle, who can't or won't do a thing to help her.

Emma's thoughts torture her. What day is it? Did she miss the funeral? Who looked after Jess's body? She didn't have many friends in the community. She should have stayed with Jess. She should have stayed. They should have taken her to hospital the day of the storm. On and on her thoughts whirl and buzz in her head. She's chewed her fingernails to the quick.

The car stops. Aunt Petra orders her out, then climbs out

herself. They stand on the sidewalk in front of a tall grey brick building while Uncle Derek parks.

When Uncle Derek joins them, they enter the building and climb the stairs. Emma reads the nameplate on the door they enter: Arthur Drake, LLM. A lawyer's office.

"Mr. and Mrs. Visser?" the receptionist's cheery voice seems jarring. "Please take a seat. You're a few minutes early. Mr. Drake's with another client."

They take seats in the waiting room, which is empty except for them. Emma's stomach rumbles. She can't remember when she last ate.

Uncle Derek gets up. "Here." He hands her a paper cup of water from the cooler and a sandwich that he must have brought from home because it's wrapped sloppily in wax paper. She sees it's cheese. Her favourite.

"Thanks." Emma risks a glance into his face, but he's already turning away. Aunt Petra's frowning even more. Emma takes a bite of her sandwich, chews slowly, swallows, chews some more, as if she's a mechanical doll. She crumples the wax paper into a ball when she's done. Uncle Derek takes it from her and his hand brushes hers, lightly.

The door to the office opens. "You can go in now." They follow the receptionist down a narrow hallway and enter the lawyer's office. He's a tall bald man with a large belly. He greets each one of them by name.

"Mrs. Visser? Mr. Visser?" He shakes their hands. "Miss Emerald Lake Visser?" He pauses on Emma's name, bends toward her and waits until she nods. Then he nods back at her and smiles ever so slightly before turning his attention back to her aunt and uncle.

"Not much seating here. Please, Mrs. Visser. Here. And Mr. Visser." They take the two seats in front of his desk.

"Miss Emerald? Would you be so kind as to sit here?" He clears some papers off a chair beside his desk.

"Terribly sorry for the cramped quarters. Small office. We'll be moving in a month." As he talks, he adjusts his lamp so that it shines directly on Aunt Petra and Uncle Derek, just enough to illuminate their faces but leaving his in shadow. And Emma's.

Out of the corner of her eye, Emma sees him studying her aunt's face, her uncle's, taking in Aunt Petra's pinched frown, Uncle Derek's downcast eyes. The lawyer's glance is sharp, astute. He cocks his head slightly and sends a sideways glance at Emma. Winks. She squirms uncomfortably. It feels as if they have a secret but she doesn't like it.

"Ah…" he clears his throat. Shuffles the papers on his desk. Clears his throat again, then holds up a file. Puts it down. Picks up another. Adjusts his glasses. Like he's killing time.

"Mrs. Visser, Mr. Visser. I've called you here … ah … as Emerald's guardians … ah … to hear and witness the last will and testimony of Mrs. Jessica Lake." Shuffle, shuffle go the papers.

"Lake? That's MY name." Emma jumps up.

"Sit down and behave!" Aunt Petra orders Emma and points to the chair like she's a dog.

"Mrs. Visser, please." The lawyer turns to Emma. "Emerald, your grandmother went by her mother's maiden name in the community. Farnsworthy."

"*My grandmother?*" Emma can hardly breathe. "My grandmother? Jess is … was my grandmother?" She rounds on her aunt and uncle. "You never told me. She never told me?" She slides slowly back into her chair whispering, "Jess, Jess," over and over.

"Stop that, Emma!" Aunt Petra can hardly contain her anger. "Stop this nonsense! She couldn't keep you." Uncle Derek puts his hand on her arm, but she shakes him off. "You're ours." She leaps to her feet and pushes her red face toward Emma. "Ours."

Emma's eyes open wide and she shrinks back in her chair. She looks at her uncle, then at Mr. Drake.

"Ah …" Mr. Drake cuts in and starts to gather up the papers. "Perhaps we should reschedule."

"No!" Aunt Petra's breathing hard. She calms herself with an effort. "Carry on, Mr. Drake." She sits down and smooths her skirt.

Out of the corner of her eye, Emma notices Mr. Drake slipping an envelope out of the file he's holding and sliding it under the blotter on his desk. He raises a finger toward her just a touch, as if to warn her. He knows that she's seen, and he wants her to see.

He clears his throat, stops shuffling paper—as if shuffling papers was just a distraction—and reads, all business-like now.

"Now, then. The will states the following, and I quote: To Emerald Lake Visser I leave my house and my boat, the *Edge*..."

"No!" Aunt Petra's on her feet again, hands fisted on her purse. "There's a mistake!"

"No mistake, Mrs. Visser." Mr. Drake taps his pen on the desk.

"The *Edge*? She left me the *Edge*?" Emma cuts in.

"We want no boat. I forbid this..."

"I want it." Emma grabs the lawyer's arm. "Mr. Drake, I want it!"

"We will not accept this boat." Aunt Petra's voice has risen again. "That's an end to it."

Keeping his voice low, Mr. Drake turns to Emma. "Your aunt and uncle must respect the law. The boat is yours." Emma watches as he turns to Uncle Derek. "Mr. Visser, if you and ... Mrs. Visser..." he pauses on her name, "will not accept the responsibility of the will, I have it in my power to replace you as guardians. Please let me know if that would be your wish."

Uncle Derek speaks for the first time. "We accept the terms," he tells the lawyer. "My brother would have wanted us to."

"You lost your brother when he married Peggy Lake and started running drugs," Aunt Petra spits out. "Why do you care what he would have wanted?" Her face is pinched.

Emma's body jerks at the words. Her father was a drug-runner? This is the first time she's ever heard anything about him and this is what she hears? Can it be true? She stares at her uncle. It's his brother Aunt Petra's talking about.

But Uncle Derek just sighs. Clearly, they've had this conversation before. "Please carry on."

"Also, I leave her all the remaining money from my estate, which will be held in trust in an account in her name." Mr. Drake pushes the file toward Uncle Derek. Extends a pen. "Please sign here as record that I have properly discharged my duty."

Uncle Derek nods. Emma is stunned, looking from face to face. Clutching at straws, Aunt Petra tries to delay him. "She wasn't sane. She was a bad influence. Just like your mother..." She rounds on Emma, pointing at her. Emma doesn't move a muscle. At mention of her mother, Emma feels a fierce anger building in her chest.

Mr. Drake interrupts. "I assure you, Mrs. Visser, Mrs. Lake was of sound body and mind when she made this will. You'll be wasting your time to try to contest it. As Emerald's guardians, you will help her care for the property and finances until such time as she reaches 18 years of age. At that time, her guardianship will be handed over to the one who is paying you to look after her. As I said, it is the law. The boat is her property. Not yours."

"We'll sell it." It's a statement, not a question.

"The boat can only be sold with Emerald's consent," the lawyer confirms. Emma sucks in a breath.

Aunt Petra pauses, turns toward Emma, considering. Then she says to the lawyer. "How much money do we have...?" She corrects herself. "I mean ... to manage?"

Emma almost chokes. She watches Mr. Drake as he opens a folder.

"Three hundred and seven thousand, four hundred and fifty-nine dollars. The money is held in stocks and bonds and an advisor at the bank has been named to oversee the investments." He steeples his hands.

Emma's eyes are wide. Where did Jess get all this money?

She was rich, but she lived in a run-down cottage. Except for the *Edge*, she lived like a hermit.

"Is there anything else, Mrs. Visser?" Mr. Drake is looking at Aunt Petra through narrowed eyes.

Aunt Petra clenches her fists around her purse. "All right then." Her voice is calmer now, slicker. She stands and turns awkwardly.

Uncle Derek stands also. "Where do I sign?" He signs where the lawyer indicates and holds the pen to Aunt Petra, deliberately. She leans over and signs, then pushes him roughly out of her way and rushes out the door. Uncle Derek leaves the room right after her.

"Emerald," Mr. Drake says the minute they disappear, putting a hand on her arm to hold her back. "Your grandmother wanted me to give this to you privately." He swiftly slides the envelope out from under the blotter and hands it to her. Then he opens a drawer and takes out another bulkier envelope. "Also, I am the co-signer on your bank account. She authorized me to take some money out for you at this time. The bank has all the records of the withdrawal."

"You better go now." He gives her arm a squeeze. "If ever you need my help, my card is in the envelope. There are those who want to help you. Take care."

"Who wants…?"

"You'd better go," Mr. Drake says shaking his head. "Contact me if you need anything."

Emma stuffs the envelopes into the waistband of her ugly, grey skirt, pulls her sweater down over them and leaves the room. She hurries down the hall to the reception area just as her aunt and uncle are stepping through the doorway.

BACK IN THE CAR the air is thick with all the questions Emma wants to ask but can't. She knows they won't be answered anyway. She leans her forehead against the window.

Her grandmother? Her grandmother? Her grandmother?

The words are screaming in Emma's head. The *Edge*? The *Edge*? Trust account? Trust account? She's rich. She's a rich girl. The envelopes burn her skin. Who's helping her? Who? What's going on?

The minute the car stops, she's out the door.

"Where are you going?" Each word feels like a bullet. Emma ducks her head.

"To my room."

"You will not keep that boat. It will be sold immediately. There will be no discussion."

"No, you will not." Emma turns her back on her Aunt and takes a step toward the house. She's not going to listen. She knows now that she can refuse to agree to this.

"Look at me when I speak to you."

Emma stops and turns making certain to keep her face utterly blank.

"Do you understand?"

"Aunt Petra, you will not sell the *Edge*." Emma repeats, staring at her aunt. She doesn't see the blow until it comes. The smack across her cheek is swift and accurate. Emma's forced backwards by the force of it.

Holding her hand to her cheek, Emma runs up the stairs to her room, closes the door. Then she flies into action. She tugs the envelopes out from under her shirt. Her hands are shaking when she rips the letter from Jess open. A yellow crinkly newspaper clipping falls to the floor. She bends to pick it up.

It reads:

Last month, well-known Toronto artist Peggy Lake reported her husband Ivan Visser was lost at sea when their sailboat was caught in a storm off the Bahamian island of Mayaguana. Lake appealed to Canadian authorities to help her find him. She stated that she would remain in the Bahamas until his body is recovered but she is now reported missing. Bahamian police have declared that the Kingston native is a prime suspect in what may be a drug-related murder. All recent attempts to locate Lake have failed. She was last seen on Mayaguana. Any information about her whereabouts should be directed to local authorities.

Emma slides to the floor. The words rip through her like a storm. Murder? Drugs? Lost at sea? It's like a movie or something. The clipping is dated from eight years earlier. Emma quickly calculates that she would have been five years old. It's torn from a part of the paper reporting on well-known people.

Emma puts the clipping down on the floor beside her and unfolds the letter from Jess.

Jan. 2012
Dear Emma,

By now you know I'm your grandmother. Yes. Your mother is my daughter. She and your father ran away before you were born and I never saw her again until she brought you to live at your aunt and uncle's. It was what she had to do under the circumstances, and she paid a terrible price. She would have left you with me if she could have, but the agreement prevented it.

Two years ago, this clipping arrived in a plain envelope with no postage stamp, and no markings. But who sent this clipping or why, I have no idea. That's when I came to find you. You remember? I broke my promise but I knew it was what I had to do. At least I could see you from time to time, even though I was not allowed to tell you who I was. Oh, that broke my heart.

But now Emma, my beloved girl, I'm sick. I didn't know how to tell you or if I should. The doctor told me I didn't have much time. If you're reading this letter then I'm not on this earth with you anymore. I'm sorry I couldn't tell you, prepare you. I love you to pieces my girl. I'd hoped to have longer with you, but your aunt would have found a way to stop us anyway. It was just a matter of time.

I hope you can forgive me someday for agreeing to what was forced upon you. Even now I can't tell you, because you must be protected. It's what we all agreed to do – to protect you at all cost. Your aunt blames your mother for this obligation and she has punished you because of it. I'm sorry for that too, because I didn't do more to try to help you understand.

I can tell you one thing you can know that may help explain your aunt's bitterness. She was your father's sweetheart, or at least she thought she was. I know that's hard to believe, but she was a beautiful young girl. She never had a chance, though, after he met your mother. Petra was from the farming community and your mother was like a dream, astonishing. Under it all, your father was wild and your mother fell in love with his wildness, where Petra wanted to tame it. When they ran away, she married his brother, your Uncle Derek, and their two farms became one. They never could have children, and when you came perhaps Petra felt she could care for you because you were Ivan's, but in the end her bitterness and anger has eaten away at her to make her the woman you now know.

The authorities never found your father's body. Go find your mother, Emma. She'll tell you what the others won't. The Edge is yours. You can sail her down there. You have what it takes. It'll be the best way. You'll need a boat down there anyway—someplace to live, and a way to get around the islands. I'll be rooting for you. And remember, I love you always. Jess.

Emma's stunned. She lifts her head, but her eyes are staring at nothing. *It's crazy.* Life has gone suddenly crazy, crazy, is all she can think.

She hears footsteps outside her door and still she doesn't move. The bolt on the lock outside her bedroom door clicks shut.

5. ESCAPE AGAIN

THE CHAINSAW WAKES EMMA EARLY. There's a sound of boots on the gable roof outside her window. A soft tap on her window. She waits. The rap comes again. She rolls out of bed and crosses to the window, twitches the curtains aside just a fraction. It's Adam. He's signalling the latch, telling her to open. *Hurry*, he mouths.

Emma shakes her head, no.

Adam slaps a piece of paper against the pane.

She reads: BOAT FOR SALE in bold letters at the top. She scrambles for the latch on the window, opens it a fraction. She's surprised it still opens. Probably Aunt Petra doesn't think she can get down from the roof again, once the tree is gone.

"Give me that!"

Adam slides the paper through the gap. Emma grabs it, scanning the words. Her boat, the *Edge*, her aunt is selling the *Edge*. She has no right. The lawyer said so. Emma raises her eyes to Adam's, devastated. He nods. He understands.

There are shouts from below. Adam signals that he has to go. He turns to pick up the chainsaw. Then pauses.

You! he points at her. Then mouths the word, *Go!* He forms a fist with his hand. *Go!* he mouths again. Then he presses his finger on the trigger so the motor revs loudly. He shimmies to the edge of the roof and begins slicing the green branches off one by one.

There are footsteps outside Emma's door. The lock rattles as she lowers the window swiftly, quietly, and lets the curtain fall into place. She stashes the paper under the bedcovers just as the door opens. She's trembling.

Her aunt drops a tray on the dresser. "Breakfast. If you don't eat it, I'll feed it to the pigs," she says and leaves.

Breakfast is a bowl of cereal and a banana. Emma barely tastes it. Her aunt is selling the *Edge*. Against the lawyer's instructions. And yet she's doing it. Emma's going to lose the *Edge*. But the *Edge* is her only hope for finding her mother. She has to do something. But what? What if she could leave? Run away on the *Edge*? How would she do it?

She remembers Adam signalling her, "You! Go!"

There is a thunderous crash outside. The tree has fallen. Her heart falls too.

IT'S THE MIDDLE OF THE NIGHT and Emma hears a light tap at her window. *Tick. Tap. Tick.* She gets out of bed and crosses to the window, pulls back the curtain. The night is pitch-black. She can't see anything.

Tick. A pebble hits the glass.

"What the...?"

It's Adam. The floodlights should have come on, but everything is dark. She can just make out his shape in the shadows. He knows when she sees him, signalling with his hand for her to come down.

Is he nuts? Emma thinks. There's no more tree. She'll have to jump. The dogs will set up a ruckus. She'll be caught for sure. And then what? Her mind is a blank. It's impossible.

Or is it? What's the worst they could do?

She goes back to her bed and sits on the edge. Then, her body acts without her mind being quite there yet and she's getting dressed in the grey skirt, blouse, and sweater, tying the laces on her sneakers. From under the mattress she takes Jess's letter and the envelope with the money, stuffs them into her waistband and moves to the window. She opens it and slides over the ledge, heart pounding.

Every noise is amplified in the night.

Her feet crunch on the roof. She freezes. Surely someone will hear her. She waits but no one comes. She waits for the dogs. Nothing. Adam must have tied them up out back.

There's a kind of pulsing silence.

She creeps over to the edge of the roof and looks down. There's Adam. He's got his arms up to catch her, this strong as an ox boy who wants to help her. She takes a breath and jumps.

"Umph!" Adam catches her but they both tumble onto the ground. "Not quite James Bond," he says with a grunt.

Emma tries to pull away, but he holds her still and shakes his head. He puts a finger to his mouth. "Shhh!"

"What's with you? Why're you helping me?"

"Cause," he whispers, his lips close to her ear. "'Cause it's bad, how they treat you. It's wrong."

Emma feels tears start to fill her eyes. "I've gotta go." This is so weird. A friend. She didn't know. And now she's leaving.

"You gonna get in trouble?" She shifts slightly, studies his face.

"Nah. They like me."

She gets to her feet. "Thanks," she mouths.

He nods. Emma turns and slowly, stealthily, heads for the road.

Once she gets to the road Emma runs like a crazy person. She runs through the night. She's going to the *Edge*, hoping against hope that it's docked where it always is. Every nerve is on full alert as she hides from any traffic on the road, skirts sleeping houses with dogs out front. Finally, she's at Jess's house. She rounds the bend and there, tied up snuggly, just like Jess must have left it, is the *Edge*. Emma almost cries with relief.

There's no time to waste. She hops on board and opens the hatch, puts her envelopes in a safe place in the chart table. She pulls off the skirt and tugs on the jeans Jess had bought her for the boat. She starts the motor, leaving it in neutral, then jumps onto the dock to untie the lines that are holding the *Edge* firmly in place. She jumps back on board, taking the lines with her. She gathers them quickly, not worrying for the moment about how neat they are. She stows them out of the way knowing she'll tidy them later. She pictures the passage away from Jess's and on out into the lake.

Luckily the water's dead calm—there's no wind at all. The only sound is frogs croaking noisily. As she's seen Jess do, she puts the engine into forward and pulls gently away from the dock.

Her heart's singing. She's escaped! And she's leaving tonight to go find her mother. But first things first: she's got to find a hiding place, where they won't find her. Once her aunt and uncle discover she's gone, they'll for sure check the *Edge*. And when they find the *Edge* gone, they'll start looking for her. Probably alert the police.

She nudges the *Edge* out into the passage, picking her way carefully from buoy to buoy in the pitch black. She tries to conjure up the shoreline in her mind. She knows Jess has endless charts on board, but she needs to go somewhere easy. Someplace she can get to in the dark. Charts won't help her.

Soon she's out in the open water. She feels the big water under her, the rolling waves, slow, undulating. The last few days have been windless, and the lake's quiet now. A thought begins to form. What if she motors as far away as she can get? If she heads due west, she'll be moving toward Deerhurst Island. It'll be easy to identify even in the night because of the lighthouse on the far point.

No one knows about the powerful motor Jess has put on the *Edge*. Unlike most sailboats she can motor as fast as a speedboat. The police won't expect that. Even boat people have no clue about the Macgregor boats. They think it's a dumpy little boat only suitable for day outings. Emma lets a secret satisfaction bubble up inside her.

If she heads to the other side of Deerhurst and tucks into the reeds or a small cove, she'll be able to rest and plan for the next part of the trip. It fills her with hope.

One step at a time, she tells herself. One step at a time. She checks to see the water in the ballast tanks have been emptied, flicks on the running lights, and cranks up the speed. It's time to put some distance between her and the past.

DAWN IS BREAKING when Emma finally approaches a small cove that looks promising for a hideaway. Lined with tall pines, it will hide her mast. The rough beach is more mud than sand, so there is little reason for swimmers to come here.

She's tired. Instead of racing along like she thought she would, she soon discovered that she could do no more than half the speed at most. In the dark, the risk simply wasn't worth it. She's taken much longer than planned.

She motors closer, searching for a place to sleep without worrying that she's going to be disturbed. As she creeps along, a creek reveals itself. Secluded, hopefully deep enough to get away from passing traffic. Emma motors slowly up the narrow waterway until the undergrowth starts to become too dense. She turns off the motor and lifts it out of the water. She unsnaps a paddle from its spot under the gunwale, grabs one of her mooring lines, and climbs up on the bow to bring the *Edge* in as close to shore as she can. Rather than dropping an anchor, she's going to tie off to shore. She curses softly as she has to untangle the line she hadn't stowed properly, but it finally comes free and she attaches one end to the forward cleat, jumps into the shallow water, and wades ashore to secure the other end to a tree trunk.

The water is icy cold. Her feet make soft *pock, pock,* sucking sounds in the muddy river bed. There are probably leeches. She cringes. She hates leeches. She'll have to check her pant legs and her skin when she gets back to the boat.

Emma untangles the second line and secures the stern. When she's sure the *Edge* is snuggly tied up, she jumps back on board, takes the keys out of the ignition and hangs them inside the cabin, then strips down to her underwear and shirt. She rinses off her feet and legs, sloshes her pants in the water and hangs them to dry over the lifelines. Two clothes pins on each leg in case a wind comes up. No leeches.

It's time for her to rest. She's travelled more than forty miles away from the farm. From here on, maybe for the rest of her life, home is wherever she is, wherever the *Edge* is. Everything she does now will be about looking after herself and her home as best she can.

Emma takes a close look at her refuge. The place she has found is a sweet haven. The aroma of pine is heavenly. It smells like safety. The sun has barely crested the horizon. The sky is streaked with pale pink and orange against the morning blue. She yawns hugely. The stillness of the woods seeps into her cells. She can feel her tired body shutting down, begging for sleep. She ducks inside the cabin, closes the hatch behind her, pushes all manner of gear out of the way to make a nest for herself in the V-berth, and plunges into the deepest sleep she's had since she last saw Jess.

IT'S NIGHT AGAIN when Emma wakes, eyes blinking in the inky dark. She wonders at the sleep that has swallowed her for a whole day and she's almost sucked back under. She forces herself to stretch, reach out and touch the switch that will bring light into the cabin. This cabin. This boat that is her home now.

Outside in the woods, the hoot of an owl fills the air. She needs to check her jeans. The only pair she has. A June bug bashes its body against one of the portals, its body making a cracking sound. The light is attracting the moths and mosquitos to her. They'll be vicious. She needs to pee.

She uncurls her body from the nest of the berth, goes to the toilet, moves across the small space to the hatch and peers out into the night. The light inside the cabin makes the outside world invisible.

Her stomach gurgles suddenly. Everything she feels and thinks is unfurling in slow motion, like a nature movie with stop motion photography. She's not sure she likes this, but she's so tired.

Food, her stomach growls again more insistently this time. What's on the boat? She stubs her toe on the foot of the table when she goes to reach for the cupboard door. The pain shoots up through her leg bringing a rush of adrenalin, waking her up fully now.

It's a good thing. Adrenalin is what will keep her alive in this adventure she's going on, in this sailboat she owns now. She has a lot to learn. When she was with Jess she treated everything she did with Jess as fun, a kind of summer vacation.

Lazy, she thinks as she opens a can of soup. *I was lazy. But I didn't know. I didn't know this would happen.*

She lifts the top of the chart table and digs through Jess's charts, soup can in her hand, eating it cold. It tastes good. There are charts of all the Great Lakes, the St. Laurence. There are charts of the Atlantic coast of America. And there are charts of the Bahamas. It slowly dawns on her that Jess must have been planning on doing this trip herself? Before she got sick, maybe she was planning to leave all along.

She puts the charts away and lowers the top of the table. She's going to have to remember everything Jess said, any hints, things she mentioned that Emma didn't take seriously. If she's going to sail to the Bahamas she's going to have to pay close attention to everything, learn fast, and be smart. Starting now.

Mayaguana, Bahamas. That's what the newspaper clipping said is where her mother was last seen. That's where she's going.

"This is completely insane!" she murmurs out loud, startling herself. Oh, oh. She's talking to herself.

"I'm going to find my mother," she says out loud to the night, to the bugs. This time the noise of her own voice calms her. She spoons up the soup chewing, chewing. Each mouthful belongs to her. It is night. She doesn't have anywhere she needs to go, tonight, at least.

The tall trees are silent sentinels. The water in the little cove is perfectly still. She turns off the light in the cabin and lets her eyes get used to the dark. The mosquitoes outside buzz madly, hungry for her blood. If she steps through the hatch she'll have to be fast about it. But she doesn't want to use her precious drinking water to rinse out the soup can, the spoon. And she sure doesn't want to attract weevils into the boat from left over food.

She rehearses the moves in her mind—hatch off, crawl through, grab can and spoon, close hatch fast behind her. She fumbles a bit. The body needs practise to learn its way efficiently. She knows she'll have plenty of practise in the months to come. But she's outside in the cockpit now. The mosquitoes attack her viciously within seconds. She moves to the stern, bends down and rinses the can, the spoon, as fast as possible in the dark. She grabs her jeans off the lifeline and struggles back inside, dropping the hatch twice, and banging her elbow badly.

Back in the cabin, she sits down on the settee to wait for the mosquitos that snuck in to make their move. She feels like she's run a mile, so deep is the weariness. The buzzing starts and she takes a good twenty minutes flicking the lights on and off every time she hears one close to her. She doesn't get them all, but she's had enough. Fatigue is dragging her down under again now that her stomach is fed. She crawls back into her nest, lets sleep claim her.

Tomorrow she'll start making her plans. Tomorrow is soon enough.

6. DISGUISE

THE *EDGE* LOOKS LIKE a hurricane hit it. Cushions are strewn everywhere on deck. Inside the cabin, all the storage spaces that are normally hidden under every seating spot or berth are propped open. Emma is upside down in the portside storage space counting:

"Fifty cans of soup (variety)," she says, making notes in a logbook she found in the chart table. "Seven plastic containers of rice, five containers of macaroni, cheese packets included. Yay Grandma Jess! One container full of hot chocolate packets. For me?" Emma grins and holds up the container as if it's a trophy.

Her grandmother! Grandma Jess. She's trying out various names—Grams, Granny, Granny Jess—saying them out loud, testing how they sound, and since no one is around to hear she figures it doesn't count that she's talking to herself. She's mostly settled on Grandma Jess. It gives her a sense of belonging, of warmth, deep in her belly.

She holds up two containers of weird looking packages, takes one out and shakes it.

"Freeze-dried meals. Just add water," she reads, rifling through the other packets. "Beef Stroganoff. Chili con carne. Chicken gumbo. What's freeze-dried?"

She turns over one of the packets. There's a ton of writing about the nutritional value, but the ingredients sound positively weird: hydrolyzed corn, torula and brewer's yeast, wheat gluten, soy protein. Yikes! But she figures they'll be good in a pinch, as a last resort. She notes them down and puts them back.

There are dried soups, packets of oatmeal, and bags of tea and instant coffee.

"Ah Grandma Jess, you sure loved your instant coffee."

Then it hits her. Emma pulls her head hurriedly out of the storage space, smacking her skull on the edge. As if the bang on the head has dazed her, she looks around her like she doesn't know where she is. But it's not the bang that did it. It's the strangeness of all this unknown that's dazed her.

What the heck is she doing? The madness of her adventure comes over her like a big wave in a storm. She can't sail to the Bahamas. What's she thinking? She doesn't have a clue about ocean navigating. What about storms? What about getting caught by the authorities?

She stumbles out of the cabin and up on deck. She leans against the mast. Her heart is racing. She feels nauseous, like she's going to be sick to her stomach. It's a huge panic attack.

She takes long slow gulps of fresh air to try to calm down.

One thousand, two thousand, three thousand, four...

Her heartbeats start to slow. The birds in the woods are riotous. She leans back and stares up at the sky as if the birds can give her some clue. A big blue jay swoops in and the smaller birds scatter. Just like—she's going to have to scram soon. Move from her safe little cove. She can't hide out here forever, even if she'd like to. She'll be found and then she'll be forced to go back to the farm.

But she can't go back. It's not even an option.

"This is all too weird," she says to no one in particular, and no one answers her. Not that she expected an answer, but still.

Emma lowers herself slowly to the deck. She's going to have to start her voyage sometime. It might as well be tomorrow.

From the charts and masses of notes Jess left, Emma's learned that she can make her way to Florida mostly by inland water-ways. In Florida, she'll have to wait for good weather to cross the Gulf Stream to the Bahamas. There were bold underlines and circles around the words "Gulf Stream." Clearly something she needs to pay attention to. But she only vaguely recalls what it is. And it feels way too far off to worry about now.

NOW is the problem.

It's probably two thousand boating miles between Kingston and Miami, Florida. Emma figures she might as well be charting a voyage to the moon, so strange and unreal all her grandmother's notes seem. For the moment, the only thing she can manage to encompass is her next step, which is to cross Lake Ontario and make it into the States, past border officials at Oswego and into the Oswego Canal without being spotted. Seven locks and twenty-four miles of dug-out ditches, some parts still dating back to the 1800s.

Jess's notes say that the border guards clear boats through customs only between nine o'clock in the morning to six o'clock at night. If you arrive after six o'clock, you have to clear customs the next morning. Once you've cleared customs, Jess has written, the lockmasters never check your papers again.

That's kind of all nice and trusting. But Emma's going to break that trust. She's not going to wait. She's going to be an illegal immigrant, like the ones she read about in class, who cross the border into the States on foot. Only Emma's going to do it in a boat. Because she's not going to clear customs.

She can't! She doesn't have a passport.

She's under age and she's a runaway. And by now the police will be looking for her. She's an outlaw in Canada. And now she'll be an outlaw in another country. Another wave of nausea washes over her. She leans her head back against the mast.

Breathe. Breathe. After a while, her brain starts to work again. And then a rush of adrenalin surges through her with the list of things she must do to get ready.

She has to take the mast down. She can't go through the locks and under the fixed bridges with a mast up. All sailboats have to take their masts down. It's a struggle for most sailboats, but not hers.

Emma scampers to the front of the deck and fiddles with clips and shackles, unwraps the smaller sail from around its roller furling mechanism, returns briefly to the cockpit to release the halyard from the cleat. In no time the sail is lowered and neatly folded.

Emma takes a breather and grunts to herself. Is it possible that only last summer she had no clue what to do with any part of a sailboat, let alone raise and lower the mast single-handed? A memory surfaces. How she'd battled with Jess over learning the task of lowering and raising the mast!

"THAT WAS AWFUL!" Jess' voice was laced with impatience. "Do it again!"

"What for?" Emma planted her feet, hands on her hips. "When am I ever going to need to know how to do this so fast? It's not a race!"

"What if it is?" Jess snapped back. "What if you needed to get this mast down in a hurry?" She huffed back to the cockpit and sat down, rubbing the heel of her hand hard against her chest.

"Raise it and start again. And this time do it faster and neater."

Emma remembered wanting to tell Jess to shove it. She even opened her mouth to do so. But one good look at Jess silenced her. There was worry written all over Jess's face. It was a weird kind of worry. Frowny and sad all at the same time. And she looked pale. Emma felt spooked and a shiver travelled up her spine, like a premonition or something.

Emma turned back to the rigging and focused. Okay, she thought. I'll just show her!

Methodically and swiftly she reattached every fitting, shackle, and turnbuckle, raised the mast and started again. Within minutes the rigging was down, every line was neat, halyards were bound so they didn't flop around, and the mast was secured to the deck. It was as if some other part of Emma's brain had taken over and her hands knew what to do by themselves.

"Hah!" she heard from the cockpit. "That's it, Emma my girl. That's it!"

Emma looked back at Jess and their eyes met. Instead of seeing a smile, again she saw the same seriousness. It gave her stomach a hollow feeling.

And then Jess laughed out loud as if nothing at all had happened.

"Okay sailor, raise the damned lot and let's go for a spin!" And she leaned back on her elbows as if it was nothing but a game. But Emma knew what she'd seen and felt. Something was not right. Something was coming.

AND NOW THE SOMETHING had come. Jess had been sick and had never told her. That's what it was. A sob bursts out of Emma's mouth as the realization of how sick Jess was hits her, but she forces it down. There's work to be done. She hooks up the mast winch and undoes the stays holding the mast in place. Inch by inch she lowers the mast onto the deck and ties it in place. She'll no longer be a sailboat. She'll be a motorboat with a stick glued to the deck.

As an extra precaution, Emma leans over the deck and peels off the boat name on the side of her boat so no one knows its name. The *Edge* will be an anonymous boat going through the canal on the way to who knows where, for a vacation or something. She'll have to make up a story.

She's figured out her plan. She's going to slip into Oswego after dark and motor right up to the first lock. Go through with the early birds before the lock master has had his second coffee. Grown-ups are often sloppy in the morning, she's noticed, and that will help confuse things.

That, and the fact that she, Emma, will be a *he*.

LOG ENTRY: *June 7, 2002, 10:30 p.m. Light Wind. It's warm. At anchor.*

Emma's hanging on a hook in a backwater ahead of the first lock of the Oswego Canal. Her plans have worked so far. She's crossed Lake Ontario with no mishaps and arrived in Oswego when the harbour master had gone home for dinner, just as she planned. She tied up at the dock as if she was going to wait till morning to clear customs, but after dark she snuck away from the harbour. Her plan has worked perfectly.

Now she's tucked away out of sight and busy heating up some Mac and Cheese. She catches her reflection in the portal over the galley and runs her fingers over the ragged ends of her hair. She's cut off the long braid of blonde hair, so that her hair is short like a boy's. What's left looks messy and unattractive. That suits her just fine.

When her dinner's ready, she heads up on deck. She's sheltered by a stand of bull rushes. It's one of the things she loves about the *Edge*—that she can hide so completely. She can sneak right into the bushes almost on shore. Pull up the centerboard and pull up the twin rudders, tip up the motor, and paddle deep into the reeds.

After eating two helpings of Mac and Cheese, she takes her dishes to the stern of the boat to give them a good rinse. Again she catches her reflection in the water and rubs her hands hard through the shaggy mop. Then she shakes her head vigorously. The feeling of short hair delights her. Now she knows why guys keep their hair short. It's a lot easier. Ha! Best kept secret. And why she had bought into the long hair thing, she didn't know. What a load of crap. Not for her anymore. Never again. She grins and her reflection grins back at her.

The quiet of the night is amazing. She's sprayed on repellent, so the mosquitos are less of a problem. She surveys her surroundings. A small sleek night heron is standing sentinel-still in the shallow water near her. The frogs are just starting up their chorus. A slight breeze is rising, making the air cooler and fresher. Beautiful. This is what she can look forward to, night after night. *If* she can get through tomorrow. She shakes off her dread. Maybe she's going to be okay. She heads back inside the cabin and closes the hatch. Time to catch some sleep before the next day begins.

7. FIRST LIES

IT'S SEVEN IN THE MORNING and Emma's positioned with other early risers in front of the first lock waiting for it to open. Her mooring lines are ready on deck for quickly attaching to the chains that hang down the sides of the locks. As the water in the locks rise, she'll slide her mooring lines up the chains and her boat will rise too. Without being attached to the chains, the rush of the water would shove all the boats crashing into each other. So it's important to be well-secured before the water starts to flow.

Emma has placed big rubber gloves next to the mooring lines. She recalls Jess telling her about their own local Rideau Canal between Kingston and Ottawa, how the insides of old locks are like dank slime-covered dungeons. The fenders dangle from the sides of the boat covered in odd bits of cloth—her grey skirt on one, an old T-shirt of Jess's on another. The fenders will keep the *Edge* off the slimy walls of the locks and keep her from getting scratched from the concrete or banged up from hitting other boats, if that happens.

The lock begins to open and as soon as there's enough space between the doors Emma slips forward. It's tricky going. She's agile and prepared but a big 36-footer beside her is not. The man yells and the woman with him shouts back. Emma realizes that a lot depends on luck: getting the timing right and being in the right spot to grab the chains quickly.

One sudden bow wave from a pushy motorboat sends all the boats bumping into each other. It's a speedboat with an attitude, a boy at the steering wheel. Someone shouts at him, but he just glares at Emma as if she's to blame. She wastes no time on him. She motors her boat forward and to the right. Since she's single-handed she's going to handle the bow and stern mooring lines from the middle of her boat.

She slows to a stop and slides a line behind a mossy chain with the motor still running in neutral, then sidles up to the side wall of the lock. Holding onto the line secured at the bow, she moves to the stern of the boat and slips the second line behind another slimy chain. She can just reach it. With the two lines in her left hand, she turns off the motor. Now all she has to do is to wait for the lockmaster to come by and collect the fee.

"Hey," A voice jeers from the other side of the lock. "What kind of tugboat is that?"

Emma looks up. It's the speedboat boy.

"A fast one," she answers curtly and looks away again, not wanting to start a conversation.

"Yeah?" he taunts. "Want to bet I could beat you, loser?"

"I know you could, till you ran out of gas. And then I put up my sails and leave you behind."

"That's a sailboat? UUUUGLY!" The boy grins and goes back to fiddling with something on his boat.

"You fishing today?" he calls. He's smiling now.

"Maybe," Emma says. She's getting nervous about the conversation. She's already said too much.

She intends to go on to the next lock as quickly as possible and do at least five locks that day. From looking at the charts that seems doable. Maybe more, if she can swing it. A lot's going to depend on the opening times. Lockmasters won't be likely to open for only one boat. But the last thing she wants is for some speedboat driving idiot to be tagging along with her.

"Except I've got to get back home at lunch time to babysit my kid sister."

"You're such a loser," the boy sniggers.

Emma shrugs. Above her head the lockmaster appears.

"You going on to the next lock, young fella?"

"No sir," she replies. "Gotta babysit my little sister later."

The lockmaster takes her ten dollars and strides on to the next boat.

"Loser," the boy says. There's a smirk on his face.

Emma could care less. She tips her cap down and braces herself for the rush of water into the lock. She hasn't caught any attention and the lockmaster thinks she's a boy. That's all that counts.

8. INTERROGATION

EMMA FLEXES HER TIRED shoulder muscles as she stands in her small galley cooking up some soup. It's late. Well after dinnertime. But she's made six locks and is very happy with herself. The *Edge* is getting filthy and that's good too. A shiny boat can get too much attention. It's better to have a battered old tug.

Emma smiles as she remembers slowly chugging forward from the crowd when the first lock re-opened, and she was at the new water level. She had given the motor just a little more throttle, then a little more. Suddenly, the boy in the speedboat had shot ahead of her and passed her, leaving a serious wake. And within minutes she'd heard the lockmaster over the VHF calling ahead to the next lock master to stop the speedster and send the police.

When she'd studied Jess's charts she'd seen that the speed limit between the first three locks was a slow five miles per hour and the speedboat had been going at least double that. Emma's plans had been to travel as fast as possible after the speed limit rose to twenty miles per hour in the rest of the canal. Her hope was to give the police no cause to notice her. And that was even easier with silly boys like the one in the speedboat grabbing all the attention.

And here she is now, just outside the last lock on the Oswego Canal where it joins up with the Erie Canal. She'll cross Lake

Oneida tomorrow. She's heard boaters in the locks speaking about Lake Oneida as if it's a wild unpredictable body of water. She's checked the chart and the only thing she can see that could be tricky is the last part where it gets so shallow that waves can cause boats to overturn. She puts it out of her mind for tonight. She hopes to get a good night rest and have an early start in the morning.

Her soup begins to boil and she turns off the burner. She pours the soup into a deep bowl and drops the pot into the sink. She's just about to start eating when she hears the knocking.

She stops, her hand in mid-air, and holds dead still. There it is again. Someone's rapping on the hull. Her heart starts to pound. She doesn't want to talk to anybody. Her lights are on, so they'll know she's inside. She can't avoid responding.

Knock! Knock!

Cautiously she comes out to the cockpit and looks around. There's no one there. And no more knocking. She waits, but there's nothing. Maybe it's something on shore and it just sounds close. Her soup's getting cold and her stomach growls. She goes below. As soon as she sits down, it starts again.

Knock! Knock! Knock!

She comes back outside quicker this time. Where's it coming from? She looks left and right and then looks over the side, curious now, and her heart starts to slow down to normal again. All she sees are some ducks scurrying off in all directions. The knocking stops.

After waiting a while she goes back inside and retrieves her soup, taking it outside with her. She sits down and begins eating very quietly.

Knock! Knock! Knock! Knock!

The sound's definitely coming from the side of the boat where the ducks have gathered. Very slowly she leans over and peers down toward the water. The ducks are butting their bills up against the side of the boat along the water line.

Emma laughs right out loud and the ducks scatter at the

sound, but once they determine she's no threat they're quickly back at it, knock, knock, knocking as they clean the lock scum off the side of the boat. Chuckling to herself, she goes back to eating her soup. The *Edge* is a fast food outlet for ducks.

She finishes her soup outside, enjoying the night air. Crickets are chirping and fireflies are just starting to light up in the dusk. The sky's an indigo blue. The Blue Hour, Jess used to call it. She'd go on and on about how she loved the Blue Hour, when the sky began to darken and the trees were black silhouettes. Emma swipes a hand across her face as a pang of longing for Jess grabs her.

In the back of her mind she wonders uneasily what she would have done if it had been a stranger knocking. She takes a deep breath and puts it out of her thoughts. She'll cross that bridge when she gets to it. If she ever does.

THREE DAYS INTO THE TRIP and Emma is feeling mighty grateful to Jess for having bullied her into weight training. At the time, she hated every minute of it, arguing with Jess constantly.

"Why do I have to heft soup cans in the air a hundred times a day? I just don't get it and I hate doing this!" Emma grouched as Jess counted off the reps. She was flapping her outstretched arms like a big goose getting ready to fly off. She felt like an idiot, but worse, she didn't want to tell Jess the truth that her arms were aching.

"Ninety-eight, ninety-nine, a hundred! Good. You're done." Jess took the cans and put them back in the cupboard.

"I hope you're doing the exercises at home too." Her voice held a warning.

"Well, yeah. I mean, sometimes." Emma hadn't quite met Jess's eyes.

Jess waited.

"Okay. Not every day." Emma rolled her eyes to the ceiling. "I just don't get it. The stupid cans are too light and it's boring to do the same thing over and over."

Jess frowned. "Well, it's like this," she told Emma. "You're a weakling. And I won't have a weakling handling my boat."

"I'm not a weakling," Emma protested, but Jess just gave one of her looks and continued her lecture.

"The best way to build muscle mass that lasts is to do many reps with light weights. Canned soup is perfect for that and your aunt won't ask the questions she would ask if barbells suddenly appeared in your bedroom."

"Okay, okay. But she did ask about the soup cans."

"What did you tell her?"

"I told her it's for a class collection for Africa."

Jess took a bag out of the cupboard under the kitchen sink and filled it with potatoes.

"That's a good answer, except the cans aren't going anywhere. Never mind. You'll figure it out. Here. Sit down. Cross your legs and lift this bag of potatoes with your foot."

Emma did as Jess instructed.

"Umph. That's hard!"

"Exactly my point. You're a weakling! Three sets of twenty." Jess sat down beside Emma and started hefting a similar bag with her foot, counting out loud as she did so. Emma scrambled to keep up.

Now she flexes her arm muscles to warm them up, confident in how strong she is becoming. She does a bunch of stretches to limber up her back and leg muscles. It's dawn when she pokes her head out of the boat to see if anything has changed overnight.

Though she's getting used to sleeping with one ear cocked for any unusual sounds, nothing has awakened her fully in the night so far. But she's always on the alert. Something tells her to always be on her guard. She lifts the anchor, pushes the *Edge* out into deeper water and drops the motor. As she motors slowly out into the river from the little bay where she's hidden for the night she sees there's a crowd of boats already jostling for a spot in front of the lock.

Show time, she thinks, slapping her cap on over her raggedy curls.

So far her luck is holding. No one's overly curious about a boy out fishing, except she should be in school. She knows that in some counties the school year hasn't ended yet and won't end for a few weeks. The question's bound to come up, and she doesn't have an answer completely figured out to explain why she's out puttering around in a boat on a school day.

As she nudges her way into a spot in the crowd of boats, she hears a voice hailing her.

"Hey! Hi. What's your name?" a girl's voice calls out from the boat behind her.

Emma doesn't look back, pretending not to hear, and begins fiddling with some lines on deck. She peers ahead of her wondering if she can pull away and find a new spot but the boat in front of her takes up a lot of room, and another boat has just positioned itself quite snugly in beside it. She's completely boxed in.

"What's your name, you in the red cap?"

Emma reluctantly turns around. "What? You calling me?" She points a finger at her chest.

"Yes, you! What's your name and where are you from?" The girl holds up her notebook. "It's a canal project for school and I'm collecting the names of as many boaties as I can. And where they're from."

"Where they're from?"

"Yeah," the girl nods vigorously, clearly enthusiastic about her project. "And why they're on a sailboat. Are they going somewhere cool? That kind of thing. I'm home-schooled. My mom's teaching me."

"Oh," Emma replies, looking pointedly at one of her blocks, as if inspecting it for wear.

"So?" the girl's pen is poised over the page. "What's your name?"

Emma's stuck. Sure, when you have a name like Emerald Lake

you spend a lot of time making up new names for yourself. But she's never considered boys' names.

"Name's Dennis. Dennis ... uh ...Smith." She covers her hesitation by picking up her work gloves and moving them from starboard to port then back again, and fiddles with the cleats holding the fenders in place. "From Albany. I'm just out fishing."

Stupid, stupid, she thought, grumbling to herself. Darn and double darn. How am I going to get out of this?

The girl just bobs her head and scribbles in her book. When she looks up again, she carries on her cheerful chatter.

"My name's Sally Sanderson and I'm from Toronto, Canada. My parents and I are sailing to the Bahamas for the winter. I'm in grade eight. What grade are you in, and are you out of school for the summer? Or are you home-schooled too? How come you're out here? Are your parents inside the boat? Man, you handle your boat really well."

"Whoa, whoa, whoa!"

"Oh, sorry. I guess I'm babbling."

"One question at a time, okay?" Emma hopes she sounds calm, because inside she's screaming, and there seems to be no way to avoid talking to the girl. She dips her head down so her cap hides her face. Then she remembers what Jess has said over and over. *Always face what you're afraid of.*

She turns to the girl. "It's cool," she says, then dips her head again to adjust her lines. "So, tell me about the canal project. How old are these canals anyway?"

It's all the girl needs to launch into her history report. "Did you know the New York Canal system and the first version of the Erie Canal were completed in 1825 making New York the famous port it is today?" Emma nods without looking up. It seems to be enough to keep the girl happy.

"Yes, because it joined the Great Lakes to the Hudson River. New York City is at the mouth of the Hudson River. But you knew that, course, 'cause you're from here. I can't wait to get to New York City. It's going to be way cool! We're going to see the Empire State Building and..."

The girl talks until the rushing water drowns her out. She doesn't notice that Emma hasn't answered any of her other prying questions.

9. ALONE

THE BOAT IS HEAVING. The wind is howling. For some reason the *Edge* is heeling over on her side. There's a scrapping sound. Then *Bam!* Then the scraping sound again. And *Bam! Bam!* Emma's choking in her sheets, huddled up against the hull, shivering like a scared rabbit.

"Mama...?"

She wakes up. But the storm doesn't stop. It's not a dream.

"What the...?" In seconds she's out of bed and up on deck to check out what's happening, grabbing the flashlight as she goes.

Bam! Bam!

The wind slaps her backward when she emerges from below.

"WHOA!"

She holds on to a lifeline while the boat shudders and jerks beneath her feet. She beams the flashlight all around her and makes out that she's turned around and has been pushed up into the shallows way too close to shore.

She pulls herself up to the bow against the fierce force of the wind and shines the light over the side. The wind has veered 180 degrees around and her anchor line is stretched out backwards under her. The *Edge* is stuck sideways and heeling over, unable to right herself, and bashing up against something hard in the water.

Emma scrambles back to the cockpit and ducks down into the cabin out of the wind to think. She could try to push the

Edge out into deeper water, but what good would that do? It'd be hellishly difficult to manoeuvre in this wind and she'd have to re-anchor, which first means pulling up the anchor which is stuck somewhere behind her now.

Bam! Scrape. Scrape. Emma cringes at the sounds.

"Must be a boulder."

She pictures the bottom of the boat in her mind. The centerboard and the twin rudders are raised so they won't be damaged. It's the hull that's getting a beating and that can be stopped with fenders.

She's figured out a plan. She strips down to her underwear and scrambles back up on deck. She grabs a couple of fenders and drops overboard into the shallow water. With all her strength, she pushes the *Edge* away from the boulder and wedges the fenders between the hull and the stone. Then she ties them off to the nearest stanchion on the deck and wades back to the cockpit. Her legs are coated with weeds and smeared with dirt.

She grabs another fender and shoves it down between some stiff reeds and the side of the *Edge*. Another huge gust of wind slaps the boat back and Emma is knocked over into the water. She comes up sputtering.

"Stop that! Just STOP it!" she yells at the storm and slaps her hands hard down on the water. The resounding crack feels so satisfying.

She climbs back aboard and stands dripping in the cockpit, her feet planted wide apart to brace against the wind. She feels amazing. Powerful. She raises her arms in the air and lets out a loud WAHOO!

"What the heck! It's just wind! It's just a storm! There'll be plenty of these to come and you can't beat me!"

"Do your worst!" she yells to the wind. "Blow your heart out."

She shakes her head at her own wildness, and then something pops into her head—something she remembers from English lit classes … *hubris*, is it? When you tempt the gods?

A shiver runs up her spine. She shrugs it off and hurries down below to find a towel and a dry T-shirt and pajama bottoms. She makes a cup of tea and wraps up in a warm blanket then settles down to wait out the storm.

"HE'S HERE, SIR." Raymond comes to the old man and places a gentle hand on his shoulder to wake him.

"Peter?" the old man asks, and when Raymond nods he reaches for his glasses.

"I'll send him in," Raymond says and turns to leave. At the door he pauses. "Are you sure you want to do this, sir?"

"I have to know how she's doing, Raymond." The old man shakes his head. "How else will I know if I don't have her followed?" He smacks his hand on his thigh for emphasis. "I have to know she's safe."

Raymond nods and leaves the room.

10. DESTINY

THE HOURS TICK BY. Slowly. As the howling wind and incessant waves grind on her nerves Emma thoughts swirl back to the life she's left behind. To the questions she can't answer, like who is she? Who are her parents? Why did she have to go live with her horrible aunt? The mystery of her family leaves a gaping hole inside of her.

The questions pound against her head like the waves pounding against the hull of the boat. What was her father like? Was it true what Aunt Petra said in the lawyer's office, that he was a drug-runner? And what did her mother do that made Aunt Petra so angry and afraid, other than run away with Emma's dad? Who's paying her aunt and uncle to protect her? Isn't that what Mr. Drake said, that they were being paid to be her guardians? How can she ever find out the answers except to go find her mother?

And what about Mr. Flinders? What does HE want and what does it have to do with her? What did Aunt Petra mean? A shiver of apprehension travels up Emma's spine. There is something so out of place about what she overheard in the kitchen only a few weeks ago. The Mr. Flinders she knows is just a stranger. A big deal in the community. Something to do with shipping. And everyone at school says he's rich. But she doesn't *know* him.

A large part of the farm was devoted to strawberries. Emma's job was to stand behind the cash register on weekends during the season. Most everyone in town bought their strawberries from the farm. Including Mr. Flinders. He never picked his own. He always bought one of the baskets ready for the rushed customers or the customers who were just passing by.

The last time she saw him he behaved the same as ever. But he had a stranger with him, some boy a bit older than Emma, and she remembers thinking he must be from somewhere south because he was so tanned, too tanned for springtime in Canada.

"And how's Queen Emerald today?" Mr. Flinders asked sending her a big wink, like he always did. Mr. Flinders made his question seem like a joke they shared. But the joke is on Emma. She doesn't have a clue why he acts like that. And it kind of creeps her out.

"Fine, Mr. Flinders. Anything else?" Emma said, being polite as she could. She hated that he called her Queen Emerald and she always hoped no one heard. Emma had darted a quick look at the boy to see if he'd noticed, since he was the closest person to the counter, but as soon as he caught her looking at him he turned away, almost as if he didn't want to be noticed.

The storm continues to howl and rage. When will it stop?

"Guilty! Guilty! Guilty!" Emma's heart starts to ache, and it takes her a while to calm down again. She feels trapped. There's no escaping the storm. No escaping her thoughts about what she's put into action. Aunt Petra and Uncle Derek will be so angry about what she's done. How will they face the community? Aunt Petra's always so preoccupied by what people think. Now Emma's done the worst thing she can do to them.

Then there's the school. The principal will have been notified. There'll be a blow-up about how it's illegal for a fourteen-year-old to leave school. The police have probably already started searching for her. Someone will have noticed that the *Edge* is gone. It won't take much for them to figure out that Emma has run away—sailed away! And the Coast Guard will be called.

The police will soon begin to wonder what happened and determine how far they should search. When no trace of Emma and the *Edge* is found on the Canadian shores, it's possible they'll start State-side.

Would someone link Emma with a random boy out sailing for the day? If anyone has noticed, would they make the connection? The *Edge* isn't your typical sailboat. What if they hand out a good enough description...?

Emma's breath hitches as fear rears its ugly head. If they find her....

Emma finally gets it. She gets the enormity of what she has done. She can never go back. Never, as long as she lives. She'll never see her aunt and uncle again. She'll be punished and ... it would destroy her. No. She'll never go back.

The rain pelts down hard. Emma tries to go back to sleep but the violent rocking and the howling keep her awake. Her nightmare hovers in the dark waiting for her. The storm. Her mother shouting for her father. She pushes the monster back down, slams the door on it.

But she can't shake the feeling that something will happen any minute and she goes over and over in her mind that she's safe. There's nothing to do but wait out this storm that slashes around her.

There's a sudden CRASH against the hull.

"Aack!" Emma races to the porthole to peer out. She sees a large branch sweep by swirling and whipping past. She huddles back down in the berth. She clutches Jess's goofy cat-shaped pillow against her chest.

"I'm safe. I'm safe," she says over and over. She abandons all effort to get back to sleep and flicks on a light.

She can see signs of Jess's presence everywhere. She snuggles deep under the colourful wool blanket Jess knitted. Wedged securely in small spaces all over the boat are Jess's books and mementoes: a piece of driftwood that looks like a frog, dried seedpods stuffed in a tiny wooden vase.

Emma remembers the plain white bed in her plain white bedroom back at the farm.

"Everything works better if it's clean and neat! Everything has to be in its place!" Aunt Petra would yell as if Emma was deaf. But it didn't work that way for Emma. There were so many rules for her to break, and it seemed that just when she figured some out, new ones got added.

So here she is, in Jess's boat. No, it's her boat, now. To distract herself, Emma pulls down one of Jess's books on sea legends. She opens it and a piece of paper drifts to the floor. She leans down and picks it up. It's an old photo. Dog-eared, very worn. Her hand trembles as she studies it.

There's Jess, looking much younger than Emma ever remembers seeing her. There's a pretty young woman with long hair. And a child. The child's clutching the woman's hand and leaning against Jess. Emma studies the photo carefully. She turns it over. The words "Emma, Peggy and me" are written on the back.

Emma's heart starts hammering in her chest. She's never seen a photo of herself as a child. Never seen what her mother looks like. So, this woman is her mother. They were together. Of course, it makes sense. But together with Jess? How could Emma have met Jess and not remembered? This must have been what Jess meant about the last time they were together. Before she was brought to live with her aunt and uncle.

More unanswerable questions start to swarm into her head. Tears well up and she wants to scream out her frustration. Instead she squeezes her eyes shut, listens to the rain rattling on the deck above her head.

After a while she gets up and pulls out the letter Jess left her, reads the newspaper clipping again. As she reads, she fingers the small purple stone Jess gave her on her thirteenth birthday. At last she can wear it openly. At least at night when other boaters won't see. She could never wear it at the farm and had kept it carefully hidden from her aunt. Amethyst, Jess had said. A stone for dreaming. She reads again how her mother was last seen in Mayaguana before she disappeared. When Emma had looked it up in the school library, she'd discovered it was the last inhabited island of the Bahamas archipelago that stretches 1500 miles out into the Atlantic Ocean. How will she ever make it there? The trip seems so daunting. Overwhelming. What makes her think she can DO this? Here she is cowering while she's pummelled by a storm and she's only on a measly river.

Her thoughts drift back to Jess, their random meeting. It was Jess who convinced her to go back to the farm with the promise she could return to visit her anytime. What if it wasn't such a random meeting after all?

Why didn't Jess ever tell her she was her granddaughter? What stopped her from saying anything? Something feels all wrong. A jittery thought creeps into her mind that Jess and Aunt Petra and Uncle Derek had all agreed to keep her in the dark. That Aunt Petra must have known she was visiting her grandmother, and that it was okay as long as Jess didn't say anything. As long as all she did was treat her like any ordinary visitor.

It was Jess who showed Emma that a home could be lovely, and that it could include colour and messiness, stones and driftwood collected from the beach, reclaimed wool in baskets ready for knitting into sweaters, and books piled everywhere. And a sweet old cat who leaves hairs on the couch.

"Whiskers!" Emma sits bolt upright, appalled that she hasn't given Jess's cat a thought until now. "What happened to Whiskers?"

She throws off the blanket in a rush, reaching for her hoodie, her jeans.

"STOP!" She's bare-footed, standing in the centre of the cabin.

"What am I doing?" She holds the jeans in one hand, her sweatshirt in the other, out in front of her as if to ask how they got into her hands.

"What am I doing!" she yells at the storm. The agitation that spurred her out of the berth drains out of her and she's limp with a kind of confusion that makes her head spin.

"Who looked after Jess's cat? Who organized Jess's funeral?" Emma's head begins to ache again. It drives her crazy that she doesn't have answers to the questions whirling inside her. She crawls back into her cozy berth and covers herself with the blanket again.

The hours continue their slow passage.

"I'm truly alone." The thought threatens to swamp her, and her heart sinks like a stone. But as soon as that sinking starts, she has another thought. A startling thought. It comes out of nowhere, like a quiet calm voice deep inside of her, buoying her up like a life jacket.

And that other thought is this: *What if I'm part of everything around me? What if I'm part of the birds that are sheltering from the storm, and the black night sky, and this wind that's howling, and the water I'm floating on, and the trees on the shore? Maybe Jess is part of everything too. Even now. What if she's right here with me on this adventure?*

She has no clue where the thought comes from. And it's followed just as freshly by another one: *What if everything that is happening is happening for a reason?*

Emma takes one of the deep breaths that have helped calm her in the past.

I ran away because there is something I need to do. And that thing is this: I need to find out what happened to my mother.

And with that last thought, something inside of Emma stops and becomes very still. It's as if Jess has reached out and put a hand on her shoulder and said, YES!

II. THE SONG FOUND

11. ALMOST CAUGHT

LOG ENTRY: *June 13, 2014, 8:30 a.m. Next leg Little Falls to Fort Hunter. Lock 11 on the Erie Canal.*
Emma leaves Little Falls about nine thirty, after finding the filter clogged with muck. The motor runs smoothly now. The lift lock at Little Falls is very impressive. The lift raises above her head and rains water down on her as she passes under it. The water in the lock empties so fast it's like a mini Niagara Falls on the other side.

Out of the blue, the Lockmaster asks to see a few passes. Emma freaks out. She doesn't have a backup plan if anyone asks. But luck's with her.

"You single-handed, young fella?"

"Yes sir!" Emma holds up the lines she's holding in both hands, to show she's got her boat secure and under control.

"You got your pass?"

"Yessir! I got a pass, but... " she nods with her head towards the cabin.

"Okay. I don't want to make you let go yer lines to get it." He tugs on his earlobe, considering her.

"I'll jus' take yer word for it. 'Sides the locks open in a minute." He waves a hand to point.

"Just remember, young fella', ever'n we find out ya' ain't got a pass we'll keep you in our lock til'en ya' git un. Hear now?"

When Emma nods, he shakes his finger at her.

"I'm gonna call ahead to the next lock. You have your pass ready, hear?"

Emma tips her head to show she's understood and then moves on through the lock out into the Mohawk River, which is part of the Erie Canal system.

Slowly she formulates a plan. She's going to hide out for a day or two before going on to the next lock. She figures by the time she gets to the next lock, the lockmaster will have forgotten. This is the first time anyone has asked for a pass. Even the other boaters seemed surprised. This guy's the exception, she decides.

She's champing at the bit to get going. But she can't take the risk of having to show a pass. So she bides her time. All her years spent on the farm have taught her patience and she finds things to occupy her while she's waiting for the days to pass.

She finds paper and pens tucked in one of the bookshelves. She used to sketch all the time in grade school. Her teachers praised her to the sky. But Aunt Petra didn't let her take art in high school and she wasn't allowed to do any art at home. Aunt Petra said it was a waste of time when she had other real school work and chores to do.

Emma has no camera, and she decides the sketches will be her record of this trip. She decides to sketch whenever she can because there's no one to stop her now. She likes doing it and it makes her feel good. She'd forgotten how much she enjoys it.

The river meanders under bridges and overpasses. It's strange to be the one in the boat being waved at by kids in cars. Her highway is the water, theirs is the road.

River barges pass her, slowly chugging along. There are the small ones, and ones that look like tugboats. And larger ones with old fashioned rope fenders. They're working away cutting trees and clearing away storm debris. She drops anchor to take a pee. Since she's stopped anyway, she makes quick sketches in her logbook.

For a while she's accompanied by a pretty hawk. She holds up her sketches to the sky as if it could see.

"Hey Aunt Petra! Even a hawk likes my sketches." As if to confirm, the hawk swoops down showing its white belly, brown and black wing feathers, then flies off.

She listens to the weather report. A cold front is coming in and the weatherman blames it on Canada, calling it a high pressure area out of James Bay. It feels funny to be blamed for weather.

That night she stops in a quiet cove in a wooded part of the river. The rains come and she's glad she's going to lay low for a while. She cleans the cabin, reads, waits. She pulls out *Chapman's Piloting and Seamanship*, a heavy tome Jess calls the boater's bible. She pretends that it's homework and she's studying for a test. This whole trip is going to be a test now. One she doesn't want to fail. She starts with Chapter One, *Boating Basics*.

Emma unearths the many notes Jess made in preparation for what looks like her own trip to the Bahamas. Did she already take this trip once, Emma wonders? Right across an old road map of the Eastern seaboard and Caribbean, Jess has written in capital letters: HURRICANE SEASON—JULY TO NOVEMBER. STAY NORTH OF NEW YORK CITY UNTIL SEPTEMBER.

Emma considers what she's just read in *Chapman's*. She's never thought about hurricanes before. If she goes south too fast, she'll be in the hurricane zone. It means hanging out in the northern part of the States for the whole summer. But that puts her close to Lake Ontario, and it means she'll have to stay out of sight as much as possible in case someone is looking for her and the *Edge*. But she's not going to risk a hurricane. She tells herself she'll figure it out.

She waits it out for three days and then she heads back out into river traffic again. Her prediction holds up. None of the other lockmasters ask for her pass. One by one, she makes her way through the locks of the canal. It's cool how the locks all raise the boats until, at a certain point, they start lowering the boats. She realizes she's gone over a mountain range and down the other side.

And the day comes when the final locks are right in front of her—the Waterford Flight. Five locks that join the Mohawk River to the Hudson River at Waterford. It's a one hundred and fifty-foot drop from the uppermost lock to the bottom lock. As she enters the first lock, the lockmaster warns the boats that there's no stopping in the Flight. A boater has to do all five locks in one fell swoop.

Emma stands in the cockpit of her boat holding onto the lines that secure her to the lock's walls, waiting for the water to lower. She can see the locks ahead of her stretched out like a gigantic set of stairs facing downward.

She studies the boats in the lock with her. There are sailboats and trawlers of varying sizes and shapes, some new, some older, each one a home for their owners, even if only for a little while. The weather has turned incredibly beautiful. Now that the storms have blown over, the sun is shining brightly, warming the weary boaters.

Passengers who aren't doing the lock-work are sunning themselves and chatting. Many are complaining of the storm that caused so much havoc: objects flying off boats, fenders and lines being loosened and letting go. One boat lost its mooring and crashed into the boat behind it. The drama of the stories makes for good sharing while the slow process of lowering the boats through the locks gets underway.

"I can't understand which way to face when I'm in the locks, can you?" An older woman in the next boat calls to Emma, raising her arms and looking vaguely forward and backward at the lines. She's on the bow of a double decker motor yacht that towers over Emma.

Emma just shrugs and tries to appear nonchalant. She doesn't want to start a conversation.

"And everything is so dirty. So filthy. I hate it!"

The woman keeps talking but Emma can barely hear her over the rush of the water. She needs to concentrate on what she's doing. She simply nods her head at whatever the woman is saying. Finally, the woman turns to another boating family who give her the attention or distraction she needs.

Still, the woman is right. It's going to be great to get rid of the filthy gloves and strip the tattered slimy coverings off the fenders. She herself could use a good shower rather than the quick dips she's been taking in shallow water in the various bays where she's anchored at night. Most of the locks are set up with great showers and washrooms. But she can't go into the women's showers looking like a boy and she's sure not going into the men's.

As soon as Emma passes through the gates of the last lock, she motors away from the crowd and puts some distance between her and the other boaters before pulling out of the main river traffic into a small creek for the night. There's rain coming. AGAIN.

The good weather didn't last long, she sighs. She can hear loud thunder rolling in the distance. It sounds just like the saying "angels playing bowling balls in heaven." She hurries to get settled for the night before the storm hits.

But her great intentions aren't all that easy to fulfill. At first, she drops anchor too close to shore. It's clear that if the wind shifts she'll be bashing up against whatever rocks or logs that are buried along the shoreline. She has to haul it up and try again. She drops it a bit further into the middle of the creek and realizes she'll block any boats going past if she swings in the night. There's a strong current, but that can work against her if she gets blown sideways against the current.

She studies the shore. It's wooded, pine trees mixed with bushes and lots of undergrowth. She decides she can tie her stern off to a tree. She makes sure her anchor is well set by backing down on it with the motor, then quickly changes into shorts. Taking a line with her, she swims ashore and scrambles through the bushes.

She ties the line to a sturdy tree trunk and swims back to the boat to tie it off to a stern cleat. Slowly she tightens the stern line at the same time as she lets off the anchor line, so her stern is pulled close to shore but not too close. And now she's tied off, she won't swing into anything unexpectedly. She's happy with her spot. Her home is secure for the night.

She congratulates herself on her good work. It's the first time she's tied off fore and aft, a kind of tricky thing to pull off. It occurs to her that she figured it out instinctively. As if she had the knowledge stored somewhere inside of her. It sure wasn't from reading *Chapman's* that she learned this. She hasn't gotten far enough along for that.

But her mother was a sailor. And her grandmother too. Is it possible that sailing is in her DNA? The thought makes her happy.

About two hours later the itching starts. She's been dozing in her berth and she catches herself scratching at her arms and chest. She sits bolt upright and flicks on a light lifting the sheets and checking for something that's biting her. There's nothing. But the itching is worse.

She strips off her T-shirt and discovers that her chest is covered with sores. She gets Jess's first aid book out and looks up rashes. It doesn't take long to figure out she has a case of poison oak! Arrgh! She rummages in the cupboards and finds an old bottle of calamine lotion and spreads the pink liquid on her sores.

Overhead the thunder begins its cacophonous roar and the rain clouds open. RUMBLE RUMBLE RUMBLE. At least there's no lightening. She settles in for a dreary, itchy, sleepless night.

12. ROBBED

EMMA'S LAID UP just outside of Troy with the nasty rash for almost a week. When she's finally ready to go, she plans to make it to the next town in the Hudson River before raising her mast and setting up her sails. But when she looks carefully at the gas tank, she realizes it's lower than she likes. She decides she better fill up now rather than take a chance.

She turns the *Edge* around and motors back to the dock, tying up to the wall next to the gas pump. The attendant comes out to give her a hand with the lines, but she's pretty much done by the time he offers his help. She's getting expert at tying up single-handed and she's pretty smug about it.

"What can I do for you, son?" he asks cheerfully.

"Could ya' fill up my spare tank and fill the main tank too. Thanks." Emma hands him her spare tank and jumps back into her boat to get her money pouch, which she pulls out from inside the chart table and climbs back onto the dock.

She extracts a wad of twenty-dollar bills and a couple of hundreds fall out at the same time, fluttering onto the wood. She catches them in the nick of time, bending down fast to pick them up but her loose shirt flops up. She yanks the shirt down, holding it close to her chest. She hopes nothing showed. She didn't put on a T-shirt because of the itchy blisters and sores.

She doesn't notice the skinny man, slumped in a nearby motorboat, till later. But when she finishes paying for the gas, she feels a prickling along the back of her neck. He's eyeing her when she glances over at him, but he quickly averts his eyes, pretends to be digging for something in his cooler.

Emma thanks the gas attendant and pops below decks to put the pouch inside again and then unties the *Edge* and casts off. It's late afternoon. She doesn't go far but is pleased when she finds a good place to anchor for the night.

She's in the cockpit tidying up lines and taking a few minutes of the remaining daylight to remove the filthy covers off the fenders when she hears the sound of the engine approaching. It's a boat coming directly toward her.

She waits, listening carefully. She has a sudden sense of foreboding. In a short time, she can see it clearly and she recognizes the dishevelled man who was at the gas pump. She didn't like the look of him at the time and was thankful to leave him behind. He must have followed her.

He comes closer and closer. She catches a glimpse of something in his face. A shiftiness. A hardness. But then she sees him put a smile on his face.

"Hello, little girl. How're you doing?" His voice is raspy.

A chill shoots up Emma's spine. If he thinks she's a boy then he's being insulting and he's trying to get a rise out of her. If he knows somehow that she's a girl, she's going to have to be very smart. She sits very still and fixes her eyes on his face.

The man moves his boat alongside of the *Edge* and put his hands on the gunnel. He isn't as old as Emma had first thought. Maybe only in his twenties.

He leaves his engine humming in neutral. Emma feels a ripple of fear travel up her spine. Her eyes dart to the winch handle in its cubbyhole, but it's out of reach. Her hand closes more tightly on the fender as she continues to pull the filthy cover off it. "Do for you, mister?" she asks.

"Oh nothing. Nothing. Just want to say hi is all."

Emma notices he's staring below decks.

"What's a pretty little thing like you doing out here all alone?"

She sees that his hands on the side of the boat are trembling. Even his arms are trembling, like he's shivering. But it's not cold out.

Emma takes a deep breath as she feels the fear pump through her veins. He looks sick. He looks weird. She let the air out of her lungs gustily. "Nice night," she says tugging hard at the cloth. Suddenly the material rips in two and the soaking sludge-covered hunk of cloth is in her right hand.

At that very moment the man makes a sharp movement. He pulls a gun from his waistband and points it at her. Emma's whole body jerks at the sight. Her heart starts to pump hard and her mind races.

"Yeah, sure. Nice night for giving me your money. I saw your pouch. And I see it now. On the table there. Now go get it and I'll leave you alone." He growls the words. His hand holding the gun is shaking, but he bares his teeth as he cocks his chin in the direction of the cabin.

In the distance Emma can hear another boat motor coming close. The man hears it too.

"Hurry up!" he barks. "Give it to me NOW!" He nearly screams it.

He's not going to shoot her. She just knows it, somewhere in her gut. Otherwise he'd have done it. He's as scared as she is. He's sick, very sick. Probably from drugs by the looks of it.

And in that split second, Emma makes a choice. She ducks into the cabin and grabs the pouch. When she comes back up she rushes at him.

"Here! Take it. Now GET OUT OF HERE!"

The man grabs the pouch from her and stuffs it down his pants. But he sways awkwardly. Emma sees her chance. She lunges at him, shoving the slimy cloth she's still holding straight into his face. The move topples him off-balance, so he falls back into his boat and the gun spins out of his hand into the water. She turns and reaches for her portable VHF radio holding it up so he can see.

"GET OUT OF HERE!" she yells at the top of her lungs. "NOW! Or I'll call the coast guard!"

She can't call the coast guard, but he doesn't know it.

"GO!" she screams at him again. "Get to a hospital. You're sick! Sick! Now GO!"

The man stares at her from where he's fallen on his back dazed, disoriented. Emma pins him with her glare. And then a strange thing happens. His face crumples.

"Sick," he repeats shakily from the bottom of the boat.

"Need help," he says almost to himself, his voice very faint. He gets to his seat, revs his motor and speeds away just as the other boat chugs closer.

It's an older gentleman and his wife. They stare at the skinny man as he passes by and then motor up closer to Emma and wave at her curiously.

"Nice night out," they call not as they pass.

She nods and waves back, then sits down on one of the seats and begins cleaning up the mess left by the filthy fenders as if nothing happened. She keeps her head down hoping they'll just leave her alone. They motor on, their curiosity over the commotion seemingly satisfied. She's glad they didn't notice how hard she was breathing.

As the sound disappears, Emma stops pretending. Her legs and arms start to shake and she lets them. She lets the shock work its way through her body. She can't make out if she did a stupid thing or a brave thing, but it feels like she just passed a major test of some sort.

When she starts to get chilled she goes down into the cabin and wraps a blanket around her shoulders. The shock shakes her some more, but she focuses on her breathing. Before she curls up on her bunk, she pulls up the corner of the mattress and checks on a plastic container down deep in the food locker. She pushes it deeper into the shadows. It holds all her money. She'd only left a couple of tens in the pouch.

13. ONE BLACK PEBBLE

EMMA WAKES THE NEXT MORNING with the sun full on her face. It's a complete surprise to her that she's slept so late because she's been rising at dawn since she was a young girl. Her farm chores always had to be done before breakfast. Since she started this boat trip, she's been so determined to get away and make it through the locks that she hasn't even considered sleeping in. She blinks her eyes and swipes a hand over her face. She feels sticky and smelly.

Yesterday's events come flooding back. What an experience! What was she thinking, rushing at that sick guy like that and pushing the gun out of his hand as if she was some kind of super-hero?

She rolls out of her berth and climbs the steps, out into the blinding heat of the day. And comes face to beak with a big gull perched on her motor. It flaps its wings and squawks loudly at her, startling her completely awake and scaring her half to death so she stumbles backward and lets out a loud "Whoa!"

The bird takes off, leaving her stunned on the deck. Her blood is pumping now. When she calms down again, she takes stock of her surroundings and it hits her. She's made it to the Hudson River! One part of the journey completed.

The sun beats down on her. It's going to be a scorcher; summer has arrived with a vengeance. She stretches her arms over her head and yawns. Then looking around to make sure there's no one's close, she strips and dives into the water stark naked.

The water's just getting warm and it feels like silk on her itchy skin. Delicious! She strikes out with a strong crawl in the direction of the far shore. She's going to have a real swim, not just the quick dips she's been allowing herself so far. This is a full out play-in-the-water episode. She stops and floats on her back for a while, admiring the bright blue of the sky. Then she plows forward again, swimming fast and hard until her shoulders ache. Finally, she turns around and does the backstroke all the way back to the side of the boat.

It's time to raise the mast and set up the rigging and sails. She has work to do.

THE HUDSON RIVER HAS A TOTALLY different character from the Erie Canal. It's wider and much busier, with shipping and the fast traffic of everyday boaters who are going from town to town by river of instead of road. A kind of boating super highway.

With the mast up she unfurls the jib whenever the winds are going her way. But she's disappointed that the heavy traffic and the many sudden bends in the river make it difficult to go for a sail. So, mostly she motors.

Once she took a chance and put out both sails just to get the thrill of the lift of wind power. But immediately the wind started to come from all over the place because of the high cliffs around her. She had to tighten and loosen the sails constantly and it was too difficult to steer with one hand and adjust the sails with her other.

As she motors along, she notices turrets and towering roofs of mansions peeking through the trees. They look like castles. In fact, she realizes, they are castles! What are castles doing on a river in America? It's like a whole other kind of world than the one she's used to.

She passes lighthouses that look like old Victorian houses stranded on islands in the middle of the river. Emma can't imagine how they're still standing. She makes more quick sketches in her logbook.

Finding secluded anchorages is getting harder. Private boat docks dot the shoreline. And even though her retractable centerboard makes it easy for her to tuck in close to shore, she often feels she's too close to people. She's nervous about being questioned, and she's worried she'll forget she's disguised as a boy and do something that draws attention to her.

"Hey, sailor!" A friendly couple in their dingy hail her. As they motor toward her she flies into a panic. She starts to veer away before she stops herself and slows down to let them to approach.

"Just so you know, there's a shifting sandbank." They point in the direction she's going. "It extends way beyond the marks on the chart. You're better to go on to Kingston and anchor under the second bridge. You'll see it. There'll be other boats there. Take care."

They wave and putter away in their dinghy. She tells herself her nervousness is getting out of hand, but it takes her a while to calm down.

She finds her way into Kingston following their warnings about going the wrong side of Coxsackie Island. It's funny to be spending the night in a town with the same name as the town she's left behind in Canada. Of course, there's no one share this curious coincidence with. It makes her lonely, so she pushes it from her mind.

She takes a chance to go into town for a carton of fresh milk curious to see what this other Kingston looks like. Long-life milk doesn't taste the same as fresh milk. And she wants to spoil herself with some bread, too. She's getting tired of crackers.

She still has plenty of the American cash that Jess left for her in the envelope. Thank goodness! She wonders what she'll do when the money runs out. She hasn't figured it out but tries not to worry about it. She hopes she'll be far enough away from Canada to not attract attention when she has to go to a bank to change her Canadian dollars.

Emma ties up at a little rickety dock some distance from a series of brand new expensive private docks. It's run down, but a sign says, "Town Dock, Free Mooring". She locks up the boat and follows one of the windy paths up-hill. When she gets to the top she sees what looks like the entrance to someone's house. There's a gate and beside it a small stone gatehouse.

"Can I help you?" A man dressed in a cap and uniform steps out.

She hesitates, and then decides she can't ignore him. "What's this place?"

"The Vanderbilt's summer estate." He frowns at her and she realizes how ragged she must look. She rarely combs her hair and that morning she hasn't showered or bathed.

"Can you tell me which way to the nearest grocery store?"

The man points down the road.

"Won't be open on Sunday though."

Dang, Emma thinks. She's lost track of days.

"But the gas station has a store," he adds. A phone begins to ring and he steps back inside the gatehouse to answer.

Emma finds the gas station and collects her bread and a carton of milk. While she's waiting in line she picks up a neighbourhood newspaper. The stories are all local. Names like Stuyvesant, Willemsen, and de Witt dot the pages. She recognizes that they're all Dutch. Her own name, Visser, is Dutch. Even Vanderbilt's a Dutch name. And Roosevelt, now that she thinks of it. That's Dutch too. Her uncle told her once that their family had emigrated from Holland when her uncle and father were just boys. When Emma started asking him more questions about her father, Aunt Petra put an end to the conversation.

"Lots of Dutch names here," She says to the check-out lady as she pays for her groceries.

"Yup. This was all settled by the Dutch. Back in the 1600s." She starts to put Emma's things in a plastic bag but Emma stops her, indicating that she'd rather use her backpack.

"I work part-time up at the museum, so I have to know this stuff. You visiting?"

Emma realizes she's made a mistake in talking to this lady and now she's stuck. She can't be rude. She scrambles for an answer.

"Yes, um … yes."

"Well, you should go see the museum while you're here. Who're ya' visiting? I know most everyone in town."

There's an awkward silence. Emma chokes on the question. She's about to make up something random when the door swings open. It's a boy, blond, very tanned, about Emma's age. He jolts suddenly when he sees Emma, then spins on his heel and walks out the door.

Weird, thinks Emma.

Grateful for the distraction, she quickly finishes stuffing her groceries in her backpack and says goodbye.

Once outside she grumbles to herself. At least she didn't have to make up some sort of story for the cashier. But she makes a promise to herself to get some reasonable story together for the next time the question comes up. As she knows it will. And she's got to stop acting like she's running from something. She wonders again about the boy who sped away when he saw her at the cash. Why'd he do that? And why did he look vaguely familiar?

She doesn't notice the perfectly round, small, black pebble sitting on the starboard seat right away. When she does notice it, she doesn't think about how it got there. She simply tosses it overboard.

14. HUNTED

EMMA NOTICES HERSELF CHANGING. Her confidence in her boating skills grows over the summer months living on the water. And she's changing in other ways too. She sees it in the mirror. She's becoming someone she doesn't recognize. She's not the girl who ran away in June. Her skin is as brown as a smooth plank of wood. Her cheeks are angular and lean, and her arms are strong.

She's likes her boy-look and makes sure to keep her hair cut short. When she has to get off the boat for gas or groceries or whatever, she always wears one of Jess's denim shirts with the sleeves rolled up and a ball-cap. She walks with kind of a swagger, which is how she imagines boys walk. She keeps her voice low and doesn't smile when she talks to anyone.

But in spite of this new-found confidence in her abilities and her disguise, something more than nervousness starts to creep into her thoughts and dreams that eats away at her. Something insidious. Something hard to control. She becomes filled with the certainty that someone's looking for her.

She can't pinpoint when she's started to feel this way. It just kind of sneaks up on her. It begins to haunt her. She starts to pay careful attention to how people look at her. Are they studying her face? Are they measuring her against some picture on a missing persons poster?

She develops a kind of reactive behaviour to people. What

was once only skittishness, becomes a kind of paranoia. If a dinghy passes too close to the boat, she hurries inside and closes the hatch, even if it's blisteringly hot out. From inside she watches until they've passed, peering out at them through the porthole. She scans boats at anchor through her binoculars to see if someone is watching her, observing her back. When she notices a familiar boat, someone she's seen at other anchorages, she studies them closely to find out if they could possibly be seeking her. She's constantly on the lookout for anything suspicious.

One evening when she's just cleaning up after dinner, she hears a knocking on the hull. It sends her scrambling to a porthole, heart racing, trying to see who's there. When the knocking happens again, and again, and again, she grabs a knife and charges up on deck. No one there. She recalls the ducks nibbling scum off the hull back in the Erie Canal and peers over the side of the boat. She sees a branch that's been swept down river and gotten caught on her anchor line. She feels like an idiot, but her heart is pounding hard. Get a grip, she tells herself, but it doesn't help. She doesn't like the fear, but there seems to be nothing she can do to control it.

At the same time paranoia takes over her life, she becomes obsessed with the need to know what happened after she escaped the farm. If she can just find out, maybe she can free herself from all this worrying and suspicion. The tension between needing to hide and needing to know what happened is exhausting. When her obsession wins, it pushes her out of hiding, like a hand on the middle of her back.

One day her obsession draws her over to the boat of a trawler couple who are buying gas. A huge Canadian flag hangs off the flagstaff. The name of their boat is written in fancy letters on the stern—the *Y-Knot* from Kingston, Ontario. Her home town. They're whispering to the attendant and as Emma feels their curious eyes fall on her, she realizes she's been staring. She looks quickly away, pretends to study something on her mast.

Her edginess is outweighed by the fact that these folks might know something. When they're done paying for the gas and are back on their boat, she approaches them. She squares her shoulders and strolls past the trawler. Pauses.

"From Ontario?" she asks the man on the bridge casually, pointing at the name.

"Yup." He's an older man. He lifts his eyes from behind the wheel where he's fiddling with some knobs on the instrument panel.

"You?" He flashes her a friendly smile, ready for some chitchat.

"No," Emma steps back and shakes her head vigorously. Maybe too vigorously. She tones it down.

"My cousin is, though." She shrugs a shoulder. "I heard something weird about her being missing. You haven't heard anything about a missing girl have you?"

"Harry? Who're you talking to?" a woman calls pops her head up from below. "Oh, hello. What's that you were saying? Someone's missing?" The big woman climbs up the steps and sits herself down heavily on one of the plastic seats.

"Her cousin's missing," the man says, and goes back to his fiddling.

"Where'd you say she's from?" The woman fans herself lazily with the cleaning cloth she's holding in her hand. She's ready for a good old chat.

Darn, thinks Emma, her nervousness growing again.

"It's nothing. Nothing. Probably made a mistake." She tips her cap down and turns to leave.

"Harry, where'd we see that news?"

The woman's words stop Emma cold.

"Was it in the *Kingston Whig?* About that young girl missing with her sailboat in Lake Ontario?"

Emma turns slowly.

"Harry! You read it to me!" the woman snaps. Harry looks up at her and frowns. Then he looks over at Emma and shrugs.

"I forget. Sorry," he says.

"Think! Way back in the early summer." The woman eyes her husband then gives a huff, clearly annoyed. She turns to Emma again. "How old did you say your cousin is?" She levers herself slowly up from the seat and goes back down the steps without waiting for an answer.

"Just a minute."

Emma hears her rummaging around. She comes back up with a big bag overflowing with newspapers. Emma almost salivates with eagerness to dig through them for anything at all that might mention her. The woman starts shuffling through the bag.

"We've been on the boat all summer, but we get our mail sent to us from time to time. We got a load of mail back in Albany." The woman struggles to lift the overfull bag up onto the seat beside her. "For gawd's sake, Harry. Give me a hand!"

Her husband comes to help but before he can reach her the bag bursts. Papers fly everywhere, picked up by a sudden gust of wind. There's a mad dash as all three of them grab at the pieces before they sink, but most of the papers are sodden when they scoop them out of the water.

"Jeez, Harry. What a mess!" the woman barks, blaming her husband even though he's not responsible for the mess.

With a sigh Harry goes below and comes back with a black garbage bag, starts stuffing the soggy mess into it.

"So, your cousin's from Kingston, is she?" His face is bland, but he eyes Emma sharply.

Emma's ready to bolt, but she meets his stare. "No. She … she's from Toronto. I guess that's not close to Kingston, is it? I've never been."

"It's close enough," the woman interrupts. "But the newspaper certainly wouldn't confuse the two." She moves closer to Emma and sits down at the table under the shade of the canvas bimini, fanning herself. "You want to come on board and have some juice or something?"

She's studying Emma too now. Emma's edginess rears up on its hind legs.

"Thanks, but I've gotta get back. The folks are waiting for the groceries, 'n all." She tips her cap. "Have a good day." She strolls back to the *Edge*. Slowly. Even though she wants to run.

As she unties the lines from the dock and motors away she feels the hairs on the back of her neck prickle. She felt sure the man had been looking at her oddly, like he didn't buy one word of what she'd said.

ONCE AGAIN, EMMA TUCKS BACK into the small, secluded anchorage where she's been staying for the past few days. Private little coves are getting harder and harder to find on the Hudson River but she needs the solitude. It's the only time she feels safe. It won't be long now before hurricane season's over and it'll be okay to start heading south in earnest. But for now, she stays out of sight as much as possible.

She plays over in her head what the couple said. So, there was news of a missing girl. In an old newspaper. Of course, there was. News is what sells newspapers, her social studies teacher told her. Any story that has adventure and disaster and possible gossip will be in the newspaper. But old news isn't news any more. She's old news.

She repeats those words over and over to herself.

"I'm old news. No one cares about me anymore. No one's looking for me now."

She goes back to her daily routines. She's been keeping track of small chores, noting things down in the logbook like: *Checked batteries, water's good, July 12, 2002*, or like: *Cleaned scum off bottom of the boat, August 23, 2002*. She's doing it to remind herself later because she's noticed that time on the boat seems to pass at a different speed. It feels as if she's leaving a note for herself, or as if she's talking to her future self. Some people might think it's weird, but it just feels like good business to her.

The morning after her conversation with the couple from Ontario, she's cleaned the boat. She's got some laundry hanging on the lifelines: T-shirts, her one pair of jeans. She checks the fuel lines to the motor and finds a loose bolt that needs tightening. She's just finishing up giving the head a wipe down after greasing the pump when she hears the sound of a motor coming close. Too close. She gets ready to grab the hatch and shut herself inside.

"Ahoy. Boat at anchor in Kreeley Bay. Permission to come aboard." The voice is coming through a megaphone.

Emma freezes.

"Ahoy. Permission to come aboard," the voice is louder. The boat is almost on her.

She can't hide now. She shoots out of cabin into the blinding sun grabbing her cap and throwing on a shirt over her tank top. She buttons up quickly as she squints at the approaching boat and what she sees makes her heart leap out of her chest.

It's the U.S. Coast Guard!

She's speechless. She watches with absolute dread as the boat powers toward her. Three men and one woman stand at attention. They're wearing flak jackets and in the holsters at their hips Emma sees the butts of guns.

They motor over to her and take their time rafting up with her boat.

"Y ... y ... yes?" Emma stammers. She wonders if she is as white as a ghost. She reaches out for the line one of the men is holding to her. She ties their boat to hers as she knows he is expecting.

"Routine check for safety devices. Permission to come aboard," the first one of the group asks again, though it is clearly not a request, but an order.

"Safety devices?" She feels the breath come back into her body.

"Floatation, flares, regulation stickers." The man stands at attention in the cockpit, waiting. Emma realizes he's waiting for her to show him her safety gear.

"Okay. Be right back."

She ducks back into the cabin and quickly stuffs the precious photo of Jess, her mother and herself under a tea towel. Then she brings out the safety harness, the flares, and the life preservers. In her neat-as-a-pin boat it takes no time to locate everything they ask for. When they come below, she shows them where the fire extinguishers are hanging.

The man checks the dates on the flares and passes the box back to her.

"Regulation sticker for disposal of oil?"

"What?"

He repeats, a touch of annoyance in his voice, as if he's used to this. His face is stern. There's no joking.

"For disposing of your diesel fuel. You have to have the sticker displayed. It's the rules." His frown deepens.

"But I don't have a diesel engine." She points to her outboard motor.

The man looks at Emma and over to the outboard. Then he beams widely. "Just wanted to check if you know what you're doing." He turns back to his colleagues who give him the thumbs up.

"This was a training session. Thanks for helping." He tips his head to her and climbs back over the side of the boat onto his boat.

The woman undoes the line attaching their boat to Emma's. "Nice day. Be safe out there," she says.

Emma stands very still until they've sped out of view and then slowly lowers herself onto the nearest seat. She can't believe what just happened. She leans her head back to let the sun warm her cold, cold face.

15. MOURNING

IT TAKES HER TWO MORE WEEKS to reach Nyack, a town just north of New York City. There are no other quiet anchorages this close to the big metropolis. The sprawl spreads north and fills the shore with houses, businesses, factories and warehouses. She uses some more of her precious dollars for a mooring ball at the marina.

Overnight the weather changes, and the air that morning has a sharp bite. The sky's clear and there's a cold breeze picking up. It's autumn. She can stop dawdling now, she tells herself. She gives herself a pep talk. Hurricane season must be winding down. She wants to get going. She wants to start on her way to the mouth of the Hudson River and the ocean. Doesn't she?

Jess's charts are clear. From Nyack she'll have to cross the bay to get over to Sandy Hook marina on the New Jersey shore. She'll be sailing right through New York harbour, past the Statue of Liberty all in one go. From Sandy Hook the long voyage down the coast to Florida will begin.

"I'm ready, I'm ready, I'm ready," she repeats as she leans over the bow of her boat and unties the line attached to the ball. She zips back to the stern of the boat to take the wheel and steer out into the river.

Once she's out of the protection of the bay, the wind is much stronger than she'd thought it was. A sudden gust flicks her cap off. She whips the boat around immediately and leans over to grab the cap before it gets sucked beneath the waves, but she's too late. She hurries to get the boat hook. No use. By the time she circles back again, the beloved red cap has sunk out of sight. Gone forever.

She brings the boat back on course, but in a few minutes of motoring against the wind and the growing waves, she starts to worry. It's not looking like it's a good day to try to sail across the bay to New Jersey. She makes a snap decision to return the mooring ball at Nyack and ride out the storm that's obviously picking up. She veers the boat around and heads back to where she came from just in time to see her ball claimed by another sailboat.

Darn! Maybe if she reasons with the man. She motors over close enough to hail him.

"Um. That was my ball last night. This wind…" She gestures to the sky. "…Kinda want to stay here again tonight." She smiles and nods as if he's already agreed.

"No way!" He shakes his head, eyes focused on the ball he's picking up. "Sorry buddy, you left it." He flicks a glance over his shoulder at the woman at the helm. "My wife can't stand this wind!" He jogs back to the cockpit of his boat, ending the conversation.

Finders keepers, Emma reminds herself. She'd have done the same. Still, it doesn't make her happy. She turns the *Edge* back out into the river. The waves are slapping against the hull and the wind is blowing hard. She kicks up the rpms, glad she has such a powerful outboard.

At the Tappen Zee Bridge she shoots a quick look up to see if there are any jumpers. The bridge is known for its suicides, according to Jess's guidebook. It makes her feel kind of creepy. She hurries under.

She's one of the few sailboats out. Recreational traffic has dwindled to no more than a trickle, but tugs and barges are still going about their business, solid and heavy enough to withstand all kinds of terrible weather. The wind continues to rise, making it slow going for her little boat. It's as if a roaring turbine has been turned up to full speed, it's that powerful.

The next bridge she comes to is the George Washington Bridge and the Palisades Cliffs. It's taken her more than two hours hard slogging in the messy turbulent river waters. She's hunched over the wheel of the *Edge* and has her engine at full throttle. And still this is the slowest she's ever travelled with the engine flat out.

She rounds a bend and the New York skyline comes into view, making her gasp. Tall buildings line the Hudson River on the New York side and equally tall buildings stand on the distant New Jersey shore, to the west. She can just make out the Empire State Building. It feels surreal. She's sailing into New York harbour. Little Emerald Lake Visser from Kingston, Ontario, is in New York City. Wow.

And then she sees it—an empty mooring ball! Coming up on her left. She motors over and around it, trying to figure out how to get her hook on it without losing control of her boat. She circles and circles like an animal circling its prey. This mooring ball is HERS! No way is anyone going to take it from her.

If she comes up on the ball from above the wind she'll be blown off it before she can grab it. She has to position her boat below the ball and let the wind push her onto it so she can grab it as she passes.

She readies the end of a mooring line and sets the boat hook close as she manoeuvers the *Edge* below the ball. Letting the momentum of the boat carry her forward she sets the motor in neutral and leans over as far as she can from the cockpit to grab the passing ball. She has to time it just right. Her heart is racing as she hooks the eye at the top of the ball with her boat hook.

SNAP! The boat hook flies off into the water. Quickly, heart pounding like a drum, Emma snatches up the rope at the top of the ball. Just as the wind sweeps her past the ball, a miracle happens, and she's able to snag her own rope through the loop in top of the ball. She wraps the line around a cleat fast, before the tension rips it from her grasp. As the *Edge* comes to the end of the slack, she swings wildly but holds. Emma struggles against the force of the wind to get the rope tied off securely. She nips back to the stern, panting but pleased, turns off the engine, grabs the keys, and heads inside closing the hatch behind her.

Outside the wind is a raging mad thing tearing at the *Edge*, tearing at the river and everything in its path. She wipes at the water on her face. The spray from the water is salty. She sits down on the bench with a *thunk*. The realization that she's near the ocean sinks in.

She turns on the VHF radio but all she gets is static. She kicks herself for being an idiot and not listening to the weather reports. She's started to rely too much on just looking outside the window in the morning and figuring the weather is good if the sun is shining. She's going to have to start planning better. She's on the North Atlantic coast now.

An hour passes. She waits, reads, studies Jess's charts, reads more of *Chapman's*, particularly the section on weather. She goes above and ties another line to the mooring ball just to be on the safe side. The wind is still howling, but the sky is clear as clear can be. Weird.

Another hour passes. She hears a knock on her hull. She waits. She hears the knocking again. She cracks open the hatch and pops her head up. There's a man holding onto the side of her boat. His grey hair is standing straight up in the wind. There's another man at the wheel of the sturdy channel boat. Emma realizes they must be from the marina. His next words confirm it.

"Ya' plan to stay the night?" he shouts against the roar of the wind.

"I guess so."

"Reckon yer a lucky one. Fella on this ball jus' up en left before you came along." He points over toward the shore, squinting against the wind.

"Guess he thought he'd head to one of the bigger marina's, but they're all full."

He's yelling now over the roar of the wind. Even at that, she can hardly catch his words. She hangs a fender overboard to keep his heavy launch from banging up against hers.

"Hurricane's hittin' hard. Lucky for us this is just the tail end."

Hurricane. Yikes!

"How much?" she shouts.

"Fifteen the night." He takes Emma's money and the other man gives her a thin receipt that tears as he hands it to her.

She goes back down below, tunes the radio to a local National Public Radio station. And lo and behold, it's the September 11th anniversary ceremonies. September 11th! Emma wants to smack herself on the forehead. She has not been keeping good track of the days.

September 11th. Here she is, in New York City. On this day of all days. As the *Edge* bucks and rears against the waves, Emma listens to the stories people share about where they were when the twin towers came down, what they remember, who they lost. Later that day, she goes above to check that the *Edge* is secure. She gets her binoculars out and searches for where the twin towers would have been.

Her heart aches for these people she doesn't know. Suddenly history isn't just a lesson in school. It's something that happens to people. Real people. Something they'll live with for the rest of their lives. Their children will live with it, and their grand-children. That's what makes history.

Once in bed she pulls the photo of herself, her mother and her grandmother out from its safe place under the mattress. This is her history. She needs to know what happened to them. She doesn't want to lose their stories. They are her stories, too, and she needs them to know who she is.

16. CLOSE CALL

THE ANCHORAGE AT SANDY HOOK is crowded with boats waiting to make their way out onto the Atlantic Ocean. It's the first leg of the trip for boats going south—destination Cape May, at the very southern tip of New Jersey.

"*Splendour! Splendour! Splendour!* ...*Silhouette*, here. Do you read me? Over."

Since the hurricane scare, Emma has her VHF radio turned on all day and evenings, to catch the regular weather reports and to listen for coast guard reports. But it's also to listen in on the boaters chatting to each other.

"*Splendour* here. Go to 26, *Silhouette*. Over."

She's becoming an expert eavesdropper. Why not? she thinks. The VHF is kind of like a phone for boaters to hail each other. A very public phone. Everyone has their radio set on Channel 16. It's the hailing channel. Boating friends call each other on Channel 16 and then switch to one of the other frequencies to chat. Emma tunes in. It's a great way to pick up tips.

In this bay, everyone's discussing the coming trip. One of the options is to make a couple of short hops, stopping in Barnegat and Atlantic City. But Emma overhears some boaters saying how expensive it is in these two harbours and there's no place to anchor, which means you have to pay for a mooring ball. Emma knows she has to watch her money, so she's going to take a chance and sail overnight directly to Cape May. This will be her first ocean sail, and her first overnighter. She's terrified and electrified at the same time.

She departs at dawn the next day. She's the only boat to leave harbour and she wonders about that as she motors out into the huge harbour following the buoys in the well-marked shipping channel. She's studied the charts and got her hand-held GPS working. She figures there's no use being scared. She just has to get going.

As she looks around her for any other sailboats, she wonders if she's just leaving earlier than everyone. It is dawn, after all. Or maybe she got the weather report wrong? It said fog and light winds. Sounds perfect to her.

The farther out she gets the foggier it becomes. She slows down. The channel is well marked, but the fog they called for is rolling in off the ocean. She's never seen fog like this before. It's a thick wall.

She squints, peering hard out to sea, wondering if it's just a patch, if it will pass, or lift, or dissipate—whatever fog does on an ocean. She has no clue. Back home, an early morning fog would lift off the lake, but you could tell it would pass. You could see through it. This fog is thick like soup.

HONK! HONK! HONK!

Three long honks! One of the ocean-going freighters leaving harbour is barrelling down on her fast.

HONK! HONK! HONK! HONK! Anyone in the channel get out of my way!

It's a clear message. Emma barely has time to veer off to starboard before the freighter speeds by. She guns her motor to counter the waves it leaves behind it. She's sloshed about like a little cork. Heart beating hard, she holds the *Edge* steady.

She watches as the big ship leaves the harbour and is swallowed up entirely by the thick fog. That caps it. She turns back to Sandy Hook harbour and drops anchor again. The fog follows her back and swallows the whole bay.

She pulls out *Chapman's*. She listens carefully to the coastal weather report again. This time when she hears the word "fog" she understands why the other boaters didn't leave when she did.

TWO MORE DAYS PASS. Emma's getting impatient, afraid she's going to lose her nerve if she doesn't get going. To pass the time, she fiddles with theGPS, entering waypoints and noticing how the distances read out in degrees of latitude and longitude. She makes a note of the Cape May waypoint and then, just as an exercise, she puts in the waypoint for Miami, Florida, and compares the two. She has over a thousand nautical miles to go to get to Miami and her average speed will be about five miles an hour! She does the math. With fewer daylight hours, that's going to take her about twenty-five days. And those are long days with no stopping. It's September. She could be in Florida by October. She feels a surge of satisfaction. She can do this

Finally, on the third day, she and six other boats make their departure. She decides even this small number of boats is a good sign. It means she's understood the weather report correctly this time. There's going to be a weather window— good winds. Not too much, but not too little. And no storms, and no fog.

She clears the harbour and makes her way past the last buoy. There won't be any more buoys marking her way for a while now. She's going to be too far out on the ocean. As the land falls away, the sea swells rise and fall. On Lake Ontario there was sometimes a long swell like this. It feels familiar. She holds onto that thought fiercely. She can do this. She can!

She's grateful for Jess's GPS. She remembers how proud Jess was when she bought it at Walmart. Back then Emma had no idea what Jess was going on and on about. She just played along, happy for Jess, but secretly shrugging her shoulders. Now she gets it.

Out on the water there's nothing to sail toward. The buoys are only there to mark some hazard, something cargo ships have to avoid so they don't crash on rocks or reefs, where their goods and the crew will be at risk. And heaven knows that's not good for business. But where she's going now, there's nothing to hit. Just water and more water! Deep, deep water.

While she was waiting to leave Sandy Hook, she had discovered something on the GPS called a trip feature where you can enter the waypoints into the GPS as if it's a route to follow. When she reaches her first waypoint out on the water and her GPS beeps confirmation.

"YEAH!" She raises her fists in the air. She feels the satisfaction keenly. She did her homework right. But she's out on the wide-open ocean. No one to hear. No one to laugh at her. She revels in the moment of success.

"HA! I can DO it." She does a little jig in the cockpit she's so thrilled.

It's something to be proud of.

Her satisfaction is short lived. Her depth meter has stopped reading. Her heart begins to race, and then, just as she's starting to panic she understands that the water is just too deep. She remembers the chart said it's thousands of feet deep where she's sailing now. She tries not to think about it. There's no danger as long as she knows where she is.

The only possible danger, she tells herself, is when she has to land. She has to know exactly where she is so she doesn't hit reefs or rocks, or anything else close to harbour. But she has keyed in the waypoints for the harbour entrance at Cape May and she's pretty certain the whole thing will be a piece of cake.

Emma gives the GPS a big noisy kiss.

"MWAH! I love you! You are going to make my life so easy."

Her next triumph comes when she figures out how to get the autohelm to work, so she doesn't have to steer by hand all the time. She needs to leave the helm sometimes to go the bathroom and check the charts, and she can't drop anchor like she did in the rivers.

Getting the autohelm to work is a huge relief. It's hard to steer a steady course manually with the big long sloping waves out on the ocean. She sometimes overshoots too far to starboard and then too far to port as the swells lift the *Edge* and drop it down into the long sloping troughs. But the autohelm seems to have no problem. So, Emma settles comfortably down on a seat and lets the *Edge* sail herself. Her only job is to keep a close eye out for freighters that might not see her.

Through the binoculars she sees huge container ships making their way up the coast. They're far out to sea. She remembers the enormous one that almost ran her down in New York Harbour. It saw her only because the captain was hand steering out of harbour. Or maybe it didn't even see her. They blow their horn and the rest is everyone else's business. The freighter traffic rules on the ocean.

Chapman's explains that at night or on long passages these big freighters are always on autopilot. If her course crosses theirs, they'll run her over like she's an ant. She won't even be a blip on their radar, she's so small. They'll never see her. It's her job to stay away from them.

She watches her sails to make sure they're not flapping with any wind changes. Lucky for her, there's a light but steady breeze from the northeast about five knots and the sails require little or no adjustments.

As back up to her GPS, Emma marks her position on the paper charts as she goes along. She decides it's important even though it's tedious. In Sandy Hook she overheard some people saying that they never use paper charts anymore, but she doesn't think that's very smart because what if your GPS battery dies, or whatever, then you don't have back up. She likes back up. She's got spare batteries. She's keeping track of her course on the paper charts. She's thought of everything.

For a second, just a second, she feels as if Jess is right there with her, nodding and beaming with pride. *Wooo!* Emma thinks. That's a bit freaky. She doesn't want to start getting all spooky on herself. But she feels proud of herself and even gives herself a little pat on the back.

Emma rereads bits of Tania Aebi's book, *Maiden Voyage*, about sailing around the world when she was eighteen years old. Her resilience and resourcefulness inspire Emma. She can do this trip south, she just knows it. It's only a trip to the Bahamas, after all. Not a trip round the world. Like Emma, Tania had never stepped foot inside a sailboat until two years before she set off in her 26-foot sailboat, *Varuna*. And like Emma, she'd never sailed solo when she made her maiden voyage from New York to Bermuda.

"If Tania could do it, so can I," Emma calls to the sea gulls skimming past her searching for their dinner. Gazing out over the vast ocean she tries to imagine the whole coast of America she'll be travelling down before she gets even close to the Bahamas. But she can't. It simply doesn't compute. Right now, she's here. There's a nice breeze, and everything seems fine.

"Here's to you, Mr. Ocean. You be nice now, hear? Nice to a girl out on her little sailboat. Nice!" She stands up in the cockpit grinning like crazy and spreads her hands wide as if to say, AH! Yes we can agree!

She tidies the cockpit making sure all the lines are neat, the winch handle is stowed in its cubby hole, and there are no other loose items. She picks up a small shiny black pebble off one of the seats, rubs it between her fingers and studies it curiously. Hadn't she…? No, no. She slides it into her pocket and doesn't give it a second thought. She goes below to get a snack.

ALL THROUGH THE DAY the waypoints keep coming up perfectly. Emma becomes a bit smug that she figured everything out first time. She lets more and more time pass before she double checks the GPS and marks her position on the charts.

The sailing is beautiful—simply beautiful. The ocean is undulating, and the winds are great. She eats her supper as the sun is setting and the display of colours takes her breath away! And then something occurs to her. She's not scared anymore. She's not scared at all. Where did it go? In its place is a deep contentment.

As far as her eyes can see there's only ocean. Her home is this tiny boat and her life depends on her ability to sail it. Instead of panic, a sense of freedom fills her. And for the first time, she notices how the horizon curves. It CURVES! Even the earliest sailors must have known the earth wasn't flat. It's easy to see the earth is round when you're on the ocean.

She can go anywhere on the whole planet with her sailboat. Her body hums with the power of this. Looking around her at this new-found world, she is absolutely certain all the wisdom of the early sailors is in within her. As the moon rises, the feeling thrums through her like the notes of a song.

On into the night she sails. When she can't keep her eyes open, she sets her watch for a twenty-minute nap. After a while the moon sets and her only reference in the inky black of the night are the lights on her steering podium that send a faint glow into the cockpit.

The sound of the ocean is a quiet kind of *swoosh, swoosh, swoosh*, lulling her as the water brushes against the hull. It's been like that all day, too. The minutes and hours pass so slowly.

Even though she's supposed to be alert, she dozes on and off.

But at about two in the morning her VHF barks to life. "Sailboat near Barnagat, sailboat near Barnagat. You're off course! Over."

Emma sits up. She's not near Barnagat. Or is she? She hears something that she shouldn't be hearing. It sounds like the crashing of waves to starboard. But it can't be!

"Sailboat near Barnagat, sailboat near Barnagat. You're off course! Do you read me? Over."

Emma's heart starts beating hard. She's supposed to be a mile or more off shore. So the sound of crashing waves is very, very wrong. She peers toward the sound but can't see anything. The crashing of the waves is getting closer.

Instinct has her revving the motor and turning the *Edge* away from the sound before she even forms an actual thought. Not caring that the sails are flapping, she cranks the wheel hard over and veers abruptly away to port.

And there, ahead of her now in the distance, so surprisingly that she kind of chokes, is the light marking the entrance of the breakwater at Barnegat. She remembers from the charts that it's a long breakwater extending far out into the ocean.

She grabs the VHF. "I hear you. Thanks for the warning. Over."

No answer. In stunned astonishment she approaches the light, then slowly passes it by. In the on/off glow of the entrance marker she can see the enormous rocks she would have crashed up on. Their dark ominous shapes mock her.

"Sailboat near Barnagat. Carry on. Over and out."

Emma looks out over the water to see who helped her. In the distance she sees the starboard lights of a sailboat. It seems too far away, but maybe it was them. They never said their name. Well, nor did she.

As she makes her way out into the open water she faces an awful truth. She almost crashed her boat! She almost crashed her boat!

"How could I have been so close to shore?" she asks herself as she tightens the sails, steadying the *Edge* against the waves that are slapping against the hull.

No longer sailing with the wind coming over her stern, the *Edge* heals sharply then slopes away down the troughs of the dark water.

"How could I have been so close to shore?" she repeats to herself as she slowly makes her way out into the deeper water.

It takes her a while to figure it out, but when she does, she's horrified. She must have subtracted instead of adding when it came to calculating the longitude and she put that particular waypoint on land. And because she had the *Edge* on autopilot, it just went where it was supposed to go. Toward *LAND*!

Now she's well out on the ocean, but she has to correct her route and start the calculations all over again. It's not easy to plot a new course out on the water in the middle of the night with the boat rocking awkwardly and the sails flapping while she goes below decks.

She sets the autohelm but because she's moving against the waves now instead of with them, the boat is bobbing and swaying back and forth awkwardly. She keeps the *Edge* pointed out to sea, not wanting to take a chance on her directions until she's sure she's on a good course. She sets the motor on slow speed, to try to steady the boat but it doesn't help much.

When she's down in the cabin the rocking makes her sick. She can only stay down for a few minutes before she has to run up on deck and puke her guts out. She wretches and wretches till there's nothing left. Even with an empty stomach, she feels sick each time she goes below.

Still, there's nothing for her to do but keep on. It takes about five trips to the cabin in short spurts to reset her course. Once she's on the way, she stays up in the cockpit except for quick bathroom trips.

She makes a note to self: ALWAYS double check. No! Make that TRIPLE check her waypoints. The rest of the night goes smoothly. She doesn't nap. The near catastrophe sent so much adrenalin into her body that she's wired. From time to time her hand strays to the black pebble in her pocket and rubs it absently.

The hours tick by until finally she arrives at Cape May just as planned. She made it! But somehow the triumph feels a little hollow.

In the early morning light, she picks out where she's going, and hand steers her way in through the channel marked by red and green buoys. When she finds a spot in the busy anchorage she drops her anchor, strips off her salt-encrusted clothes and crawls into her bunk. Just before drifting off, she tucks the pebble under her pillow and goes to sleep for twenty-four hours.

17. GIANTS OF THE SEA

IN THE C AND D CANAL THAT connects the Delaware River to the Chesapeake Bay, Emma has her second up-close and personal experience of the menacing giants that ply the oceans. The cargo ships moving slowly down the canal are as massive as entire apartment buildings stuck together, and they loom over her. Her eyes pop out of her head when her route takes her close to them. She knows she's moving, but instead it feels like she's dead in the water as the mountain-sized ships move past her. It takes a while for the odd feeling to pass and it sinks in that these giants of the sea are passing her by at twice her speed.

As she makes her way cautiously forward it occurs to her how much of the world's goods are shipped across the ocean and into cities through ports. She's never thought about it much before, but now she comes face to face with the fact almost on a daily basis. It's something to think about.

Out of the blue, old Mr. Flinders pops into her head. All she's ever known is just that he is "in shipping," but now she wonders what exactly he does.

"No matter. He's nothing to do with me now," she murmurs. She shrugs and focuses on her sailing.

As the canal ends, she veers quickly off to get away from the big ships. She watches them making their way toward Baltimore and up the Delaware River to Philadelphia. Then, after they part ways, she thinks no more about them. She simply feels relief that they are far away from her, now.

Her days in the Chesapeake Bay are filled small moments of joy. She's entranced with the world she discovers there, watching the fish and fishermen, the water birds and the waves. She loves waking up early in the mornings and come on deck to see the watermen nearby check their crab pots, surrounded by flapping sea gulls waiting for handouts.

She loves the glowing gold of the grasses that line the banks of the bay, and the ducks that greet her at every anchorage. She watches the vast numbers of Canada Geese flying in their V-formations overhead. It's almost an invasion, there are so many of them, fattening themselves on the rich growth of the bay water plants before heading even further south.

From Jess's book on birds, Emma learns about birds she's never seen before. Black-winged cormorants that look like pterodactyls perch on wood posts holding out their wet wings to dry. Kingfishers search for fish with determination using their great long beaks. They wait alongside regal Blue Herons. She passes trees filled with what looks like big white blooms, but they turn out to be white ibis. Emma wonders how the trees can hold up the huge numbers that fill their branches.

The whole bay is strewn with the bright-coloured buoys that mark the fishermen's crab pots. Sometimes Emma feels as if she's sailing an obstacle course as she weaves her way between them, her heart stopping as she veers above and below the buoys. She keeps her fingers crossed, hoping she doesn't snag one of the lines.

In a small village where she stops to gas up and fill her propane tank, Emma overhears a woman at a crab shack telling one of the customers that the story of Pocahontas is originally about Captain Smith and a group of Aboriginal people who lived in Maryland.

"The Pocahontas part of the story is mostly made up for Hollywood, 'course," the woman continues as she slaps two enormous soft-shell crabs on a paper plate and hands them to Emma.

"You eat'm shell 'n all, dear." The woman nod and grins.

"That's right," a man beside her chimes in. "Soft as butter." Emma smiles and sits down at one of the picnic benches.

"Don't you believe everything you see in the movies," the man continues to the woman across from him. "No, no!" He chews thoughtfully for a few slow minutes. Everything is slow in the Chesapeake.

"Sure, she was a kind of princess, the daughter of the Chief of the Powhatan tribe. That part's true."

"And the part she played in the ritual that made Captain Smith a member of the tribe," adds the lady at the counter. "That part's true, too."

"But the part about them falling in love's not true. No, um."

"Didn't she marry a Rolfe?" Another woman at a nearby table asks.

"Rolfe. That's it. But the Rolfe's all moved away now. You'd find nary a one."

A table of local men and women all join in then, remembering folks who've left and folks whose kids have left home. *Like me*, Emma thinks. She's left home and she's never going back. No one can make her.

Emma bites into her crab. It's soft and sweet, so delicate it tastes like she imagines an expensive meal might taste in a fancy restaurant. But it's served on a paper plate and she's surrounded by locals who could care less about a young boy out enjoying his evening meal.

It's dusk when she climbs back aboard the *Edge*. Right away she knows something's wrong. In the dim light, she sees dirty footprints all over the cockpit. Heart beating hard, she checks to see if the hatch lock has been tampered with. No. It's okay. She scans the other boats tied up. There's no movement whatsoever. She turns back and there on one of the seats is a small round black pebble.

"I must have dropped it," she thinks to herself.

She tries to remember if her feet were dirty when she left the boat. She opens the hatch carrying the black pebble in her hand and lays it on the chart table where she thought she'd left it. That's odd. The one she'd found back in Sandy Hook is still there.

This is another pebble. A second one.

And then comes the memory of tossing a pebble just like this one overboard, back in the Hudson River. Three round black pebbles. All the same.

She sits down hard. Her stomach feels a bit sick. She rubs the pebble between her fingers. Not a marble, but it could be one except it's smaller. What's going on?

Emma climbs back outside. She sees the footprints are too large for her feet. They aren't hers—she knew it all along.

Why are there footprints on my boat? Why is someone leaving me pebbles? A shiver runs up her spine.

She takes a last look around before closing up the hatch behind her. She goes to bed, but she doesn't sleep well. She wishes she could have left the dock. She always feels safer at anchor, away from other boats. Every creak and every footstep on the dock wakes her.

The next morning at dawn she leaves the mouth of the James River and starts across the bay towards Norfolk, Virginia, where she enters the Intracoastal Waterway. She wants to get away from whoever is following her as quickly as possible.

18. BEING FOLLOWED

THE WEATHER CLOSES IN completely after she leaves Norfolk and starts her voyage down the thousand miles of Intracoastal Waterway that lead to the Florida Keys. The first leg is through the Dismal Swamp. And it's as dismal as its name.

The rain starts with a vengeance, sheeting down her face and the back of her neck as she motors over water the colour of molasses. Old growth pine, oak, and hemlock tower on both sides of the narrow waterway. She feels their dark presence hovering over her.

Her first stop is in Elizabeth City, where the Wright brothers made their famous first flight, sparking aviation history. She ties up at the town dock and locks the boat before going to the local hardware store to purchase some fittings to make another boat hook.

Her second one had sunk to the bottom of the Chesapeake. She'd been sailing wing on wing through one of the fields of crab pots and had tacked too quickly, so her boat hook, which was serving as a makeshift whisker pole, flew overboard. Upset by how much a new one cost when she checked the chandlery in Norfolk, she's concocted a plan to use a broom handle with a hook fastened on the end.

In spite of the rain her spirits are high. She whistles a silly tune as she returns from her outing. And there, wedged into the locked hatch cover, is a folded piece of paper. She pulls the paper out and unfolds it. Another black pebble just like the other three falls out.

"*You're doing great. Take care,*" the note says. A shiver passes through her. With the piece of paper clutched tightly in her fist, Emma studies the boats nearby to see if anyone meets her eye or looks suspicious.

Who's watching her? Where are they? What's going on?

She quickly unlocks the hatch and stows her purchases below. Then she casts off and motors away from the crowded dock all the while peering over her shoulder for signs that someone is watching or following, her but no one moves on any of the boats. No one that she can see, at least.

When she's out of sight of the town dock and away from the houses that line the shore, she drops her anchor. She feels safer out here, away from people. But why should she? Why is it safer here? She doesn't know the answer. She just knows what she feels.

From her hiding place in the shadow of a huge cypress tree

she watches the water for any approaching boats. The dripping branches hang down to the water and the tree's roots extend like dozens of bony fingers into the mud. Anyone coming close will have to push past the cavern of the tree. The rain pelts down and Emma huddles inside on the bench, her arms wrapped around her knees. She goes over in her head what just happened.

Another pebble. And now a note. Why leave a note? It must be because whoever it is wants her to know for certain that she's being watched, followed.

Followed! Followed! The words churn around in her head. This is insane! Nuts! Anger boils up inside her. She was so proud of her disguise, her escape, and now she realizes she hasn't escaped. Her disguise didn't fool this person, whoever it is. Panic rises up in her throat. And swiftly anger flashes through her again like a roaring flame. It burns itself out in a few seconds leaving behind a kind of blank stillness.

Four black pebbles and a note giving her a compliment. *She's doing great.* Emma considers her reaction. Has she been so paranoid about getting away that she considers only the sinister, only the threatening side of everything that happens?

She lets the question sink in. What if this person is an ally? A friend? But who could it possibly be?

Not her aunt or uncle. Could it be her mother? Impossible. She doesn't even know if her mother's alive.

Adam? He's the only other person she can think of who'd offer help. But what does he know of sailing? She brings the image of Adam to mind, doing the farm chores, helping her uncle, catching her in his arms when she jumped from the roof. At that memory, her heart does a little skip. A friend, yes. But not a sailor. A small pang of loneliness hits her, but she pushes it away.

After a while Emma gives up trying to find the answer to her endless questions. She gets up and warms a can of soup for dinner then crawls inside her sleeping bag. She closes her eyes, but she's too wound up to fall asleep. She rolls over onto her back.

There's condensation on the ceiling of the cabin over her head. Now that the cold weather's here, there's no way to keep the boat warm and dry. The damp permeates everything. She lies in the darkness and thinks about the note. Every once in a while a water droplet falls onto her face. She turns over and grabs the plastic tarp she's been using to cover her berth and keep her sleeping bag from getting totally soaked, and she pulls it up over her head.

She has no idea what's she going to do now?

EMMA WAKES AT DAWN to a golden sunrise. As she pries open her eyes, she finds it hard to believe that she slept. She gets up on her knees and peers out the porthole. No one in sight. Her spirits lift slightly and she gets out of bed and cooks herself some grits, now her favourite hot cereal for starting a cold morning. It comes in small paper packets like oatmeal back home and all she has to do is add hot water. She gobbles it down and heads out on deck to haul up the anchor.

If she can make good time today maybe she'll be well away from whoever's following her and that will be an end to it. She lifts the anchor and then hurries to the stern as she always does. She presses the starter button on the motor and nothing happens. She presses the button again. Nothing!

The *Edge* is drifting back into the dense undergrowth of the tree with the current. She grabs a paddle and pushes herself away from the tree and out into open water. She runs back to the bow and drops the anchor again to stop the boat from drifting and give herself time to figure out what's wrong. This is the first time the motor hasn't started instantly.

She checks the gas tank to find out if there's a leak, but everything's fine. She can't smell any tell-tale whiff of gas. Then she traces the slender rubber hose that joins the motor to the gas tank and there it is. The hose's disconnected!

Did the person who came aboard to leave the note take the time to pull the hose off? Why would they do that? Such a simple trick wouldn't go unnoticed for long. The motor had had just enough fuel in the reservoir to get her to her overnight anchorage, but if she'd travelled further, she'd have discovered the loose hose sooner.

Is this a prank? It isn't something to cause her danger. Only annoy. She feels as if she's being tested. The back of Emma's neck begins to prickle and she looks around as if she'll be able to spot the culprit.

Fat chance. They know how to keep out of sight.

She reconnects the slim hose and primes the motor. When she presses the starter button this time, the motor springs to life. She puts the motor in gear and heads off down the waterway.

But now she knows she's not alone.

No. She's not alone, and it creeps her out.

19. TORNADO

LOG ENTRY: *October 7, 2014. Beaufort, North Carolina. Winds blowing hard 25 knots from the NE. Nor'easters tracking in more often now. Nights are colder. Even though I'm further south, the sun barely warms the air during the day.*

Emma's getting tired. There've been no more signs of anyone following her. No more pebbles either. She starts to feel herself relax. She sails from Elizabeth City to Albemarle Sound, from there to Pamlico Sound, inside of Cape Hatteras and The Outer Banks. In the Sounds, she's able to put out her sails and enjoy some sailing time. It's so peaceful with the motor off. The winds are from behind her so she puts the *Edge* on a nice reach and skims along over the water. She'd almost forgotten she's on a sailboat, it's been so long since she's had a real sail.

AFTER THE CAPE, the landscape changes again. She notices shrimp boats everywhere. The metal frames of the fishing rigs make them look like alien robots. The big rig arms lower into the water when the shrimpers are fishing. They squat awkwardly where they sit and the thumping of the generators boom out across the water.

The days are becoming noticeably shorter and shorter. The sun rises at around seven in the morning and darkness starts to close in at around four thirty p.m. She's only able to travel

for about eight hours a day in total, including the stops for pee breaks and a rest. She can't use the autohelm because the path from buoy to buoy in the Waterway curves and twists continuously, and there are so many boats to dodge.

The Intracoastal Waterway is just like a river in that way. There's a speed limit of five to ten knots an hour and she calculates she's travelling about sixty miles a day at the most. She estimates that she'll be in Florida in about three weeks, if all goes well.

But she's going to have to take a breather soon. Exhaustion is starting to set in. She's got to get groceries and fuel and do some laundry. It always takes a long time to find the grocery store and the local laundry place. With the cold and damp, she can't do laundry on the boat anymore. The clothes never dry.

Her money is dwindling with each fill of the gas tank. She's going to have leave the Waterway and do an outside sail on the ocean like she did along the New Jersey shore. The idea makes her nervous but she'll save on fuel. The American money from Jess has almost run out. She has some Canadian money and she's going to have to get up the nerve to go to a bank and change it. But it won't last forever. She's going to have to find a way to access her Canadian bank account soon. She still has the lawyer's number and she's trying to decide if she should call him.

When she arrives in North Carolina, she tucks into a small anchorage near some reeds. She makes herself a simple meal with leftover spaghetti sauce. Since the motor incident nothing more has happened. She heads to bed, tired from the long days of non-stop motoring.

During the night, something wakes her. Owls! She's never heard so many in her life. Their hooting fills the still dark air. She lies stiffly in her bunk as they cry out with a strange kind of insistence. Then right behind where she's anchored she hears a loud mechanical whirring and chugging. Glaring lights pierce the darkness sending Emma to the cockpit in alarm. It's a shrimper passing extremely close on its way to its shrimping grounds, which explains the hungry and eager owls.

The bright lights illuminate the whole anchorage. Visible only for a brief moment, is another small sailboat at anchor. A man stands in the cockpit with his binoculars fixed on her. He lowers the binoculars and their eyes meet. The man tips his head at her before the black night once again swallows him. Emma realizes with a shock that she hadn't heard him come into the anchorage and would've had no idea he was there if the shrimper hadn't come by.

She goes back to bed but her sleep is fitful and uneasy. Her plan is to wake up early and get a better look at him, but when she rises at dawn, the man and his boat are gone.

Fear roars through her like a bush fire. There'll be no stopping now. She'll make do with what food she has in her storage locker. She's got fuel in her spare tank. She'll only stop when she's forced to. Her clothes will have to wait.

She studies the charts to see if she can head out onto the ocean right away, but the weather is bad. Too bad to risk it. She's being followed and she can't escape him. He knows where she is, and he knows where she's going, unless she finds a way to go inland and hide.

She plays this option over in her head as she continues her slow, tortuous route through the Waterway along the coast of North Carolina. But it doesn't make sense, somehow, to go inland and hide when in a few weeks she can be in Florida and make her way over the Gulf Stream to the Bahamas. In the Bahamas, she'll be able to completely disappear. That's what she needs to do. That's what she needs to focus on.

Dark clouds start to mass as soon as Emma makes this decision. The VHF radio barks out reports fast and furious about a possible tornado. It names various counties where the bad weather's building, but Emma has no idea what county she's in.

She keeps a close watch on the black sky and hopes the weather will track westward the way they're predicting. She doesn't want to slow down unless absolutely necessary, but as the wind begins to pick up she realizes she may have no choice.

The voice on the VHF becomes urgent, cautioning small boats to take cover. Emma rounds a bend in the Waterway and sees a flotilla of boats aiming for a nearby marina. She tries to hail the marina as she slows to a crawl.

She hails the marina again and then switches to a less-used channel to see if they were monitoring that. But there's still no answer. She sees a few of the boats coming out again and taking off in another direction. It's a sure sign there's no more room. So she turns the *Edge* around and heads back out into the Waterway.

The clouds are now as black as night, forming a dense wall and aiming directly toward her. Emma makes a snap decision to set anchor and just ride out whatever's coming. She puts the motor in neutral and runs to the front of the boat to drop the anchor overboard and WHAM!

The wind hits with such force that she's flung onto the bowsprit. The metal stanchion catches her in the chest. She feels something crack. She crumples to the deck. Groaning she levers herself onto her knees and throws the anchor overboard. But it's too late.

From where she crouches on the deck she can see the anchor plop onto the mud beside the hull. It takes her no more than a minute to realize that the *Edge* has been lifted by the force of the wind and dropped high up onto a mud bank. She's aground. Good and stuck!

She holds on to the lifeline as the wind continues to howl and slap at her. And then just as quickly as it hit, the storm moves on. The black wall carries on its destructive path, leaving the Waterway behind.

Emma lies down on the deck. Huge shudders shake her body and her chest burns fiercely. She can hardly breathe for the pain. Strangely, the sun suddenly bursts out from the remaining clouds and shines brightly down on her.

After a while, she struggles to her feet to survey the damage. One of her cushions lies in the muddy grass behind the boat. Her new cap's lost. She studies the mast and sees that the main sail's still wrapped in its straps and the jib has remained tightly furled. Luckily she hadn't any sails out or they would surely have been ripped off.

Her anchor lays useless in the mud beside the boat. She grimaces at how the hull is embedded in the muck. The force of the tornado has picked her up and dumped her up on the mud bank. The hull of the *Edge* is wedged in deep.

Within a few minutes a fishing boat comes by and tries to pull her off. But there's no budging the *Edge*. She's just too deep in the mud. The fisherman tells her to call Tow USA, but she's heard over the VHF chatting that even just calling them to come and look at your boat will cost hundreds of dollars. Surely there's some way she can do this herself.

Emma makes her way back to the stern of the boat. The motor was down when the tornado hit. The prop is stuck in the mud. Deep. She's going to have to lift the motor and find out if there's any damage. She tugs on the motor but it doesn't budge. It's stuck solid. She scrambles painfully overboard to see if she can push it up from the side, but it doesn't budge an inch.

Her chest aches horribly. She rubs the heel of her hand over the spot and wonders if she's cracked a rib. When Uncle Derek got kicked in the rib by one of the horses, the doctor told him there was nothing he could do for a cracked rib except be patient and careful as it heals. So she'll just have to be patient.

She tries again to dislodge the motor but there's no way she's strong enough to lift the heavy thing, especially with her injury. She needs to use her brain to figure this out.

As she's considering the situation a small sailboat motors by, then circles back and comes close. The skipper hails her and asks if she needs help.

She eyes the man. He's got a cap pulled down over his face and sunglasses on so she can't quite see him. Her instinct tells her to avoid asking for help, but she ignores it. "Trying to figure out how to get off this mudbank without calling Tow USA. Prop is stuck."

"Maybe you can rig some form of lift using the main halyard," he says and points to the mast.

She eyes the mast and thinks of the forces on the main sail. The halyard's strong enough to hold up a sail under heavy weather. Perhaps it can be used to raise the motor. It's a good suggestion. She nods and sends him a thumbs up.

"Give me your anchor," he calls.

"What?" Emma's surprised. The *Edge* isn't drifting, that's for sure, so why does he want her anchor. Her radar is on high alert again.

"Give me your anchor," he repeats. He motors as close as he can and passes near her to explain. "I'll take it out into the river and drop it. Then you winch yourself off the mud bank. It's the only way." He nods at her as if to emphasize his confidence in this procedure he's describing. He circles around again while she processes what he's suggested.

"You kedge yourself off the mud bank using your winch," he continues, when she hesitates. "You know, just like old ships used to do." He scratches his head and waits until she nods. "I'll take the anchor out into deeper water. Otherwise you'll have to swim it out."

She nods again. He flashes her a smile and she sees that he's younger than she had first thought. His grin looks vaguely familiar. But maybe it's just because he's being friendly. She quickly jumps over the side of the *Edge* and retrieves the anchor from the mud where it lays and hands it up to him when he passes by in the deeper channel just outside of where she's stuck. She cringes in pain as she lifts it up to him.

"You okay?"

"I'm fine."

He shoots her a doubtful look, but she doesn't want him hanging around getting chatty. "I'm fine," she repeats, and smiles in spite of the pain.

He takes the anchor quite a way out into the river and lets it drop. Emma climbs back aboard the *Edge* and tightens the rode until the anchor's well set. He lifts his hand signalling goodbye and she waves back. She watches him for a minute, once again puzzled by why he looks familiar, then turns back to her boat and starts crafting some sort of sling for lifting the motor out of the mud.

She gathers up the extra straps she has and wraps them around the body of the motor. Then she winds the main halyard through the straps and fastens the shackle. She wraps the rope end of the halyard around one of the winches and starts to crank the handle. Slowly but surely the motor starts to move.

First there's a small shift, and then there's a wobble. And then plop! It lifts straight out of the muck.

Emma feels a surge of pride. She's done it!

She gets down out of the cockpit and goes over to check the prop. If it's bent, she doesn't know what she's going to do. She's hugely relieved to see that everything's okay. The soft muck hasn't damaged it at all. She lets the relief sink in as she realizes the most important part of the operation's been accomplished. Now to get the *Edge* back in the water.

She wraps the anchor rode around the winch and starts painfully, slowly, cranking the winch handle, around and around. Every turn of the winch is an agony and still she cranks. The *Edge* starts to inch forward slowly down off the mud bank and out toward the deeper water. She's doing it! The rush of elation pumps adrenalin into her arms and gives her strength to keep going. She cranks harder, ignoring the pain. Slowly, slowly the *Edge* inches forward and suddenly she can feel it. The *Edge* is floating!

Emma strips off her filthy clothes and bundles them in a big garbage bag for washing later. She throws buckets of water over the deck and into the cockpit flushing out the mud and debris she's tracked in. And then she's underway again sending a silent word of thanks to the kind stranger whoever he was.

20. OUT TO SEA AGAIN

"SMALL SAILING VESSEL TO STARBOARD of *Navigator!* Stay your distance." The VHF barks to life shocking Emma into complete alertness. Is she being hailed by the hulking freighter in front of her?

It's dawn and few sailors are about. She's progressing slowly out of Charleston Harbour and uncertain of how to get around a huge ocean freighter that's manoeuvring in what seems sporadic and uncertain moves in front of her, blocking her way first on one side of the harbour, then on the other side.

Emma grabs the VHF. "*Navigator, Navigator.* This is the *Edge.* Do you read?"

"Roger the *Edge.* Is that you to my starboard? Over."

"Must be me. What do you want to me to do? Over."

"Stay back while I make this rotation. You could be sucked up in my thrusters. You sure are small. One of my crew spotted you at the last minute. Over."

"Roger that. I'll stay back. Thanks for the warning. Over."

"Roger. Good luck to you. Over and out."

Over and out. Emma puts the *Edge* in a quick arc away from the freighter. After motoring a good distance away, she sets the motor in low gear and watches.

It's pretty amazing that the big ship noticed her, and kind of the Captain to hail her. She's the size of a flea as far as he's concerned. Emma shakes her head as it sinks in.

The next leg of her trip's going to be an overnighter. Rather than motoring down the windy and long Intracoastal Waterway through Georgia, she's chosen to plot her course on the outside from Charleston to St. Mary's Inlet at the top-most corner of Florida. After the tornado blasted through, the winds have lessened.

The weather will hold. She's counting on it. The low-pressure area hasn't budged for the last twenty-four hours. When the low veers north again, the storm that's above it is certain to be nasty with the amount of pressure that's building. Emma's gambling that she'll be safe at anchor when it hits.

Emma puts her motor in gear and starts forward, following the freighter as it heads out to sea. As she follows *Navigator*, she realizes she isn't as alone as she sometimes feels. And this connection's a friendly one. That small connection with the Captain mattered to her. His *good luck* wishes were nice.

She's still puzzled by the note on her boat from the unknown stranger in Elizabeth City. And she's still spooked by the stranger watching her in North Carolina. But could it be that they aren't the same person? Maybe it was just a fluke that she saw the man watching her through binoculars? Even she has studied boats with her binoculars.

As the last buoy leading out of the harbour comes up on port side, Emma looks back at the South Carolina shoreline swiftly receding in the distance. It's time to start sailing. She lowers the twin rudders and drops the centerboard, then presses the switch to fill her centerboard with water and give her the water ballast she needs if she's going to sail. She turns the *Edge* into the wind and quickly raises the main sail, falling off and setting course south. When the westerly wind fills her mainsail fully, Emma unfurls the jib and feels the *Edge* lift in response. She cuts the motor and raises the prop.

The *Edge* is sailing again. It's been a long time.

An hour later Emma's tucked comfortably in a corner of the cockpit. The ocean's rolling its velvety curves in a steady rhythm. It's a perfect day for sailing. Emma sets the autohelm and picks up her GPS to recheck her course. She tweaks the autohelm once or twice and then settles back into her seat to enjoy the vast calm vista that presents itself to her.

There's no one in sight. It's just her and the sea, the beautiful sea. When it's calm it's beautiful, and when it's not, it's horrid. Today you could be in love with it, and tomorrow you could hate it. No one who lives on the sea likes a storm and sailors most especially. Even a large vessel like the freighter would take a beating in a storm. For a small boat like Emma's, a storm could be lethal.

Like the storm that stole her father's life.

That memory of the nightmare still haunts Emma. And this open ocean passage will bring it closer again. She'll be far off shore—farther than she had been when she was off the New Jersey shore. The weather's more risky and the ocean more vast. Thousands and thousands of feet of ocean lie beneath her small boat right now.

Emma drags her thoughts back to the present moment. She's calculated the trip will take under thirty hours. She gassed up in Charleston, did a bit of laundry in the marina right at the town dock, and picked up a few groceries at a nearby corner store. That ate into her cash supply. She's tried to work out a budget and figure how much longer her cash will last. Considering the hundreds of dollars that the gas is costing, if her trip's going to last another six months, she'll run out of money soon. She'll have to break down and contact the lawyer. Find out how to access her account.

What was it he said again? *There are those who want to help you.* Something like that. It seems so long ago now. Who could he be talking about? It didn't sink in at the time, because so much was happening. But what could he have meant? Who even knows about her? The same old questions start their buzzing in her head. She just can't figure out the mystery. And she doesn't even want to try. All she wants now is to find her mother. She wants to focus on that.

And what'll she do after her trip is over? When she's found her mother and all her questions are answered. That fleeting thought ends in silence. She has no idea. No idea at all.

She turns her attention to the tasks at hand. She adjusts her sails for a faster speed, letting off the jib a bit and easing the main. She wants to use all the wind there is to its best advantage. When she's finished fiddling with the sails, she attends to other chores. She cleans the rust that's growing on the stanchions and metal fittings. She's discovered that stainless steel is not rust proof in the sea air, no matter what the manufacturers say.

After the rust busting's done, she bakes. Her favourite recipe is for muffins. She's still got flour in the big ten-gallon container tucked under the starboard bench. And she has some cornmeal from the last shopping trip. She makes her muffins in a small six-muffin tray and they taste heavenly just out of the oven and still hot to the touch. She gobbles them down.

One chore after another, and some fun activities in between and still the time passes slowly. That's life on a sailboat. There's always maintenance. Emma decides that a creative person can find things to do, but the truth is, life at sea is one of two things—easy and rather too peaceful, or dangerous and too scary.

While doing her chores, Emma always has one eye on the horizon for freighters and other large ships or hazards. She thinks about how much courage and stamina it would take to sail around the world single-handed. Are those sailors lonely? Are they bored? And what about the long distances when they can't get any long hours of sleep for weeks on end? They can only get catnaps. She decides they must be totally sleep deprived and exhausted.

Unexpectedly, a butterfly lights on her shoulder. In the next second, it lifts off again and flits from one end of the boat to the other as if checking everything out. Emma watches its tireless wing motion, waiting for it to perch somewhere and rest, but it never does. By its orange and black markings, she knows that it's a Monarch butterfly, on its way to South America for the winter—so many miles there and back again. Every year it makes the voyage.

"Amazing," Emma whispers as she watches fascinated. And then, just as suddenly as the butterfly had arrived, it's gone.

She gets to her feet and goes forward to the bow of the boat sending a silent *thank you, Otto,* which is what she's nicknamed her autopilot, for giving her the freedom to move around without always having to steer. She hasn't learned to fully trust Otto in heavy weather, but it works great in fine, calm weather like she's enjoying today. Halleluiah!

She plops herself down on the bow and lets her legs swing over the side. She rubs her ribs. They aren't as painful as they were, and that's a relief. As far as she can see there is just blue, blue, blue.

A whistle to her right startles Emma out of her dreaming. There's another to her left. And instantly she's surrounded by dolphins. A whole pod has joined her boat. They swim over and under each other, careening along in the bow wave and then swimming away and back again. They roll over and show her their bellies, and it seems they are playing with her. From time to time, one of the dolphins pokes its head up and eyes her where she sits, and then drops down under the surface of the water to keep in sync with its friends. Emma watches in awe and glee.

"You're beautiful!" she shouts to the dolphins, reaching out her hands as if she might touch them. A huge happiness wells up inside of her and she feels like jumping in the water to play with them herself. The dolphins stay with Emma for almost an hour and then they turn and swim away all at once, like kids being called home for supper. As if they are all one family.

Emma's sense of aloneness returns in a rush after they leave. She sails on through the rest of the long day until the sun's beginning to drop toward the horizon and the air's cooling. After making dinner, she scrambles back to the cockpit to check her bearings and her charts. All is well. She's planned a light dinner and then a short nap before the night sail begins.

But she feels anxiety building. She talks out loud to it, saying all manner of silly things.

"Thank you, Mr. Fear for being here. Thank you for getting my adrenalin flowing. Yes, I messed up the last time. I won't do it again. Thanks for trying to keep me safe." The words are like a prayer. They keep her going through the slow hours of the night and into the dawn of a new day.

EMMA SAILS INTO ST. MARY'S INLET at six in the morning and sets her anchor like a pro. There are dozens of boats in the harbour, but she finds a spot. She's ecstatic. The overnight sail was a complete success. She didn't fall asleep. She didn't make any mistakes in her waypoints. She's a real pro now and she feels like one. It's time for a good long sleep.

She surveys the anchorage and sighs. There's no sign of the dark boat that may or may not have been following her. She takes a few deep breaths and goes below closing the hatch behind her. Nothing's going to wake her. Nothing!

21. SABOTAGED

"BOAT AHOY! YOUR ANCHOR'S LOOSE! You're drifting into us!" The yelling's got nothing to do with her. Emma pulls a pillow over her head.

"McGreggor 26. Your anchor's let go! Your anchor's let go!" The sound of feet. More shouting. "They don't hear!"

There's a sound of clattering and thumping. "Get fenders out. They're going to crash into us. Damn!"

McGreggor 26! "That's ME!"

Emma's up like a flash and pulling the hatch cover off. She's on her feet in the cockpit and reaching for the key to start the motor. The *Edge* is careening toward a boat to port of her. The people on the boat have hung fenders over the side and have their hands extended to hold her off.

The motor turns over and Emma swerves away. Just in time, she thinks past the roaring in her head and the pounding of her heart.

"Sorry" she shouts as she pulls away. "Really sorry!"

They give her a thumbs up. It happens, it happens. No harm done. They appear to be a family. The mom, the dad, a boy and a girl. She waves her thanks for their understanding. But she's upset.

Yes, Emma knows it happens. But not to her. Not this time. She had checked her anchor before she went to sleep and it was well set.

She motors away from the crowd. She has to pull up her anchor soon or it will get caught on something. She puts the motor in neutral and quickly runs to the bow to haul it up.

At first, what she pulls up doesn't compute. In two quick pulls she has the end of the anchor rode in her hand. No anchor. Just a cut rope.

The shock hits her. The rope's been cut! It's a clean cut, not frayed as it would be if it were worn. Someone cut her anchor line. And now she has no anchor.

The *Edge* is drifting again. Emma runs to the cockpit and takes the wheel. She motors around very slowly as she tries to figure out what to do. She checks her watch. It's only seven o'clock. She only slept for an hour. When could this have happened? She's going to need another anchor, perhaps will have to buy one in town. There's bound to be a chandlery in a place as big as St. Mary's. She starts considering her options.

She can tie up at the town dock, leave the boat and go to town. But the person who did this is here, in this harbour. She can head back out to sea. But she needs an anchor, no matter what. And she doesn't have a spare one.

In her circle of the harbour she motors past the boat she almost hit. They've gone below decks again. She'd hate to bother them, or wake them if they're sleeping like she was. She rubs her eyes with one hand. She's exhausted. Going back out onto the sea doesn't seem like a great idea.

Just as she's about to turn toward the town dock, the boy pops his head up from the boat. He's about the same age as Adam. Again, the memory of Adam sparks a pang of longing.

"Hey. You okay?"

"Yeah, well, my anchor line's been cut." She holds up the cut end of the rode.

The boy comes out on deck and leans toward her. "What the fu...?" he cuts himself off. "Our fenders are still out. You wanna raft?" He picks up a line ready to toss to her.

Emma raises her thumb up and comes closer. She motors

slowly alongside and the boy catches her port stay. She grabs the line he tosses at her and ties it off to a cleat. Then she hooks another line around her stern cleat. She adds a fender of her own between the two boats. By this time the rest of the crew are poking their heads out and coming up.

"Hey. What happened?" the dad asks. The girl and the mom join him in the cockpit.

She shows them the anchor rode and how it's been cut.

"Nasty." The boy scratches his head. He has boat-hair, sticking out every which way. He's grinning at Emma like crazy. "I'm Sam."

"Who'd cut your anchor loose?" the dad asks, frowning. He leans closer, examines the rope.

"Don't say that, Mark," the woman interrupts. She gives her husband a little shove. "No one would do that. It must have been a fault in the rope."

Emma listens as they banter among themselves. The boy looks at her and shrugs. She shrugs back, a ghost of a smile on her face. She can't tell them what's sitting in the pit of her stomach and making her sick. She can't tell them that it's sabotage.

"Hon, you look dead beat? You want a cup of tea?" asks the mom.

Caught off guard Emma figures it would be rude to say no, so she nods. Besides she could use one. The girl ducks back inside and brings out a mug.

"We're the Hamilton's," the mom says. "From up-state New York. I'm Mary. This paranoid idiot's Mark. This is Alison." She gestures toward the girl. "And Samuel's already introduced himself."

As the word "hon" penetrates Emma's tired brain, she realizes that she's wearing only a tank top and her pyjama bottoms. They know she's a girl. No wonder the boy is making eyes at her. She crosses her chest with one arm self-consciously.

"I'm Emma." She raises her hand in a slight wave.

"Hey, I'll dive for your anchor if you want," Sam says. Emma practically chokes on her tea. Is he being macho, she wonders, or just nice? This is her first time in a while being recognized as a girl and it feels weird.

"Ah … Sam." His dad cuts in. "It's black as hell down there and who knows what the bottom's like." He turns to Emma. "Might as well kiss that anchor goodbye." He shrugs. "But you've probably got a spare, right?"

"Yeah. I've got a spare," She lies. "You're right. That one's gone." She finishes off the tea and hands back the mug. "The tea was great." She starts untying lines. "I kinda gotta keep going, but thanks for letting me raft up for a bit."

"You can stay longer," Mary offers. "We'd love to hear about your trip and where you're going. We're going over to the Bahamas. That where you're heading?" It's typical boatie curiosity.

"Nah," Emma says. "Just out sailing for a bit."

Sam helps her with the lines. When she's free she puts the engine in gear and pulls away. "Have a good one."

As she motors away, she realizes she's made her decision. She's going to head back out to sea. For the moment, no other choice makes sense. Someone cut her anchor rode. That some-one is here right now.

She turns the *Edge* back out towards the ocean. She hasn't listened to the latest weather report but in the distance she sees ominous clouds forming. She can only hope that she has time to figure out where to head next and that the weather holds off until she gets there.

22. AGAINST THE ODDS

JESS ONCE TOLD HER, "You're stronger than you think you are." These are the words that keep Emma going as the *Edge* pounds through the growing waves on the North Atlantic. The wind's coming over her beam as she heads back out into the deep ocean. At first she's happy because this is the *Edge's* best point of sail, but gradually it dawns on her. She's going to have this wind on her stern while she navigates south along the Florida coast.

Too much wind!

But what choice does she have now? She remembers Jess telling her to trust the *Edge*.

"You're best to reduce sail and ride it out," Jess had said that long ago last day they had sailed together.

Emma turns the nose of the *Edge* into the wind and locks the autohelm. She climbs up on the deck to reef down the main to its smallest size. The *Edge*, buffeted by the growing waves, bucks under her feet like an angry bull. But she holds tight. Her safety harness is strapped on and she's tied to the lifelines and wearing her lifejacket.

Bam! A wave smashes over the bow and into the cockpit. She's glad she closed the hatch completely. Otherwise she'd have a soaked cabin by now.

Bam! Another one sweeps up and over the deck.

"What am I doing out here?" she screams out. But there's

no one to answer her, to guide her, to help her decide to go on or to go back. She's already sailed more than a mile off-shore and to turn back will take her another hour of hard slogging, maybe more, against the wind and the waves.

Better keep going, she decides. And then the skies open and the rain pounds down. Emma sweeps the bangs out of her eyes and climbs forward to reef in the jib till it's no bigger than a handkerchief. When she's got the sails down to their minimum, she makes her way back to the helm. Now will be the test.

Bam! Bam! The waves smash over the *Edge*. Emma unlocks the autohelm and bears off, putting the *Edge* on a broad reach with the wind coming over her rear quarter. And now the waves are coming mostly from behind her.

She looks back and yelps. The wave coming up behind her is as high as a truck. She sails down into a trough and the wave grows until it towers over her like a tall building. She feels its weight like a giant hand, about to slap her.

Just as she's certain that she's going to be smashed down by the mighty hand of the wave, the *Edge* lifts up and sails over the crest. Emma's heart leaps into her throat as she feels the little boat careen along and then get sucked back into a trough again. She's terrified. Her hands grip the wheel.

"This is it! This is where I die!" she thinks.

But just as she has that thought, the *Edge's* sails fill again and they pull forward and up. They start again to ride the crest, speeding along at an unbelievable rate. Her heart pounds out of control. Is it fear? Is it excitement? She's on a roller coaster ride of shocking proportions. If she does something wrong, they'll be smashed to pieces by the weight of the water.

After two more cycles of riding a wave and sinking into the trough, then riding up to the crest again and down again, she starts to get the hang of it.

"It's like surfing," she gasps. Or what she imagines it must be like to surf. The rain keeps pounding down, drenching her to the bone. And still she holds on for dear life, steering her little boat through the madness of the storm.

Hours pass. Emma is like a zombie. She's cold and starving. And she has to pee. She knows she's dangerously tired. She needs to check her position on the GPS she left safely inside. She knows she can't leave the helm in this storm with the *Edge* on the course she's on. It will be too dangerous. She remembers reading in *Chapman's* about a kind of braking system she can make with the sails. She'll have to back wind the main and set the jib so that the dual action of the wings creates a kind of stop-start—a sort of stalling.

"The *Edge* can weather any storm," Jess had said. "Promise me you'll trust her." And Emma had promised. Now's time to put that promise to the test.

Emma feels her heart pounding as she points the *Edge* into the wind and sets the sails, one contrary to the other. The boat slows immediately. The waves are horrendous, but the *Edge* bobs back each time. With frozen fingers she locks the autohelm on the wheel. She won't make any progress toward southern Florida, but the exhaustion is sweeping over her now.

Emma fumbles with the hatch and practically falls down the steps as the *Edge* jerks, tips, and rights herself. She closes the hatch as quickly as she can, but not quickly enough. A rogue wave splashes into the cabin, and everything that was dry is soaked immediately.

The salt water sloshes around her feet and gradually drains into the bilge. Emma hears the bilge pump sucking and sends a prayer of thanks that it's working. But when she surveys the cabin her heart sinks.

Bracing herself against the mad rolling of the boat she sees that everything that wasn't clamped down has spilled onto the floor. Cupboards have sprung open and emptied their contents. There are dishes and books strewn everywhere. Her papers are scattered, her charts are a sodden mess. She rescues her charts and lays them over the settee to dry. Gripping the handrail and safety handles positioned all over the boat, Emma makes her way to the head where she sees that the cabinet has flown open and the floor is littered with its contents.

The *Edge* careens over on her side, then bobs back up. The motion is sickening. Emma is slammed into the hull, banging her elbow on the basin. She wedges herself around and manages to pee. But then the challenge is to flush. She dreams of a hot shower, which is the furthest from all possible things. She drags off the wet jeans and her life vest and jacket, hanging them on the hook behind the head. Her wet T-shirt is next. She focuses on getting something dry out of her tiny clothing cubby. But all the while she feels the nausea growing. The dreaded need to vomit is rising by the second. On the floor, totally sodden and gluey are the sea-sickness pills she had bought. She bends over to pick them up and they crumble in her fingers.

Too late anyway! She lunges for the toilet and vomits. She slides to the floor and vomits again, gripping the edge of the basin tightly while the *Edge* battles on through the madly raging wind and waves.

Emma vomits until there are only dry heaves. When she's certain that there will be no more chance of vomiting all over herself, she pumps the head and crawls the short distance to her berth. She knows she's dangerously dehydrated, but there's nothing she can do about it. She curls up in a ball up against the hull, drags the wet covers around her. A fear like no other sweeps over her.

This trip will be her death. The *Edge* will not make it. She will not make it. The voyage will end here somewhere off the coast of Florida. So close to her end destination of the Bahamas. So close but too far.

Too far. She sinks into oblivion.

EMMA DOESN'T KNOW WHAT TIME IT IS when she surfaces from the exhausted sleep she finally dropped into. She blinks her eyes, feels the stickiness of the salt on her face. The *Edge* is still swooping and bobbing in the storm. Maybe it was only minutes. Maybe hours. She has no track of time, no idea where they are.

She remains curled in her little nest that has warmed her in spite of the dampness, taking stock as much as she can with her foggy head. With every jolt and drag of the *Edge*, her heart pounds. Yet somehow she's still alive. The *Edge* hasn't sunk. They're still afloat. Somewhere.

She realizes she's got to find out where they are. She needs to get to the GPS and get a reading. She unwraps herself from covers, grips the handrails against the motion of the boat, and wedges herself in the seat in front of the chart table. She takes the GPS out of its safety in the table and pulls the damp charts toward her, spreading them out in front of her to read.

As she waits for the GPS to power up she realizes something astonishing. She's not sick! She's finally gotten her "sea legs." There's not much time to celebrate this triumph before the device beeps into alertness. She takes a reading. The numbers make no sense. She matches the numbers to the chart. It can't be.

The *Edge* heels over and rights herself as the waves crash over the deck and she rides down a trough and up another, then heels over practically lying in her side. Emma braces herself against the table and studies the GPS again, and then the charts. She can't believe she's been blown so far off course. She's been pushed farther north than she would have thought possible and is now positioned off the coast of Georgia. She must have sailed far enough out into the Atlantic to pick up the edge of the Gulf Stream and be swept north with it.

She grits her teeth and takes a breath. There's no use in being angry. This is her life now. She has no one to rely on but herself and the *Edge*. It's her life. This was her choice. Whatever challenges come her way, they're hers now. And that's what counts.

Emma surveys the disaster of the cabin. The mess can be cleared away a bit, but the bulk will have to wait till this storm is over. The time on the GPS tells her she slept for five hours. She needs to go above and check for freighters and other hazards. It's a miracle that she's still safe.

Emma drags on her rain gear and life vest and heads out to do a horizon check, closing the hatch behind her as quickly as possible. Nothing. No freighters. No other boats. Nothing. The grey rain shrouds the Atlantic. The wind howls and the steel-grey waves that rise and fall are enormous.

Emma takes the biggest chance she's taken so far. She resets the sails and locks the autohelm back on a course south. This will be the first time that she has trusted the autohelm to steer a course in a storm. That means the *Edge* will be sailing herself mostly, with Emma only coming out for horizon checks every half hour. After one last look around, she scurries below.

23. GIVING UP

L OG ENTRY: *October 27, 2014. South Florida, Winds light, beached the* Edge.

Emma puts the pen down. What she doesn't write is how she's feeling—the words going through her head. She should be so proud she made it to Florida, but she's punch drunk with exhaustion and only registers her own craziness.

"It's over. I can't do this anymore. Whoever's chasing me, I give up. Come and get me. I can't run anymore. I don't even believe in why I'm on this trip anymore. I don't care if I find my mother. I'm lonely and scared. I stop here. I'll just wait right here. It's my birthday. I'm officially fifteen years old. Who cares?"

She has hauled the *Edge* up on the beach under a bunch of palm trees. Out in the open. Where anyone can find her. Like the good sailor she is, she checks that the sails are properly stored, and that all the lines are neat. But inside the *Edge* is a mess. She just doesn't have the energy to do anything about it. She grabs her cap, cramming it over her shaggy hair, and tumbles down from the cockpit, exhausted. The beach is deserted. In the past, this would have reassured her, but she no longer cares.

Dinnertime, she guesses, and flops down on the sand to stare out over the Gulf Stream that stretches between Florida and the Bahamas. Her eyes can hardly focus. All she knows is she needs to get off the boat, get away from the constant stress of this trip.

She should be excited and looking forward to the next adventure. But after almost five months of living on the *Edge*, Emma has lost her direction. She puts her head down on her knees. She's come to a full stop. She's beyond hope. She's finished.

She no longer wants to keep trying to find the perfect hiding spot for the night. She no longer knows if she believes in her search. She's beyond sleep, and beyond caring. She can't think straight. She knows she's probably beached the *Edge* on private property and will have to leave in the morning. All she's hoping for is one night's sleep.

But why would she go on if she doesn't know why she's going? If her mother is in the Bahamas, how will she find her? The archipelago stretches over fifteen hundred miles. Mayaguana! It's the last and the furthest of the inhabited islands in the long string of islands. The furthest, and the sailing to get there will be mostly on the open ocean, and that means overnighters.

And what if her mother's no longer there? What then?

She's tired, and so tired of not being able to talk to anyone. But she can't take the risk of having to explain to anyone what she's up to. People are always so curious. And if they know she is alone and only fifteen, they'll interfere. Everything is a risk. She's being watched and followed, and she's even been sabotaged.

Emma's heart feels as heavy as a stone. It hurts. Absently, she presses the heel of her hand against her chest and rubs hard, as if she could rub the pain away. It hurts way more than her broken ribs ever did.

Suddenly there's a nudge at her arm. "What's...?" Tucked into the crook of her elbow is the long slender snout of a dog. She yelps and jumps up in alarm.

The dog leaps back and plants all four feet delicately on the ground right in front of her, giving a yip and nodding its head.

Emma's heart is pounding, but she laughs at the sight. Is she being spoken to?

"Esperanza?" Emma can hear a woman calling. "Esperanza! Oh, there you are!"

Coming out of the palm tree grove is a tall woman accompanied by three more slender dogs, clearly the same breed as the one called Esperanza. She looks like some kind of apparition, a kind of mystical being in her long flowing dress.

"I'm sorry," the woman says softly as she gets closer. "I hope she didn't startle you. I'm Vicki and these are my beloved children. Esperanza you've met." She gestures towards the other dogs. "And this is Riata, Serafina, and Iridessa." Giving Emma a quick welcoming smile, the woman pats Esperanza's head and turns to sit down on the sand facing the sea.

It's obvious that this is a walk she takes often, and Emma wonders if this stretch of beach belongs to her. All four dogs sit down politely and face the same direction. A stillness settles over the little group.

When Emma slides back down onto the sand, Esperanza comes over and leans against her so she feels included. Emma doesn't want to break the spell. She doesn't dare move.

After many minutes the woman breathes in deeply and sighs. She turns to Emma, "Gorgeous night, isn't it?" Her voice is musical, and full of kindness.

Emma is caught completely off guard by the quiet and comfort that emanates from the woman. She opens her mouth to reply, but no words come out. Instead, much to her shame, something inside of her breaks. A tear trickles down her cheek. And then another. And another. Until the tears are streaming over her face, dripping off her chin.

The accumulated loneliness of the past months wells up and overflows. She's mortified, but helpless to stop the tears. She's as quiet as possible, holding her shoulders rigid against the waves of grief. She hopes the woman won't notice. She figures if she's still, they'll move on and she'll be left on her own again.

But the woman doesn't move on. As if reading Emma's mind, she says, "I know," looking out at the water again. "I know," she repeats quietly. "It's good to let go sometimes."

Then she turns to face Emma and what she says next rocks Emma to her core. They are the oddest words a stranger could say and they are words that Emma can hardly believe she's hearing correctly, except the woman is looking right at her, speaking directly to her.

"I know you're feeling lost. And you need to rest. I would be honoured to offer you sanctuary for as long as you need it. Your boat is safe here. You are safe here."

Emma feels herself nod, ever so slightly.

"My house is just there." And the woman named Vicki points beyond the palms to a house that appears to glow pink in the darkening evening.

"Come when you're ready. Come have some tea."

23. SANCTUARY

SOMETIMES, WHEN A BROKEN HEART has had no safe place or time to grieve, and the right time and place finally come, the grief floods the whole world.

Emma goes to Vicki. And Vicki opens her arms and takes her in. She leads Emma to a small room she calls her healing room and makes up a bed for her, nestled in the corner near a window overlooking a magnificent garden.

Vicki cradles Emma while she sobs her heart out and finally sleeps. While she sleeps, the light of the moon comes and goes, passing like a time-keeper over Emma's weeping and sleeping body. Every day the dogs come to sit beside her bed. Every night, the dog Esperanza keeps vigil. Whenever Emma opens her eyes, their faces are close on the pillow. Esperanza raises her head and offers her eyes. Emma can see in their depths the compassion and love of complete innocence.

"How long?" Emma asks Vicki finally one morning.

"Three nights of the full moon. It's waning now. And so will your grief. I promise you. This is all good." She feeds Emma like she's a child, except for as long as she can remember, no one has ever cared for her this way. Emma opens her mouth and lets Vicki feed her spoonful after spoonful of nourishing broth.

Emma frowns at the words: *This is all good*. It's the kind of thing Jess would say and it puzzles her just as much. How could this much pain be good? And yet, in the cave of her heart she feels the same stillness she experienced on the beach. A peace that engulfs her. She sleeps some more.

Then one night Emma wakes and her whole body's shuddering. Wave after wave of fury and anger rush over and through her.

She whimpers in her sleep. And then she's dragged under again. She's consumed by fury. It feels as though it will burn her alive. Into the heart of the fury comes the image of a tall woman holding a small child by the hand.

The child is crying and begging the woman, her mother, not to leave her, not to go away and leave her alone with strangers. It's the worst fear a child can face—to lose the one person they love and trust the most. Emma's heart breaks for the child and a new fury rears its head. She knows the child is herself.

"Momma, how could you?" she cries out loud into the night, the haunted hour, the darkest hour, the hour before dawn.

Then her nightmare comes to haunt her, the boat turns over in the angry ocean again and again, and she knows she'll die, and in some place in her heart she wonders if dying is just a form of escape, but it won't solve anything. She moans and thrashes in her bed saying the words over and over again, "Momma, how could you?" She doesn't hear Esperanza growl and leave the room swiftly. Immediately Vicki is at Emma's side.

"Emma, dear. I'm right here with you," she says.

Emma struggles to sit up in bed and open her eyes. But she's exhausted and she lies back down, closing her eyes again. Vicki's voice soothes her. At last there is stillness again. Emma lies back on the pillows, shuddering.

"This is all good, dear. Very good. Now is the time for healing, dear. If you are willing."

Emma nods, not really knowing what Vicki means, but needing something desperately. She feels so hollow, and at the same time so full of pain and anger. If only she could let it go.

"Now close your eyes and imagine a campfire," Vicki continues softly. "This is a special campfire. It is a campfire of unconditional love and you are sitting at that campfire with the younger you. Can you see the campfire? Can you see the little you?"

Emma closes her swollen eyes and nods.

"And there is a special person there with you, someone you can trust, someone who loves you completely and utterly, just as you are. Can you see this person or get a sense of who it is?"

Again Emma nods. She has a strong clear sense of Jess being right there at the campfire with her. She can feel her.

"Now, is there someone you need to speak to? Someone who needs to hear what you have to say?"

Emma whispers, "My mother."

"Wonderful. So invite your mother to the campfire. Can you do that? Knowing this is a campfire of complete and boundless, unconditional love."

"Yes," Emma sighs.

"Emma," Vicki says with infinite tenderness. "If you could tell your mother now what is causing you such pain—if you could, what would you tell her?"

It's as if a dam has broken. In her mind's eye Emma turns to her mother, to speak from her deep pain, the pain she felt as a child, when she had no words to tell her it was not right, what she did, leaving her with people who didn't love her. It was not right. She pours out the loneliness, the fears, and the heartbreak. She pours her heart out until she's completely empty.

"You're doing so great, Emma," Vicki's voice soothes. "You're doing so great, dear. Now, in your mind's eye, look into her heart." She breathes in deeply. "If your mother could speak to the child you were, from her heart, what would she say?"

Somewhere deep inside of her, Emma hears her mother speak as clearly as if she's in the room. She feels the tears start to roll down her cheeks as her words of love flow.

I'm so sorry, Emma. I didn't know what else to do, sweetheart. I wasn't able to care for you and keep you safe. Something terrible was about to happen to me and I couldn't keep you with me. I had to leave you. They promised to look after you.

I could only trust that they would. I never wanted anything but the best for you. I love you completely and utterly. I'm so sorry you suffered so much pain.

Maybe this is what did happen, thought Emma. Maybe her mother was trying her best. She feels her mother's words penetrate her aching heart. She's so tired of holding onto the pain. And something begins to grow, filling the space in her body where the pain has been. Emma feels her heart swell with a feeling she's never felt before.

"But what happened to you? Where are you now?" Only silence follows these questions.

"Ask your special person," Vicki whispers.

Emma imagines Jess's presence in her heart. She listens.

This is what your journey is about, Emma. Don't give up. You have all the courage and confidence and ability you need to find the answers. Your mother needs you to find her now.

Jess's words are so clear, as if she's speaking them out loud. Emma sighs.

"Emma," Vicki's quiet voice shimmers into the room. "The greatest gift we can give ourselves is to forgive. When we forgive, we heal ourselves. If you knew your mother was doing the best she could at the time, could you find it in your heart to forgive her?"

Emma feels her whole body soften. "Yes!" She takes the deepest breath. "Momma, I forgive you, I forgive you. I know now you loved me. I feel it."

She gives another huge sigh. Warmth floods into her heart. It feels sweet and bright and shiny as if the sun is beaming down on her. She describes it to Vicki.

"It's like I'm part of everything, Vicki. Part of the whole universe. And I'm full of light."

"That's your essence, sweet one. Who you really are. It never goes anywhere. It's love. It's life force. It makes your hair grow and your eyes sparkle. It's who you really are and always will be. Breathe in the truth of this."

Emma breathes in the beautiful words as if they're perfume from the flowers under Vicki's window. As she breathes, she drifts off to sleep deeply again.

When next she wakes, the sparkling sunshine surrounds her. Iridessa, Vicki's pretty white dog, pads into the room and lays her head on the bed next to Emma's hand. Emma strokes the silky hair and it feels so good. Immediately her stomach gives a loud growl.

"That's a good sign," Vicki chuckles as she enters the room with a tray laden with fruit and toast, yogurt and juice.

Emma blinks a few times at the woman in front of her. In the sunlight, Vicki's hair glows radiant red, her long flowing dress is a rainbow burst of colours. Emma feels as if she's seeing the kind woman who has given her shelter for the first time.

Her stomach growls again and she gets busy devouring everything in sight while Vicki chats cheerfully about her dogs and what's going on in the garden, the birds she's seen that morning, and the state of the ocean.

"The wind's turning again, dear." Vicki crosses to the open window and looks out. "It'll soon be time for you to cross safely. It will all be as you were hoping."

Emma pauses in her chewing. "How do you know I'm crossing?"

"I live by the sea, dear, and I know what you sailors are looking for. You need to cross the Gulf Stream with the southwest or westerly winds."

Emma's cheeks glow pink with embarrassment. "I thought you might be a magical person or something. I feel so different today and I know we did something last night when I was having the nightmare. I just can't remember what."

Vicki tips her head back and lets out a warm rich laugh.

"It was your own magic that made the difference—your own soul speaking to you." She places her hand on Emma's. "You can have access to that inner wisdom any time you need it. It's always with you. I don't have it. And I didn't DO anything. I merely accompanied you on your own journey." She smiles warmly, gives Emma's hand another squeeze and picks up the tray.

"Vicki," Emma calls out to her. "I'm so grateful for … for all of this." She waves her hand at the bed, the dogs, and the flowers on the table beside her. "But I'm curious. Why did you take me in? Why would you help a stranger like me?"

"You're welcome, Emma. You're welcome to return anytime you wish and to stay as long as you need to."

Vicki reaches out to tuck a tendril of Emma's hair behind her ear. "As for why?" She tips her head slightly to the side and gives a small nod, as if to confirm something to herself. "It gives me joy to help someone when I can." When she raises her eyes Emma could see there were tears.

"I'll never forget you, Vicki."

"Nor I you, dear one. We're connected. Always." And her smile as she leaves the room is so sweet.

EMMA SHOWERS, puts on her freshly washed clothes. She goes to find Vicki where she's working in the garden. Vicki brings her back into the kitchen to make lemonade from real lemons. Emma tells her about her mother and father, Jess, the letter, her escape from the farm, her plan to find her mother. She doesn't tell Vicki about being followed or about the sabotage. She doesn't know why she holds back. It's as if she doesn't want to bring suspicion and fear into the room again.

"It sounds like you're on a quest, Emma."

Emma shifts uncomfortably. "I'm not going on." She looks out the window not wanting to meet Vicki's eyes. She can just make out her boat, still sitting on the beach where she left it.

Vicki says nothing, just waits, her hands in her lap, a smile on her face.

"I'm finished. Done!" Again there's only Vicki's silence in response. Finally, Emma turns and faces her. "Why don't you say something?"

"It's not for me to tell you what to do." She adjusts the fresh flowers in the vase on the table. "Everyone has choices in their life. Challenges and choices. Everyone. Yours is to turn around and go back, or to go on. Only you can choose." She brings her eyes back to Emma's face and beams at her with love.

Emma feels something shift inside of her. She stares into Vicki's eyes for a long time while she experiences this new sensation, trying to figure out what it might be. After what seems a long time, she says, "I need help."

Vicki opens her hands. "Well, then," she says grinning broadly. "Tell me what you need."

As Emma answers, she understands that all she needed to do was ask Vicki for help. One by one, the things that were worrying her are taken care of over the next two days. A friend of Vicki's buys the anchor and helps her fix the new rode to it. Together, Vicki and she set the *Edge* to rights, cleaning up the mess after the storm.

Finally, there's only one thing left to be done. Emma calls the lawyer. Her call is put through immediately.

"Emerald, I've been waiting for you to call."

Emma takes a breath. She thought she'd have to explain more than this, be cagey and evasive. After all, she is a runaway and he shouldn't be helping her. "I need more money."

Mr. Drake asks for the necessary information. It's all too easy. Again Emma feels suspicion rear its ugly head. But now she heeds it.

"Why are you making this so easy?" Emma asks. "What's going on?"

"I'm just following my client's instructions." There's a sound in the background. Voices, a door closing.

"Who?" Emma asks. "Who's your client?" There's a click. The line goes dead.

Emma runs to Vicki, shock surging through her body. She's furious. She's scared. She feels upside-down with confusion.

"Vicki," she calls as she runs. "I haven't told you the truth." She stands trembling in front of her friend, her first real friend since Jess. Hands at her side, palms facing forward, her whole body sags as if she's waiting for Vicki to get mad at her for lying; or, at least, for not telling the whole story.

Vicki unbends from where she's been plucking dead blossoms off a hibiscus bush. She turns and smiles. "Well, then. It's time to tell me what else is going on, isn't it?"

"You knew?" Emma follows Vicki past a tinkling fountain and through the garden.

"I knew something was scaring you through and through, dear." Vicki leads her to a carved bench under the palm trees. "But it was your privilege to share or not to share."

While Emma explains what else has gone on during her voyage, Vicki listens quietly.

"And now I find out that the lawyer is working for someone who seems to want to help me. But who?" Emma's frown deepens as she tries to puzzle it out.

"Emma, look at me."

Emma meets Vicki's eyes.

"If you knew who was helping you, would you change your plans to go on?" Vicki raises her hand when Emma starts to say something. "What if you can't know who it is? Right now, I mean. Will you change your plans?"

There's a long pause while Emma thinks about this.

"Do you see what I'm saying?" Vicki asks gently.

Emma shakes her head. Then changes the movement to a nod. She frowns again. "You mean, if someone's helping me, that's good. That's enough. And it doesn't matter who it is?"

"Yes. In a way," Vicki smiles. "But it's simpler than that." One of the dogs comes up and pushes her head under Emma's hand. Emma looks away from Vicki's eyes for a minute, considering. She strokes the silky head, then looks up at Vicki again.

"This is about me, isn't it?" She lifts her chin. "It's my quest and my challenges and how I choose to go on."

Vicki smiles her encouragement.

"There's something bigger going on." At Vicki's *ahhh*, Emma continues. "The answers are in the Bahamas. And I'm going to find them, aren't I? I just need to keep going and believe it. And believe in myself." Vicki smiles.

"I can do this, can't I?" She grabs Vicki's hand. "I mean, who knew I'd get this far! And now ... well, now the *Edge* is fixed up. And I have money again and some unknown person on my side, even though ... I don't know ... cutting my anchor rode doesn't seem like a very friendly thing to do."

"Yes, but it brought you here."

"Wait a minute! Are you in on this?" Emma leaps to her feet pushing the dog away.

"No, no, dear." Vicki laughs her big open-hearted laugh again.

"Then why are you laughing?" Emma's still frowning at Vicki and standing alert, ready to protest or defend herself.

"It just delights me, how the universe works." Vicki pats the seat beside her again. "Sit, dear. Sit."

When Emma sits down again, hesitantly, Vicki continues. "I didn't know you before you arrived on my beach. But life is full of mysterious occurrences like that." Vicki reaches out and pats Emma's hand. "That's the magic. Don't you feel it in your bones? How one thing leads to another and brings you just exactly where you're meant to be? The wisest of the wise say there are no coincidences."

Emma thinks back to Adam and how her aunt and uncle couldn't have known he'd help her escape when they hired him as a farm hand. He probably didn't know himself. But he was exactly where she needed him to be.

"But Vicki, that means I've got to get going, and keep going." She shakes her head as if to clear it of some fogginess. "I don't know what I'm saying, exactly. I just feel like I've got to hurry up, get a move on. Something like that."

Vicki nods and gets to her feet. She's beaming. "You know what I think, dear Emma?" She spreads her arms wide and the wind lifts her flowing dress so it floats out around her. She looks just like a colourful angel. "I think you're ready—more ready than you realize."

III. THE SONG SINGS

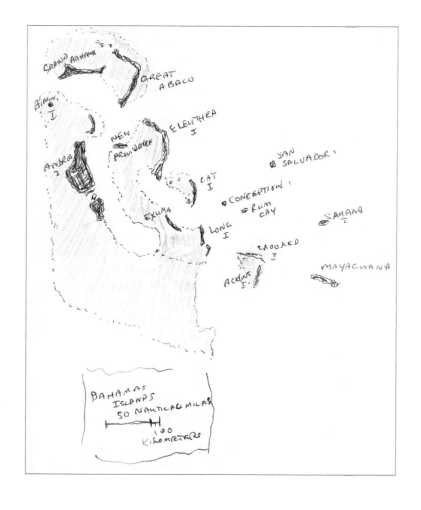

25. BAHAMAS AT LAST

EMMA SLOWS THE *EDGE* to a near standstill and prepares to anchor in the middle of a vast open expanse of crystal clear turquoise water. It's the end of a long, long day of sailing. Normally she'd look for somewhere secluded to anchor for the night, but there's no shelter out here on the Great Bahamas Bank and the only island she can see, far away in the distance, is tiny Bimini. But she won't go closer to any islands where she knows there's a Customs Office. Her grandmother's charts are clearly marked. She'll have no problem avoiding the islands she needs to avoid. Because she won't register her entry here, or anywhere else in the Bahamas for that matter. Same as in the U.S., she's just entered this country's waters illegally.

Emma's decided she has no intention of staying in the Bahamas for very long. She's going straight to Mayaguana as quickly as possible. She's going to find her mother and get all the answers to all the questions. And then ... well. She doesn't know exactly. But she'll figure it out then. Later. When she has the answers. Right now, though, she has to get some rest. She's been awake since four o'clock in the morning.

This is her first stop after crossing the Gulf Stream. The crossing was so easy it almost seems unreal to Emma now. All it took was waiting for the right winds. The dreaded Gulf Stream changed from a monster that can batter boats to smithereens, to a silky underwater river that was no more threatening than a woman's hand caressing the *Edge* as she sailed from Miami to these shallow turquoise waters.

Everything about this place astonishes Emma. She could be on an entirely different planet. She stands on the bow of her boat and lets her new anchor plunge to the sand beneath her. She can see it hit the bottom. She watches it right itself and dig into the sand as it's supposed to. To make sure it's secure, she backs down on it gently. Then she turns off the motor and straightens. All she hears now is the wash of the waves.

Emma looks around her, taking in the warm breeze flowing over her arms, the blazing sun, the endless light blue water as it meets the light blue sky. Small clouds scud along overhead and quickly dissipate. Not far behind her is the indigo blue of the deeper Atlantic waters. The line between the dark blue and the lighter blue water marks the edge where she just crossed onto the shallow Bahamas Bank. It's like a ledge she stepped onto. And now, instead of the water being fathoms deep, she's floating in water that's as shallow as a swimming pool. A swimming pool that stretches ahead of her as far she can see.

The *Edge* gently rises and falls and the waves *slap, slap, slap* against the hull. She knows she should go get the sketch book that Vicki gave her, and her new water colours, try to capture these first impressions. Instead, she just sits quietly and takes it all in.

As her eyes get used to immensity of the pale blue around her, she begins to notice the subtle changes in hue. Bright blue, to light turquoise, to light yellowish blue. Not far from where she's anchored there's a patch of yellowish blue. When she looks closely, she sees that it's a coral head very close to the surface. These are the hazards of the Great Bahamas Bank that she's going to have to be on the lookout for. The coral heads are as hard as rock and can tear a hole in a boat hull just as easily.

"So," she says out loud. "I'll be sailing by colour now, instead of buoys."

She goes below and pulls out the charts to read them, confirming her spot and planning her next move. When her eyes begin to blur she realizes again how tired she is. She grabs a handful of nuts and heads back out on deck to decide what she wants for dinner before tucking in for her first night's sleep in the Bahamas.

Her heart swells unexpectedly as her latest triumph sinks in. She's here. She's truly here!

"RATS!" EMMA WINDS HER FISHING LINE on the piece of wood shaped like a kind of door handle and pulls up what remains of a red snapper. "That was going to be my dinner!" she calls out to the barracuda that ate the best of her fish. She throws the fish head back into the water, watches the flurry of action. *Yup, barracuda.*

This is her eighth day on the Bank. It doesn't seem like very long, but she's sailed almost three hundred and fifty miles of the Bahamas archipelago—a small fraction of the thousands of miles of sailing she's done since she left home. And she still has over a thousand miles of the Bahamas to go. She puts in the maximum hours that she can depending on winds, but it turns out she can still do only about forty miles a day, not much more than when she was up north. She simply can't risk arriving too late in the afternoon to where ever she decides to anchor because once the sun starts to set, she can't see the colour of the water properly. She can't risk sailing on the Bank at night with all the coral heads.

"Oh well," she sighs. The barracuda are hungry too. And she knew she was being too slow in checking the line she always trails behind her now.

She stows her fishing gear and concentrates on her sailing. She tacks back and forth in short bursts, hauling in the jib and snapping the boom over. She's sailing for the fun of it through a wide bay pockmarked with coral heads. But she's good, and the *Edge* responds like a racing boat. She grins and sighs. The small wave that splashes her as she tacks is warm. The sun is warm. The wind is warm. The sky is blue.

She's planning to sail overnight once she's off the Bank again and out in open water. But until then, she just puts in her full days and doesn't put too much energy in worrying. Something inside of her has shifted. Or sunk in. It's a kind of patience. She knows she's making the best time she can, and that worrying won't make the trip go faster. She tacks again, tips her head back and grins, sending silent *thank yous* to the weather gods and the boating gods and the fish gods and any other kind of god she can imagine. The *thank yous* just feel so good.

She's sailed passed Andros and is heading toward Long Island, giving the main Exuma islands a wide berth. From the excited exchanges she overhears on the VHF, they're clearly popular among boaters. Someone even called Georgetown a summer camp. Emma still finds herself avoiding the other boaters as much as possible, and especially the ones who don't have much else to do but gossip. She hears them talking among themselves over the air-waves, introducing themselves, organizing get-togethers, happy hours, and other activities she can't join. She'd stick out like a sore thumb among this boating crowd—too young, too solitary, too serious.

The locals are another matter altogether. She still doesn't mingle much, and she always seeks out the smaller less touristy islands. She's discovered that Bahamians are a mixture of white and dark-skinned people, so she fits right in. When she does her groceries, the locals are polite and give her space. No one pays her much attention and she's become comfortable with wandering in the markets of small villages, dropping into local cafés for lemonade and even sitting on the docks at night, where the everyone gathers to chat and watch the sun go down. No one seems to care if she says little and just sits with them. In the Bahamas, Emma enters a whole new world, one where she finally feels at ease.

But it's out on the water that she feels most herself. She's learning to be self-sufficient. She catches fish. The local fishermen are friendly on the water and off. They've taught her how to clean her fish and she's bought the right tools for it. In the markets, she stocks up on the local fruits like wrinkly lemons and mangos, and the various local root vegetables that last best in her food storage spaces. Her fresh water tanks are full and her gas tanks too.

She tacks again, and then once more. And then decides to call it a night. She pulls up into the inner corner of a quiet bay where she's decided to anchor. She turns the *Edge* into the wind but doesn't bother to turn on her engine. She's furls the jib and then hops to the bow to drop anchor. Backwinding the main, she sets the anchor well in the soft sand and is satisfied when the *Edge* comes to a complete stop at the point where she's tied off the rode. She uncleats the halyard and drops the mainsail, flaking it expertly on the boom, ready for tomorrow's sail. She stands up and surveys her domain, congratulating herself on finding a beautiful anchorage.

It's time for dinner. Not the fresh fish she was hoping for. She'll have to settle for macaroni and cheese or soup. It's her standard backup fare. She takes off her cap and shakes out the raggedy mop of curls. She's letting it grow a bit longer now, no longer concerned that people know she's a girl. That freedom is another relief for her.

It's the end of the day and the sun's not so harsh so she strips down to her bathing suit, tossing the man's shirt she only wears now to keep from burning under the sun into the cabin. She gazes at the water and considers whether to dive in for a swim now or wait until just before bed. Or maybe both. Why not?

As she's standing at the stern trying to make up her mind, a small boat peels out of one of the reefs and heads in her direction. For a moment she freezes. Then she relaxes when she sees it's two local boys about twelve years old who are waving at her. One stands up holding a conch shell in his hand.

"Hey miss. Have you got the time?"

By now Emma is used to this question. It seems to be the standard greeting on the water from young boys out lobstering or conching all day. They never seem to have a watch.

"Sure. It's five thirty." She greets them with a warm smile that reveals her new-found mix of friendliness and shy curiosity.

"Want some conch?" The second boy slows the boat and comes closer. Emma sees that the boat is full of the pink and cream coloured shells of the Bahamas' favourite food.

"Okay," she nods and squats at the back of the boat admiring their catch. "How much?"

"Free." Both boys say pointing at how many they have as if to say, "It was free to us, now it's free to you." She's impressed again by the generosity of the children she's met who are always so willing to share what they have. But she has some money and it only seems right to pay them for their conch.

"How about five dollars for two?" Emma asks.

The boy holding the conch smiles broadly. "Sure. If you want, I can fix them for you." It's a sure sign he thinks the price is right. The offer to "fix it" is an added bonus. Emma nods "yes" and goes to get the dollars.

Whack! She hears from the cabin. *Whack! Whack!* She comes back up, hands over the dollars to one of the boys and watches while the other boy knocks a hole in the top of the shell with his machete, inserts his knife through the hole and, in one deft twist, cuts the tendon that attaches the conch to its shell.

"You know how to cook it?" he asks, pulling the pink animal from its shell and handing it to her. There's a big sneaky grin on his face, and Emma knows he means the fact that conch has to be tenderized before being eaten and that requires pounding it hard for about twenty minutes with a hammer.

Her mouth starts to water as she thinks of the delicious unexpected meal she'll soon be eating. Even if it is a lot of messy work.

She remembers the first time she had been told how to prepare conch. She made the mistake of doing the pounding inside the boat in her little galley. Conch juice spewed all over the place and she spent hours afterwards cleaning bits of flesh and juice off the walls of her home. But it was worth it. She never forgot the flavour of that first conch.

"Yup, sure do," she replies and grins back when he hands her the second. They nod at her and wave goodbye, then head over to another boat that's just pulling into the bay.

Emma frowns. The last thing she wants is company. She narrows her eyes as the single-handed sailor sets his anchor with the same efficiency as she did. She watches him go about settling his boat away for the night. She sees the boys handing him conch in the shell. His blond hair is bleached, and he's tanned a nut-brown. Clearly a local, she decides, and turns back to her dinner.

She takes the conch below and plops them in the sink. No use taking a swim. She'll need one after she's done. She rummages in her drawer for the wooden hammer she's acquired for this task and grabs what else she needs before heading back outside to start preparing her conch.

She doesn't think about the other sailor again as she pounds away at her dinner and plans what will be the most delicious way to eat it, fried in some butter, or breaded, or with a little onion. Later she hears the *whack, whack* of his machete and the pounding sound as he prepares his own conch. Yup! Definitely a local. She's relieved he's just ignoring her.

EMMA SLEEPS, AND SHE DREAMS OF FISH under the boat. They seem to be crowding round her little home and nudging it from side to side, bumping it. She stirs and wakens, as she's gotten used to doing, always alert for changes in the wind or water. She hears nothing and wonders what woke her. She waits. Still nothing. She waits some more then slowly drifts back to sleep again.

She rises at dawn the next morning ready to have her early morning swim and start her day. She crawls out of her berth and up into the cockpit. And there on the floor in front of her is a piece of paper, weighted down by a piece of driftwood.

Her heart leaps into her throat. She looks around the anchorage and notices the boat that arrived last evening is gone. Gone! Was it her follower? Why hadn't she paid better attention?

"You're kidding, right?" she snarls in the direction of the open water. "Why don't you just come up and hand it to me?"

This is the first sign of the presence of the watcher, the follower, since she was in St. Mary's Inlet, back where her anchor rode was cut. How did he find her?

She shivers in the morning air, then bends down to pick up the note. The driftwood is surprisingly heavy. A hardwood of some kind. She looks at it more closely. It's carved in the most intricate of patterns. A sculpture of some sort. She opens the note.

"Do you know what they are?" What does this mean, she wonders, frustrated. This isn't a game now, is it? Riddles?

"*They*. What's *they*?" she says to the wind. She reads the next line.

"When you get to M., ask."

Emma shivers again. M.? Does this person know she's going to Mayaguana? Okay. Yes. Okay, it's a clue. And then she realizes that he must mean the little black pebbles. She flies back inside and digs for the baggy she's hidden in the chart table. She takes out the pebbles and rubs them between her fingers.

What are they? It's a good question. She had assumed they were simply smooth round stones. A bit smaller than marbles. They could be beads. Are they? What does it matter what they are? She studies them closer and notices they aren't exactly black. More like a dark green with black running through them. The polished wood of the sculpture is the same. She turns it in her hands. The patterns are intricate, but make no sense to her.

Who is she supposed to ask? Her mother? Does this person even know that's who she's looking for? Emma's heart skips a beat. Who is it that's following her? And how does he know so much? That's what Emma wants to know.

26. OPEN OCEAN AGAIN

EMMA NAVIGATES THE CUT through the two last islands in the group and breaks out onto the open ocean again. The water is the deepest cerulean blue and darkens to blue black as the ocean bottom falls away. She turns around to look wistfully at the turquoise pool she's leaving behind. But this is the only route to Mayaguana. She'll sail around the northern tip of Long Island and then turn southeast to Rum Cay where she'll stop for the night. She originally wanted to sail directly to Mayaguana, but the navigating is just too tricky. She read somewhere that many sailing ships during the golden years had crashed up on the reefs that ring these islands and she can understand why. She doesn't want to be another one.

The sailing is hard slogging. With the wind on her nose and the waves building, she's feeling the old anxiousness returning. Does it ever go away? she wonders. Maybe it just lurks there in the back of your mind ready to plague you when you need to be confident. She reminds herself that once she rounds the northern tip of Long Island, she'll have the wind over her beam and may even gain some time once she's on that fast point of sail.

Another wave splashes over her. She spits out the salty water.

"Oh, for goodness' sake," she yells out. It feels good to say the words as she says them again, louder this time. "For goodness sake!"

And then she starts to sing. She starts with church songs and sings as many as she remembers. Then she sings songs from school, and then songs from the radio. Then she starts all over again. She starts to make up songs, and yodels in some way she's made up for herself. Then she makes up sounds that remind her of dolphins.

When the sun is high overhead, she lays her fishing line out behind her even though she figures it's improbable she'll catch anything at the speed she's going. She's discovered that a slower speed is better. But then she's not on the Bank trawling through the coral. Maybe on the open ocean it's different. It's the first time she fished on the ocean.

She turns back to sailing, getting ready to tack again so she's not so far away from the island. She studies the outline of the island. The northern tip is visible now and she'll be able to round the island in a couple of hours. She tightens the jib, turns the nose of the *Edge* through the wind, lets the jib off at the last minute, and pulls in the starboard sheet. The main's cleated and tacks itself. When the *Edge* picks up speed again, she looks back. To her surprise, a flash of fish rises and falls behind the boat, then leaps and dives again.

"Hah! Dinner! Yippee!"

It's a big fish. Bigger than she's caught before. She lifts the wooden handle out of the cubby she's wedged it in, and is jerked off her feet, bumping her cheekbone on the wheel pedestal.

"Ouch!" she cries, but she doesn't let go. She shoves the handle back into its secure spot and assesses the situation. First off, she's going way too fast. She watches the fish fighting the line. She's got a good eighty-pound test line. The fish is working out and she knows it will eventually tire, but she can't wait too long or it'll get eaten by other predators. And right now, she knows she's a predator too.

"This is my fish. All other greedy ones stay back," she yells out to the sea.

Emma makes a quick decision. She's going to tack away and

then let the sails luff. She'll lose a bit of way, but she'll pick it up again. She turns the motor on to give a bit of steadiness and tacks once more quickly, then loosens the sails, slowing the *Edge* down to a crawl and locks the autohelm. The *Edge* bucks and yawls in the waves, but the motion doesn't bother Emma. She knows she can trust her little boat.

She focuses on the fish. She braces herself against the stern seats and picks up the handle. Wrapping the line slowly round the wood, she reels the fish in. With each leap out of the water, the fish tires. Its beautiful rainbow back glistens and glows. As it gets closer she sees that she's caught a dorado, or a mahi mahi as they're sometimes called. It's big. At least twenty pounds.

Hand over hand she wraps the line till at last the fish is right at her stern. Now the tough part will be to lift the fish into the cockpit. Emma pulls on the gloves she keeps handy for hauling the anchor. She wedges the handle into the cubby so it's secure, then lays flat on her belly so she can reach past the outboard and bring the fish alongside the boat. It fights and fights, but she holds fast.

She gets ready to yank the fish overboard, braces herself, one foot hard against the back of the seat, the other leg splayed out for steadiness. She figures if she can time it for when the *Edge* does one of her yawls in the waves, she'll use the return motion to help her with the fish.

Down, down she reaches, takes the line and hauls the fish close enough to grab it behind the gills with her other hand. Then she waits for the motion of the *Edge* to heel to the side. One, two, she pulls up and back the moment the E*dge* swings back and away. Up, up and *whap*! She has a flopping huge fish flailing and splashing in her cockpit.

"Oh!" she gasps and laughs as she slips and lands on her backside. She quickly gets to her feet and stands back. It's still caught on her hook. The beautiful rainbow life slows. Emma has the same experience she always does when she watches one of her catches tire. Reverence!

"You beautiful creature, I'm sorry to kill you. I'm grateful for your life." Emma watches it slow, no longer able to breathe. She sucks in her own breath aware that life is breath. And her life is possible only because she can fuel her body. The gift of this creature's life for hers—Emma's life—to go on.

And then, just like that, it's over. With surprise she sees the wonderful rainbow skin dull to a steel grey.

She's never seen a fish change colours like that before. It's as if she has a different fish in her boat now. With another deep breath, she starts the laborious process of gutting, cleaning, and filleting her fish to feed herself for the next few days. And as she works, she sings. She sings to the beautiful fish from the sea.

27. DESTINATION

EMMA'S TACKING BACK AND FORTH slowly in front of Abraham's Bay, Mayaguana, in the grey dawn. It's too early in the morning to risk entering the coral-filled bay without good light. Even if she drops her sails and raises the centerboard, she knows there's a risk of hitting the prop of her outboard and damaging it. So she waits.

She scans the entry. It's narrow and from the charts she knows it opens into a long and wide bay that will protect boats from the sea. Though hardly anyone comes here.

All night she'd listened on the VHF for any chatter from nearby boaters and heard nothing. At one point she even wondered if her VHF was working. The empty air was strangely spooky and made her feel very alone.

But she knows alone is just a state of mind. And temporary. She's proud that her mind doesn't trick her into panic like it did in the North Atlantic when she was still green. A beginner. She doesn't consider herself a beginner any longer. But she's not smug about it either. That's why she's being cautious and waiting for the right time to enter.

She stretches and yawns. A huge yawn. It's been a long two days and nights of sailing, but she knows she did the right thing. She's been in the Bahamas for two weeks and her goal is so clear to her now. So close.

But is it? she wonders.

She tries to imagine what it will be like to find her mother, to speak to her. It shouldn't be hard to find her. She read somewhere that there are fewer than four hundred people living on the island.

She sails back and forth, back and forth, munching on hard cookies she dug up from the locker. She examines the one in her hand—some sort of oatmeal cookie. Now it tastes like cardboard. But her body seems to be okay with that.

"Sailboat outside of Abraham's Bay, do you read me? Over." The VHF barks to life. Emma stares at it for a moment, as if she doesn't quite compute. Then she springs for it.

"The *Edge* here. I read you. Who's this? Over."

"Hello there, the *Edge*, did you say? Strange name for a boat. Over." Who is this chatty person? Emma thinks. But then, maybe she doesn't care. She needs to chat. She throws caution to the wind. If anyone here is looking for a girl from Canada who ran away many months ago she'll be surprised.

"Well, I'm living my life on the *Edge*. So the name suits. Who are you? Over."

"This is Captain Joe. And this is the mailboat, *Lady Mathilda*. We'll be leaving soon and I see you prowling around out there. Do you need help coming in? Over."

"I'm good, thanks. Just waiting for the light. Probably okay to come in now, but I'll wait till you pass. Thanks for the heads up. Over."

"Have a good day, then. Over and out." Emma has no sooner replaced the VHF in its holder when a barge bursts out of the narrow entrance and heads her direction. She turns on the motor and holds the *Edge* steady. Someone on the pilot's deck waves as they plow on by at a good clip, on route to the next island stop. She waves back.

As they pass, she gears herself up to enter the bay. No more stalling. Because that's what she realizes she was doing. Stalling. Because, whatever she's trying to tell herself, she's afraid of what'll happen when she finds her mother.

EMMA TAKES THE *EDGE* right to the dock and ties up. It's in pretty good shape for a tiny community. Two old men are sitting on a bench under a tree chatting. They glance at her but hardly pause in their conversation. It's as if she's a normal sight.

She walks up to them and waits politely for the right moment to interrupt. Finally, one of them stops and addresses her directly.

"Hello, Miss. Can we help you?"

Emma realizes she has no idea what to say to such a direct question.

"Hello." She studies the ground in front of her. What should she say? Should she ask right out? She looks up and meets the eyes of the man who addressed her. Both men are studying her avidly now, seemingly in no rush for her to speak.

"Um. I'm looking for someone who may live here. Is there someone I should speak to who could help me?" She remembers she's wearing her cap and takes it off, in an awkward gesture of politeness. She's unexpectedly shy, she realizes.

"Well, now," says the second man, his arms folded over his chest. "I'm the policeman on this island, so perhaps I can help."

Policeman! Emma goes on full alert. Thoughts speed through her tired brain. The police aren't the same as customs and immigration, are they? He won't care. He won't even know. She'll play it cool. She can't exactly make a run for it now, anyway. And she wants to find her mother.

She wipes her sweaty palms on her jeans and studies the man who says he's the policeman. He looks like a local to her. His shirt is a washed-out blue and he's wearing faded cotton slacks with sandals. It's certainly not a uniform. But maybe that's normal for a remote island. He's smiling at her, his white teeth gleaming against his black, black skin. His eyes are kind.

His eyes are what spur Emma to ask her most terrifying question.

"I'm Emerald Lake, and I'm looking for my mother, Peggy Lake."

What happens next is etched in her mind forever. The man

who says he is the policeman heaves to his feet instantly and grabs her in his arms. Emma goes rigid as a board. Too late. She's been caught! They were looking for her after all.

But then she realizes the man's embrace is friendly, not hard. She's being hugged.

"What did I tell you?" the man says, turning to the other man who's also on his feet now clapping his hands then raising them to the air, then clapping them again.

"Didn't I tell you Peggy's daughter would be beautiful?" He holds Emma out at arms' length, his hands gripping her shoulders, his eyes scanning her face as if looking for something.

"Come. You have to meet Momma!" He says finally. He starts leading Emma down the path in a great rush. Emma's being swept along the dusty road and the two men are calling out to the people they meet, to houses that seem empty, to the school that's not yet open, to the church, the store, the local café.

"Peggy's daughter's come! Peggy's daughter's here!"

People pour out from their homes in whatever state of dress, or un-dress, they happen to be. Children from their beds rubbing their eyes, women and men in hastily pulled on clothes, one man's face is covered in shaving cream and he holds a razor in his hand. The cook from the café wears an apron and carries a big bowl in his arms. He continues to stir whatever's in it as he grins and nods his head.

Interrupted in what they were doing, but stopped by what they hear, the locals of the tiny community swarm to the dusty street to touch Emma's hair, to pat her shoulder, to greet her and welcome her to their island. It's still early in the morning, before their daily business starts.

"Peggy's daughter. Peggy Lake's daughter," she hears again and again. They know her mother. They know her. Her heart soars. She's here. She must be here. It's a matter of time before she comes to say hello. *What will I say? What will I do?* The thoughts swirl around in Emma's head as she's gathered up by the crowd and led to the café called *Momma's.*

There she's hugged fiercely by an enormous woman who introduces herself as Momma. She grabs Emma's hand and leads her inside, yelling at the cook to prepare a special breakfast. A chair is pulled out for Emma, and everyone stands around her while she sits down. She scans the black and white faces for the one face she thinks she'll recognize, the one face she's dreamed of seeing for ten long years. No one looks familiar. They all look friendly, but no one is her mother. Where's her mother? Where?

And then the overwhelm hits her like an avalanche. All the many miles have brought her here to this place, to this moment.

"Where is my mother?" Emma asks once she realizes she has to ask the important question.

The room goes utterly silent. Not a person moves. Emma looks from face to face. What has she said? A fresh panic wells up. Is she dead? Is her mother dead? She starts to get to her feet her mouth open to scream.

And then she bursts into tears.

"Oh, honey!" says Momma. "Charlie!" she calls to someone near the door. "Go to the clinic. Bring the nurse. Go now."

Emma lifts her face from her hands. "No. No. I don't need a nurse."

"Here, here honey. It's all too much." Momma waves her hands at the people who have poured into the room. "Give this little girl some space." She pulls out a chair and lowers herself into it. "Now, honey. You tell Momma."

And at those words Emma starts crying all over again. How could she tell them that all she wanted was to hear those very words but from someone else's lips? How could she explain that she had built up hopes, such hopes? That her mother would be here? She knows she shouldn't have, but she did. And this island, this moment, was as far as she could imagine going. And now what?

"Is she dead?" She chokes out the words as she grabs Momma's arm. Her eyes are wide. Has this all been a wild goose chase? Her heart plummets like a bird falling from the sky.

"Well, now honey. No. She's not dead. I think she's on Great Abaco." Momma says stroking her chin. She nods at the policeman. He nods back.

"She's in Hopetown," someone yells from the back of the room.

"No, that was four years ago. She's in Little Harbour," another calls out.

Momma chimes in. "Oh yes. That's it. She opened that jewellery shop, didn't she?"

"And she helps Pete with the bar," says an older man who's sitting nearby.

"I have to go. I have to go to her, now." She stands up looking straight at the Momma who is not Emma's momma. But her legs will hardly hold her and she sits back down again.

"What's the rush, honey?" Momma's face is puzzled. "Your momma's not going anywhere?" She looks at the policeman to see if he agrees. He raises his hands, his eyebrows rise too, followed by his shoulders. He looks around the room as if to look there for the answer. Emma looks too.

"You'll stay with us for a while. Rest up. This was her home for a good long time, and it's yours too."

The room is filled with friends and families and neighbours. Emma imagines they all know most everything about each other. Here she is on this little island with a population of a few hundred. It's one of a family of islands that stretch fifteen hundred miles. By now she's familiar with the habit Bahamian people have of visiting each other by small sailboat, the only way they can afford to travel.

Children grow up and have to leave their homes to go to high school on the main islands, like Great Abaco or Exuma, far away from the islands where they were born and raised. They stay with aunts or uncles or distant cousins and only come home when school's out for summer. To them Emma's visit is as natural as that, a daughter home from school.

Now, they'll visit. They'll ask questions, share stories, and go on with life. Let Emma go on with hers. It dawns on Emma that they don't understand her need to leave in a rush. They honestly mean it when they say she's welcome to stay. They want her to stay here, on the island with them. Become part of the community. Stay and be one of them. The whole concept is foreign to Emma.

Momma reaches over and pats Emma's arm. "You're lookin' for your momma. Of course you are. But first you're going to make yourself at home with us." She pushes to her feet. "Okay, everyone, shoo!" She waves her arms at everyone and hollers. "This little girl needs food and a rest." She turns to a woman standing near her. "Rita, you fix up your spare room."

The woman named Rita nods and smiles, gets to her feet beaming at the privilege of having Peggy's daughter stay with her.

Momma says to Emma. "You gonna spend time with Rita. Your momma and Rita were best friends when she lived here. Still are." She pats Emma on the back and tugs her to her feet, nudging her in Rita's direction. "She can tell her everything about the island. Be like your lovin' auntie."

Momma stands up and waves her hands at everyone in the room. "And tonight is a party. You all come over here for a feast." She beams from ear to ear. "Peggy's daughter's come for a visit and we need to welcome her right before she sails up north to say howdy to her momma."

28. ISLAND LIFE

THE NEXT TWO DAYS PASS in a flurry of activity. The level of attention she receives is uncomfortable at first, and then she realizes just how genuine their interest is, how truly they understand her adventure, her quest. And she starts to relax.

She's invited from home to home. She's invited into the school to talk to the children about Canada. The local boys show her how to catch lobster with a net. The younger children show her their favourite swimming spots.

The mothers feed her cornmeal cakes and lobster chowder and conch fritters. The fathers advise her on the next leg of her trip, the best fishing grounds on the way north, the quietest coves for anchoring.

And all of them remember her mother. She hears: "Peggy used to braid my hair just like this." "Peggy helped me paint this shell." "Peggy made me this skirt from a dress that didn't fit her anymore." "This is favourite Peggy's recipe for coconut pie." She keeps her face so still, motionless when she hears these snippets of the woman who didn't want her or couldn't look after her. No one notices, she thinks, when she closes her eyes on the pain of longing that rises up inside her. She smiles. She nods.

"Did she?" she says to the friendly person who is sharing the treasure that they are sure will mean something to Emma. "That's lovely. When did you say she taught you this?"

But deep inside, Emma's painful sorrow over her lonely childhood grows stronger with each of these statements. She tries to keep the hurt at bay, but in the middle of the night, while the tree frogs fill the night air with their loud song she trembles in her bed. The ache in her heart is an open wound.

"Why?" is the word that wakes her and locks her in its grip. She's too restless to sleep. She quietly tip-toes from the house where she's a guest and makes her way to the dock. She stands beside the *Edge* not certain why she's there. She knows it will be rude to sleep in her own boat. She turns to leave again and sees a shadow. Someone has followed her.

She stands rock still. Out of the dark steps Mayaguana's finest.

"Hello, Arthur," she says to the policeman. The night is velvety and warm.

"Hello, Emerald." He always calls her by her full name. "Come and sit."

Emma moves to the bench where she first found him and waits. He's here for a reason.

"I've been watching you." She can feel his eyes on her, even in the darkness. "You're troubled about something."

"Why?" she turns to him. "Why did she take me to Canada and leave me behind with people who didn't love me or want me?" Her hand closes on one of the pebbles she's been carrying in her pocket.

"Your mother never forgot you." The words hang in the air between them. They slice Emma to the core.

"How would you know that?" She's astonished by these words. "What do you know of my mother?" She moves to get up. "Or are you like the others? Did she help out at the police station? Do something kind for prisoners?" She's surprised by the bite to her words. She didn't realize how much she resented hearing about her mother and all she'd done in the community. All she'd done in this place that she made her home, while Emma was alone in Kingston missing her.

"I don't want to have this conversation." She gets to her feet.

"I just want to get moving, leave, find my mother, and get on with my life." She raises her hands in the air, in hurried frustration. "Except, I don't even know what that will be now!" She drops them back down. Her shoulders slump.

She starts to leave. "I should get back to Rita's before she notices I went for a walk. I don't want to worry her." Arthur's next words stop her dead in her tracks.

"She stayed in my jail, Emerald … after she took you home to Canada." He sighs. "After she was detained, she asked me permission to take you home and I gave it." He rubs his forehead as if remembering gives him a headache. "I got in big trouble for that. Letting a suspect leave the country. But she came back, like she promised." He turns to look at her.

"When she came back and waited for the police to find your father's body…. Well, all she talked about was you. How you were safe and that's all that mattered."

Emma slides back down to the bench. "What happened?"

"When they found him, and she was cleared of the murder charge, she stayed here on Mayaguana until the talk calmed down."

Emma can hardly breathe. "What happened to him?"

"Fell overboard, she said." Arthur scratches his head thoughtfully, as if to decide whether to go on or not. "I'm sorry to say he drank a lot, your father. And alcohol is a cause of many deaths at sea here. We see it often. There was no evidence to the contrary."

"Why did they arrest her, then?"

Arthur turns and, in the darkness, reaches out to put a hand on Emma's shoulder.

"Your dad was a drug-runner, Emerald. He was in deep trouble."

She remembers her aunt's words in the lawyer's office. Under his hand, Emma shudders.

"The police needed to make sure she wasn't involved." He lifts his hand from her shoulder and sighs deeply.

"I saw something when I was a child, a baby. Only four years old. It's been a recurring nightmare, but maybe it was real." Emma gets to her feet. Despite the heat she's shivering.

"Four men," she shakes her head. "I thought they were monsters, but they were probably just wearing diving gear. Came on board and took my father, took him off the boat." She begins to pace.

"Emma," Arthur cuts in. "It might have been a dream."

"No!" Emma cuts in, her hand palm up to stop him. "I've been lying to myself my whole life. I'm through with that now." For a moment she doesn't move.

"Did your mother see?"

"No. No I don't think so. I was looking through the hatch above the V-berth and one of them saw me."

Arthur sucks in his breath. "You say one of them saw you watching."

"Yes, but I didn't know it was a man. I thought it was a sea-monster. It was so black out, and the masks..." her voice trailed off.

Could this explain it? Could this explain what her aunt and her grandmother meant about protecting her? Had she been in some sort of danger?

"Is that why didn't she keep me with her?" her voice cracks.

"I suppose you need to ask her." He rubs his chin, watching Emma. After a minutes pause he says, "You can call her, if you want."

Emma's whole body jerks. She hasn't thought of this.

"Call her?"

"You can use the office phone."

Emma's having a hard time breathing. Imagining what she would say ... it's impossible. Somehow in her mind she's seen herself speaking to her mother for the first time face to face. Not over a phone line.

"I could?"

"We can call today."

"We can call today?" Emma repeats.

"Well, yes," he laughs pointing to the lightening sky. "Come over later, after breakfast." He stands up and reaches over to pats her shoulder. This time the touch is light, friendly, as if this phone call is no big deal. "We'll make the call."

She meets Arthur's eyes. "Okay." She wishes she could put more warmth in her voice. But she just can't. Emma pulls away from him.

"You're not the only one to spend time away from your parents, Emerald." It's as if he's read her thoughts.

"You?" she asks.

"Yes," he says. "They sent me off island when I was eleven, for school."

"Did you know your mother and father were alive?"

"Yes."

"Did you know they loved you?" Her voice catches on a sob, but she sucks in her breath. She's not going to cry. Not here.

"Yes."

"Well, then it's not the same for you, is it?" She gets to her feet.

"I'll come by later, Arthur." She starts off down the dusty road, but before she gets very far, she stops, turns around, and walks back to him. She takes the pebble that she always carries out of her pocket. "Do you know what this is?"

Arthur turns the pebble over and over in his fingers. "You know, your mother had a bag of these with her in jail. She said they were her lucky bearings." He gives the pebble back to her.

Bearings, Emma thinks. What he's talking about? She hesitates a minute longer. "Arthur, you know I'm in the Bahamas illegally, right?"

Arthur nods.

"Why haven't you reported me, or whatever you're supposed to do?" Emma's hand is trembling as she slips the pebble back into her pocket.

"We have different concerns, those immigration folks and I." He grins, and she can see his white, white teeth. "You're

no threat to my island, Emerald. And that's all I care about."
Emma leans down and gives him a kiss on the cheek, then
walks away into the growing light.

29. PHONE CALL

FEAR, ANGER, TERROR, HURT ... fear, anger, terror, hurt ... fear, anger....

Emma is filled with these feelings as she makes her way to the police station. She can hardly breathe with the force of them. But she hides all the turmoil behind a face as empty as a blank page.

It's Sunday and there's a small crowd of islanders with her before going to church. People who have come to support her. Word has travelled. She's going to call her mother. She's going to speak to her mother for the first time since her mother left her in Canada with her aunt and uncle.

She hesitates in front of the low, white structure with the bright green door. No one moves or says a word. They are waiting for her, respectfully. She turns to face them.

"I'm going in now," she says, totally unnecessarily.

"Good luck, honey," someone says.

"Say hi for us. Tell her to come over soon," says another.

"Yes," joins another. "It's been too long."

Emma takes a step. Then another. Knocks at the door, which opens immediately, as if Arthur has been waiting there.

"Come in, Emma." He steps aside to let Emma through.

Emma walks past him without looking back. Her focus is all on her mother now, on what she'll say. This is way too hard, she thinks and pauses, then stops.

"It's gonna be all right, Emerald," Arthur takes her arm, leads her gently to a chair where a phone is off its cradle, clearly just put down. The island grapevine must have warned him Emma was on her way. Her mother is waiting.

She picks up the receiver. "Mom?"

"Emma," a woman's voice says. "Emma."

There's a long silence, as if neither of them know what to say next.

"Mom, I sailed here," Emma says. "To find you." Her hand gripping the telephone receiver is slick with sweat.

"Emma." The voice is soft, rushed. "I can hardly believe it. I can't believe it." Silence stretches between them. "You found me."

"Well, not yet."

"But you'll come to Little Harbour?"

"Yes," Emma nods her head as though her mother can see. "Yes, I'll come. I'll leave tomorrow."

"Oh my God. I'm going to see you!" Again silence, heavy with the weight of something neither of them can say. The line crackles and pops. The silence stretches.

"Good sailing then," Emma's mother says, finally. "Take good care of yourself."

"I'll see you soon, Mom." She twists the phone cord around one finger after another.

"Yes, very soon. Very, very soon." There's a big sigh. "I can't wait." The line goes dead.

Emma holds the receiver in her hand, staring. The cord's still wrapped around her fingers. She untwists it. She's filled with a deep sense of disappointment. What did she expect? What could she possibly have expected from a phone call? The phone starts to beep, reminding her she still hasn't hung up. She puts the receiver back in its cradle with both hands as if it weighs a ton.

She gets to her feet. But her legs are like rubber. She sits back down, heavily. She starts to tremble. Her whole body's shaking.

"Whoa," she says as the trembles fade away.

Arthur hands her a glass of water. "You did good."

"Thanks." Emma drinks and hands the glass back. "Well, I guess I'm invited to Little Harbour." She smiles slightly at Arthur, but the smile doesn't reach her eyes.

Could that be it? As simple as "see you soon?" Something doesn't feel right. But maybe that's just because there are still so many questions. Emma sighs. She looks closely at Arthur as if he could guide her, but his face is completely bland. Too bland, maybe.

Emma shakes her head. Now she's suspecting everyone. She gets to her feet and as she does, a movement catches her eye, then just as quickly it's gone? Is there someone here? Someone listening? Confusion floods her body. She turns.

"Arthur...?" she starts to say. She stops. Her eyes fall on a piece of driftwood sitting on his desk. The markings are the same as the piece of wood that had been left for her with the note. "Who made this?" she asks, picking it up and studying it. She already knows the answer.

"Your mother," he says, pauses. "She made so many while she was..." he shrugs.

"...In jail." Emma finishes his sentence, places it back on the desk, and turns to leave. Again, there's a flicker of motion in the other room. Emma takes a step toward it, but Arthur takes her hand, gives it a squeeze. She looks past his shoulder, and there's nothing now. Maybe it was just a lizard.

"I'll be leaving tomorrow." She turns her attention back to the kind man in front of her.

"I'll be on the dock to say goodbye." Now Arthur leads her toward the door and opens it. Emma has the peculiar sense that she's being sent on her way. She steps through the door into the blinding sunlight and the waiting faces. She puts a big smile on her face as she knows she must.

"Hey honey. You lookin' happy!"

"Yeah, she's happy."

Emma is swept up in the crowd as they make their way back to Momma's, the café where everyone meets to talk about the island's business. She tells them she's leaving for Little Harbour the next morning. She's going to see her mother, yes. Yes, her mother's going to come to Mayaguana, Emma lies, realizing she forgot to ask and yet she knows that it's okay. Island time is slow enough that a few more years could pass and they'd remember the invitation as if it was made yesterday.

Many offers of help mean the *Edge* is ready and restocked before the day is done. Someone fetches water to fill up her tanks. Her gas tank is topped up. Someone else gets her fresh mangos and eggs and other goods. When everything is stowed away she comes back to the village for a last night of celebration.

The next morning the islanders come to say goodbye and send her on her way north to her mother. It's going to take her at least five, maybe six long days of sailing to get there, depending on the wind direction and the winter storms.

"I'll be back," she tells them all. "I promise." And she's surprised to realize she means it.

30. STOWAWAY

EMMA'S FAR OUT ON THE OPEN WATER, her sails are set, her autohelm is locked in place, when she goes below to get her charts in order and tidy up.

"Hello." A boy uncoils himself from behind the stack of spare sails and blankets stuffed in the V-berth. He's not much older than Emma.

She rears back. "Wha...?" She stumbles and almost falls. An intruder! Is she being hijacked? She recovers and lunges forward grabbing the VHF from the chart table to call for help, but the boy's faster. He snags her wrist.

"Whoa. Take it easy." He says the words almost lazily. "I'm not going to hurt you." He pries the VHF out of her fingers and stuffs it in the pocket of his shorts. "I'm not going to hurt you. Just hitching a ride is all."

Emma pulls away from him, rubbing her wrist where he had grabbed it. She casts around to see if there's anything she can get her hands on to fend off this boy if he comes near her again. Her eyes land on the big flashlight in the cubby over the sink. She inches her way toward it.

She leaps sideways and swipes the flashlight out of the cubby and raises it above her head. But the boy chuckles and shakes his head, holds his hand out as if he expects her to just give it to him.

Emma holds the flashlight in front of her ready to fend him

off if he comes close. She grips it with two hands and waves it like a sword.

"Stay away from me!"

"Emma." He reaches out to grab it, but she snatches it away from his reach. "Give it up, Em." She brings it back in front of her. She's thinking of what else she can threaten him with.

"How do you know my name?" She holds her fighting stance.

When he doesn't answer, she inches toward the chart table. Maybe she can reach the flare gun. That'll get his attention. But she'll have to dig it out of the box and.... Maybe a knife? That's better. Keeping her eyes fixed on his face, she darts a hand out to open the top drawer. But the boy slaps his hand over hers where she fiddles desperately with the safety latch.

"Emma," he says again, with a weird kind of patience, the way an older brother would speak to his kid sister if they were horsing around and he was done playing.

"Who are you?" She spits the words out. What's he doing on her boat? Can she overpower him? He's not a sickie, like the man who tried to steal her money. She raises the flashlight to bash him over the head, but he blocks her and wrenches it out of her hand. Emma dashes away, running from him over to the chart table and flings it open, grabbing the box with the flare gun.

"Give it up, Em," the boy says again, taking the box out of her shaking hands. "I'm not going to hurt you. All this time I've been following you, don't you think I could have hurt you by now if I was going to?"

His words stop her in her tracks. "It's YOU who's been following me?" Her mouth falls open.

"Why?" she shouts. "Why are you following me?"

"It's what I'm being paid to do."

"Paid? Paid?" she stammers. "You're kidding, right?" Now he's not making any sense at all. "Who'd pay you to follow me? I'm nobody. And you're just a kid!" He must be mad. She's screaming. Hands empty now she braces herself. But there's no place to run. She studies him closely. He doesn't look like a crazy. In fact, he looks smart.

She suddenly realizes that she's not scared of him. She spins on her heal and climbs up out into the cockpit, and sits down behind the wheel. It steadies her somewhat. She hasn't lost, exactly. Maybe she can distract him and dunk him overboard. How dare he come aboard! She has to think. Think! There must be something she can do to get him off her boat.

But curiosity gets the better of her. There are too many unanswered questions starting to swirl in her head.

He follows her out to the cockpit and takes a seat, stretching his feet out in front of him and making himself comfortable. Emma grits her teeth in frustration.

"Who pays a kid to follow a kid?" Emma stares hard at him, daring him to brush her off. She cocks her chin up and squares her shoulders, drums her fingers on the wheel. No way can he be telling the truth. No way! She sends him with a look of complete disdain.

"I'm not an ordinary kid. I've been sailing my whole life."

"Okay, so you're a sailor—like I care!" her voice drips with sarcasm. "Who would bother to hire someone to follow a nobody from Canada—and pay for it?"

"Your great grandfather."

Emma sucks in her breath. "Liar!" she spits out.

"It's the truth."

"My ... great ... grandfather," she repeats each syllable slowly. Her eyes narrow to slits. "I don't know who you're talking about." Who's this guy kidding? And why does he look vaguely familiar? Why does she feel like she's met him before?

"Sure you do," the boy gives a short laugh, folds his arms across his chest. "Mr. Flinders. The old dude."

Emma goes completely still. This is too strange. "Flinders," she says again. The name sends a shiver down her spine. Her aunt's words rise up into her consciousness. *You know what Flinders wants as well as I do.*

"Mr. Flinders." She shakes her head. "Not possible. You're making this up." But for some reason, she senses he's not. Then she remembers. Last spring. The boy standing behind Mr. Flinders while he bought his strawberries. With a tan and shaggy blond curls.

"Wait a minute." Emma points an accusing finger toward him. "I recognize you." She studies him. "You were in Kingston in the spring. You came with him." She tightens her hands on the wheel. "I saw you."

He shrugs as if it's of no consequence. He reaches for the jib sheet.

"Don't!" she growls. "Don't touch anything on my boat without my permission."

"Hey!" he raises his hands in the air. "It's luffing." He points at the shimmering sail.

"Leave it." She leans forward to adjust the sail herself and returns to her position behind the wheel.

Emma narrows her eyes. Something else is tugging at her. She studies him. He's about as tall as she is. His blond hair's bleached by the sun, scruffy like hers. He looks familiar. Familiar, like she knows him. "Who ARE you?"

"Not important."

"It's important to me," she slaps her hand on the wheel angrily. She feels light-headed, reckless. With blinding speed, she unhooks the autohelm, throws the helm hard over, and uncleats the jib all in one swift movement. Then tightens up again.

Peter ducks his head in the nick of time as the boom smacks over, barely missing him. She's turned them around. She's going back to the island.

"What are you doing, you crazy girl?" He wrestles with her over the helm and she jabs him hard in the ribs. Rubbing his side, he laughs as if enjoying himself, then sits lazily back down.

"Next time I'll kick you in the balls," she threatens. She'd almost done it too, but she stopped. What stopped her? she wonders.

"I'm turning you over to Arthur. He'll know what to do."
He laughs again. "Go right ahead."

Something drives her to taunt the boy. "You might as well
tell me who you are. I'll find out soon enough." Emma leans
forward over the wheel, determination on her face.

The boy says, "My name's Peter."

"Peter." She pauses, waiting. When he doesn't say anything
more she prompts him. "Peter what?" She sends him a piercing
look to let him know she means business.

With a huff he replies, "Visser." He pauses to let it sink in.
"Peter Visser."

Emma guffaws in frustration and frowns at him. "Do you
think I'm an idiot? You made that up."

The boy looks uncomfortable for a second. "Nope. It's the
truth." Then he lifts his shoulders and flashes her a goofy grin.
"I'm your half-brother."

"AAARRHGH!" Emma raises her arms in the air and makes
fists with her hands. "Stop the bullshit. I don't have a…"

"Yes," Peter cuts her off. "You do."

There's a flat honesty in the words. Emma brings her hands
back to the wheel. She turns and looks at Peter. Looks closer.

"You're my father's kid?" she says. *Your brother's boy.* Aunt
Petra's words, spoken with such hatred in the kitchen that
long-ago day come back to her now.

Peter tilts his head in a small bow, then raises his hand slightly
and points a finger toward himself. "That's me."

Emma stares at him for a long minute. "How old are you?"

"Nineteen."

Four years older than her. She brings her hands to her head,
yanks off her cap, and gives her hair a vigorous rub as if to
sort out the thoughts roiling around in head.

"Okay, let me get this straight," she says at last, looking up
at him. "You're my half-brother that I never knew about. And
you've been hired by my great grandfather that I never knew
about. And you're accompanying me on this visit to find the

mother I haven't seen in ten years." She pins him with her eyes. "Is that about it?"

No answer. Peter just gazes forward, scanning the horizon, as if considering his options.

"Is that it or isn't it?"

"Look, Em," Peter says finally. "It's complicated. But it's not my business. I'm just doing what your GG wants. And that's it." He folds his arms across his chest as if to end the conversation.

"Yeah, sure. Stop talking to me. Like that's going to help." Emma's voice is cold. "I'll just keep asking questions." She drums her fingers on the wheel. He's still not looking at her. "I'll go get Arthur, and tell him what you did." She points in the direction of Mayaguana where they're headed again now that she's come about. "I'm pretty sure break and entry is illegal everywhere in the world. You'll be in trouble for sure, no matter if my GG, as you call him, hired you."

"He's in on it."

"What do you mean?"

"Arthur knows." Peter looks at Emma while she processes this. "That's where I was staying while you were hanging with Momma and everyone." The water swish swishes past the hull of the *Edge*. Time ticks slowly by.

"Why's Arthur in on this?" Then she has another thought. "Is my great grandfather paying him too?" Her heart plummets. "I thought he was my friend." She drops her head down on the wheel.

"Just because he's doing what your GG wants doesn't mean he's not your friend, Em," Peter says, his eyes on her.

"Did everyone on Mayaguana do what my GG wanted?" She tips her eyes up to him and there's such sadness in them, he squirms.

"Nah." He shakes his head. "No. I mean, I don't think so. No one else knew I was there." He continues. "They were just being themselves."

Emma fingers the bracelet one of the children made for her. After taking a deep breath and then another, Emma makes a decision. "Prepare to gybe."

Peter shoots her a look to make sure she's means it and is truly inviting him to act as her crew. At her nod, he uncleats the jib, gets the other line ready. Together they make a quick neat gybe and reset the sails on the *Edge's* original course. Emma hooks up the autohelm.

The *Edge* slices gracefully through the calm ocean. There's a light steady breeze. It's a perfect day for a sail. Perfect except that the whole trip has been ruined, thinks Emma. Spoiled. All her excitement about going to her mother has been overshadowed by what she's learned, by the uncomfortable feeling that she's being played with. Like a cat plays with a mouse.

"What's going on? I can't understand any of it." She rubs a hand over her eyes. "I have so many questions tumbling around in my head I don't know where to start." It's as if she's speaking to herself. She closes her eyes for a moment, to focus.

"Start with the first one that jumps into your mind," Peter offers.

She opens her eyes and studies him long and hard. Is he a friend or a foe? Can she trust him? Even if she doesn't, she needs to know the answers.

Where to start? Where in the world should she start, she has no idea. She narrows her eyes at him, asks him the first thing that pops into her head. "Why'd you cut my rode in St. Mary's Inlet?"

"Ah, that." He grimaces. "Not my finest idea. But you were taking too long. The GG wanted you in the Bahamas much sooner. He's kind of impatient."

"I hate him." The words leap out of her.

"Yeah, well, you don't know him, do you?"

"Why do you keep saying he's MY GG? He's yours too, isn't he?" Emma eyes Peter.

"Nope. Not mine."

"He's my mother's grandfather?"

"Yup." Peter nods.

"He's Jess's father?" Emma springs up, her whole body exploding on one word "NO!"

"Whoa, Em. What's the big...?" Peter leans forward. On the off-chance that she's going to send the boat careening over again, he reaches for the wheel.

Emma flings an arm out and smacks him on the face. Then she stands there stunned. She's never hit someone before. It feels awful, like an ugliness has invaded her. She feels empty too. The intense anger that had shot through her has drained away, leaving only shame.

Rubbing his cheekbone, he eyes her. "Feel better now?"

Emma crumples onto the seat. "I'm sorry." She reaches out to rub her thumb over the skin, but he jerks away from her. "I'm really sorry. I never hit anyone before." She shakes her head. "That was ... awful." She's appalled at herself. Her aunt had hit her so many times that she's lost count, but she knows for certain she'll never hit anyone ever again. "You upset me. But that's no excuse. I'm really sorry." She keeps her eyes on his.

"It's okay." He rubs his cheek, then smiles. "It's okay," he says again. "I hardly felt it."

She scowls at him and turns away, stares down at the water for a long time, acutely aware of his presence, but unable to face him.

"My grandmother was special to me." She turns to him finally. "You don't know what she meant to me. And now you tell me that he's her father?" Emma sighs. "I don't know how to make sense of this—the strangeness of a family I don't know. No one speaking to each other, or acting like a normal family? All the secrecy?"

"Hey, tell me about it," Peter says, standing up and scanning the horizon again. "Families are strange."

Minutes pass. The dark water thrum thrums past the boat. Her heart thrums, too, and with a pain she can't explain.

"What was he like, Peter?" Emma pauses. "Our father, I mean."

Peter sits down again, settles back against the seat. "I really didn't know him, Em." He tugs on his cap, scratches his head. "He was never there, you know." He shoots her a strange look, a kind of apology. "And then there was your mother."

Emma sucks in her breath. What an idiot she is. Of course, her mother … his mother. "Oh. Sorry … yeah …okay."

"Hey," she wants to change the subject. "Where's your boat, Peter?"

Peter points vaguely in the direction they're sailing.

"How'd you get to Mayaguana, then?" Her voice is flat. "Mailboat."

The mailboat she met on her arrival in Mayaguana. Hmmm.

She waits for more information. But he just stares at his feet indicating the subject is closed. She smacks her fist down on her leg. She's going to have to pry the answers out of him.

"What's going on, Peter? Why all the mystery?"

When he doesn't say anything, she feels the anger mounting. "Come ON, Peter."

"Look, Em. I can't talk about it." He meets her eyes. "What's between you and your GG, it's not my business."

"What *is* your business, then?" Emma insists, exasperated.

He pauses, closes his eyes for a moment, as if to figure out how best to phrase his answer. He opens his eyes again and peers at her from under his shaggy bangs. "I guess you could say my job is to get you to the old man as quickly as possible," he says finally.

Emma huffs out an angry breath. "Well, that's ridiculous."

Tired of the whole conversation, she jumps to her feet and lifts a locker, rummages inside for a cleaning cloth and her rust remover. She starts rubbing the rust off the base of a stanchion furiously, just for something to do with her hands. Anything to keep herself occupied while she sifts through the information—or lack of information.

She feels exactly as she does when she's trying to find her way into an unknown harbour in the dark. She's desperately looking for the next marker, and the next, to lead her in. And she can only see a few feet in front of her.

"If the old man needed to talk to me, then why didn't he just talk to me way back in Kingston?" She shakes the cloth at Peter. "I wouldn't have had to make this crazy sailing trip all the way to Mayaguana, Bahamas."

She stops polishing and plops herself down on a bench in frustration. She's beyond patience now. "I mean, I've been under his nose all these years and he's never said anything to me!"

"I have no idea." Peter says, eyeing her like she's might explode again at any moment.

When Emma glares at him, he shakes his head.

"Hey!" he says to her, "don't get angry at me—it's you who ran away. For all you know, he was going to speak to you back there."

"This is just bull crap and you know it." But something of what he's trying to say sinks in. The sun is bright overhead. The minutes tick by as Emma cleans and Peter lounges on the bench with his eyes closed.

When they've been sailing for almost an hour, Emma feels something inside her shift. They're making good progress. Toward what, she doesn't know. What's her destination now? Some tension in her loosens. But what's left is a kind of emptiness. As if she's lost some of her drive.

Up until this morning she's been clear about her goal, or at least as clear as she could be. First and foremost, she needed to get away from her aunt and uncle. And she needed to find her mother. That was her main purpose. That was her focus, what kept her going through all the challenges of this trip down the coast of America to the Bahamas. To find her mother and finally discover the truth of what happened. Now, she scans the horizon, considering his words and all she feels is confusion.

"What else do you know? Do you know about the *Edge*? Do you know about my grandmother?"

Peter sends her a bland look. "Nope. You're a good sailor by the way."

Emma flicks off his compliment with a toss of the cleaning cloth. "I just don't get it. Any of it." Emma gets to her feet and puts away the rag and rust cleaner in the locker. She studies the horizon and assesses the wind again. They should tack soon.

She peers over her shoulder at Peter, raises her eyebrows toward him as if waiting for an answer, but he just tips his head and sends her a kind of goofy smile. She's so annoyed she could scream.

"Why are you on my boat, Peter?"

"To bring you to him as fast as possible. He wants to see you in two days."

"Two days? Not possible." She shakes her head once, then again, with more determination. "Why does he think I'll go along with you, all chummy and cheerful?"

He gives her an odd look that she can't interpret. "Because it'll be fun?" he asks all innocently.

"Fun!" Emma screws up her face. "So you're here to get me to Flinders faster. If he needed to see me sooner, then why didn't he just fly into Mayaguana? Or get a speed boat to bring me to him?"

"Don't know." Peter flashes his palms up in mock surrender. "Honestly, I don't."

His off-hand manner flicks a switch in her. "You want me to believe you don't care about anything except," she makes imaginary marks in the air with her fingers, "*getting the job done.*"

At Peter's shrug, Emma folds her arms over her chest in frustration. "Okay, okay, I get it. Following me was just a job. You don't care about me." Her face is deflated.

"Em, I care," Peter says. "I did what I could to help," he

pauses, then adds almost as an afterthought, "…when it didn't interfere with your GG's orders."

Emma studies his profile. He's not looking at her. It's like he's hiding something, or stopping himself from saying more. And just like that, a light bulb goes on in Emma's head. "Was that you who hailed me back when I messed up at Barnegat?"

Peter lifts one shoulder, tips his head, as if it's of no matter. But it matters to Emma. He pulls a cap out of his back pocket and crams it on his head. And another image pops into her mind.

"That was you who helped me off the mud bank!" She reaches out and puts a hand on his arm. "I knew I'd seen you somewhere else."

Peter turns and looks at her, his eyes holding hers. Emma gets the feeling that he wants her to understand something he can't put into words.

"After the tornado." She laughs. "You had on that hat. And sunglasses, trying to hide behind a disguise. But I knew you. It was weird."

He covers her hand with his own, holds it there for a beat, before getting to his feet. "I could see you were hurt." He looks out over the bow, studying the horizon. "I wanted to do more, but…"

"But you had to follow orders," Emma finishes for him. She's stunned. Peter's been looking after her.

"You scared me, you know," she says. "I hated that."

"I know."

Then realization dawns on her. "You were trying to encourage me. Like that note up in Elizabeth City? *You're doing great—* you truly meant that."

Peter doesn't take his eyes off the water.

They sail in silence for a while. But something's still niggling at the back of Emma's mind that she just can't let go of.

"I just don't get why I had to make the long sail to Maya-guana," she says. "My mother wasn't there anyway."

A seagull flies close to check if there's any food, then flies away. "Why didn't Flinders intercept me earlier, if time's the only thing that's important to him?"

Again, Peter turns his hands palm up and shrugs.

The *Edge* slices through the water. Playing over the whole story in her mind again, as if it's not her own, as if it's a story that belongs to someone other than herself, Emma reaches down and trails a hand in the foam as it curls out behind the stern. It's a good day for fishing, she thinks almost automatically. She should put out her fishing line.

And then, with a flash of intuition, Emma has the complete conviction that she was being tested throughout this entire voyage. Tested by her great grandfather. He was testing her for her stamina and her courage. For her sailing skills. Testing her commitment to finding her mother.

"He's been testing me." She spits out the words bitterly.

"Why would...?" Peter starts to ask, but Emma puts up a hand.

"He's been testing me through this whole trip." She wants to get under this somehow. "He needs to know I'm worthy." She slaps her hand on the wheel working it out. "Worthy of something—his approval maybe."

Peter jerks.

Emma sits up straight both hands resting steadily now on the wheel as these thoughts sink in. "What?" She pierces Peter with a look.

"What do you know, Peter, that you're not telling me?"

Peter just shakes his head.

"Peter?" Emma's voice if filled with aggravation.

With a jerk of his shoulder he says, "He's rich, you know. Very, very rich. And you're going to inherit, right?" Another jerk of the shoulder.

Emma's mouth has dropped open. Never in a million years would she have considered this. Is it possible she will inherit?

"You're kidding me. I'm not..." Peter's not looking at her.

Emma decides she doesn't care. She doesn't need Peter's help to figure this out now. For one thing, she's confident that she passed every single one of the tests of this voyage with flying colours. She has nothing to fear from this old man. Nothing she needs or wants from him.

And then the memory of Jess slides into her head? Was giving Emma the *Edge* part of her great grandfather's plan? No. That's too farfetched. Jess had planned to go find her daughter herself. She didn't know she was going to die. Emma's running away just somehow fit into some other scheme, a scheme that had nothing to do with Jess. She's sure of it. She flips off her cap and rubs her hand through her curls.

Without Jess, she wouldn't have known how to sail, would she? And sailing is something she loves more than anything she's ever done. Now she finds out Mr. Flinders is her great grandfather. Well, her great grandfather wants to come out of hiding and meet her? It's about time. Emma straightens her shoulders. She's proud of what she's done, proud of who she is. And it has nothing to do with being related to some old curmudgeon who likes to play with people's lives as if they're puppets. She has a zillion questions. But now she knows who she needs to confront. And confront him she will.

She looks over at Peter who's watching the sea like the pro he is—scanning the horizon and being attentive to all the myriad boat details. "Weren't you worried about me after you cut my rode and left me without an anchor?"

"No," Peter says. He turns and meets her eyes. "Why would I be?" There's something in his voice, maybe a note of pride. "You could handle it".

"Thanks, I think. But you know very well I could have damaged someone's boat. Or the *Edge*," she continues. "That would have put a spanner in my GG's plans to speed me along." She cocks her head at Peter. She wants an answer.

He shakes his head, starts to make a small adjustment to the main sheet. She slaps his hand away and makes the adjustment herself. "You know what you're doing, Em." He turns to her, grinning. "I mean it. I've never seen a girl with such good sailing skills." Then, "Besides, everyone puts out fenders."

Emma recalls that even she had fenders at the ready. "Were you testing me, too?"

He shoots her a puzzled look. "No," he says, shaking his head. "Why would I do that?"

And just like that, Emma knows that he truly believes her to be a good sailor. It sinks in that he takes it for granted that she's resourceful—his confidence in her is so complete that he didn't worry when he did a stupid thing that would have, could have, put her into trouble.

And she'd been fine. Of course, she had. She'd figured it out. As she would figure many things out. And strangers throughout the voyage had been kind. The kindness of strangers would be there again, and again. Because she's learned, even though she resisted it, that there is kindness in the world. And people were there for her when she needed them.

"It must have frustrated you when I stayed so long at Vicki's."

"Some." Peter nods.

"I was going to quit this whole adventure right there," Emma tells him.

"I wouldn't have let you." The fierce look he gives her warms her through and through.

"What would you have done?" she laughs. "Written me another anonymous note?" She shakes her head. "No. I needed that break." She pauses, realizing. "I needed that sanctuary, that place to completely break down, and the space and time to put myself back together again."

Peter's eying her. "Who is she, anyway?" he asks. "Someone you knew?"

Emma smiles. "No." She looks away, remembering the healing goodness of the woman who opened her home and heart to her. "She was just a kind stranger."

She turns back and, from under the brim of her cap she studies him, this new stranger who's not quite a stranger. And then, quite unexpectedly, she finds she can let all the other questions she has about him go for the moment. Emma knows she's looking at her brother.

He catches her studying him and studies her right back. She realizes his eyes are her eyes. No wonder he looks familiar. When he grins, she recognizes his grin. Something inside of her clicks into place, like a piece of the big unfinished puzzle of who she is. This is her brother. And he's a kid, just like her. Maybe that's enough for now.

"Here," she says, getting up from the helm. "Take over." When he raises his eyebrows at her she just heads toward the cabin where she pauses on the top step.

"So, Bro. You want a muffin? I make amazing muffins. The best in the world, I reckon, and I dare you to disagree."

In answer, Peter's stomach gives out a loud grumble. His mouth forms a round "O" and they both laugh.

She goes below, and then has a thought. She takes the bag of pebbles out of the chart table and tosses them up to him. He catches them just before the hit the deck.

"You know what those are?" she says, opening the cupboard to pull out a mixing bowl.

He turns the bag over and studies the pebbles. Then he shoots her a crooked smile. "Weird, huh?" He pushes back his unruly hair. "He never said what they were."

31. DISASTER

I t's FOUR IN THE MORNING, the darkest part of the night when there's a cacophony of smashing, tearing, crumpling, grinding and the *Edge* comes to a crashing halt.

Emma's just come off her watch. She's drifting into sleep when it happens. With her heart pounding hard in her chest, she hurls herself up on deck. Peter's pulling himself up off the floor of the cockpit where he's been thrown by the impact. Together they rush to the side of the boat.

There in the water is a container as large as the *Edge*, submerged just below the surface of the water. The *Edge* is smashed up against it. There's a gaping hole in the hull, water gushing in. The *Edge* is sinking!

Emma races back down below. Peter's right behind her. Water is flooding the inside of the boat. She grabs a sail bag, a blanket, a pillow, anything she can get her hands on and stuffs it all in the hole. The water forces everything back out. There's no stemming the flow. She feels Peter's hands on her shoulders.

"Emma, put this on." He hands her some wet gear and her lifejacket. "Quick!" He grabs a spare lifejacket and then a jacket for himself. Then he digs in the chart table for the flares, and stuffs them in his pocket.

For a moment Emma's mind turns to sludge. The *Edge* is sinking—no getting her back. Everything she has will be gone.

"No!" she screams.

The word reverberates through the cabin as Emma springs into action. She grabs the VHF. "Mayday! Mayday! Sailboat sinking." She gives the GPS coordinates of their last position. "Mayday! Mayday! Sailboat sinking."

Peter calls. "Leave it, Em! There's no one there!"

Emma's too angry to quit. "Why doesn't anyone answer?" she yells at the VHF, shaking her fist at it. "Where are you when we need you?" she yells again and slides it into her pocket.

The *Edge* yawls to one side. Emma shoots a hand out against one of the bulwarks to brace herself. The water is up to her knees now. There are books, pillows, shoes all sloshing around her. Her favourite cap floats by. She lunges for it and crams it on her head. A pot bumps up against a cabinet making a loud bang.

She looks over and there floating away from her is the ziplock bag with the photo of her mother and Jess, along with Jess's last letter to her and the newspaper clipping about her mother. She wades after it and grabs it just as the *Edge* tips and leans even further. She stumbles, then catches herself and tucks the precious package into an inside pocket.

"Come on, Emma. We've got to get out of here." Peter calls from the cockpit. His voice is urgent.

She pulls herself up the tilted stairs and out into the cockpit. The *Edge* is listing badly on her side. Emma has to stand with one foot on the side of a seat and the other on the door of the hatch. She turns back. Something's keeping her stuck here. She's not ready to give up yet.

Peter's about to jump into the water when Emma calls out to him, "Wait!" He turns.

"If we lash the *Edge* to the container, perhaps she won't sink completely." Peter nods. Together they scramble to pull out all the lines they can find from the various lockers. Emma guns the outboard and opens the throttle bringing the *Edge* as close to the container as she can. The *Edge* is so full of water now that it's like moving cement.

Peter jumps overboard carrying a line in his hand and swims over to the container. He crawls up onto the top and lashes the line to one of the rings on the side. Emma cleats it off to the hull. They tie as many lines as they can from the boat to the container.

The *Edge* gives a terrible shudder. Emma's heart lurches. She's going down. If they haven't done a good enough job of securing her, then she'll be gone.

"Emma, jump!" Peter shouts. "Now!"

Emma leaps into the water, free of the wreck, and swims over to where Peter is standing knee deep on the top of the container. Peter takes her hand. They watch. The *Edge* tips over on her side and slowly submerges beneath the water. There's a terrible wrenching sound as the cleats take the weight of the boat. Then nothing. The sinking stops. The hull of the *Edge* is completely under water but she's stopped sinking. The container's holding her weight.

For a moment Emma slumps against Peter. "It's safe. The *Edge* didn't sink."

Then a sudden fury rises up inside her, gripping her so that her body is shaking with it. She starts to curse. She curses container ships. She curses careless crews that don't secure their cargo. She curses storms. She screams at the top of her lungs until she's emptied out, emptied out and limp. She doesn't curse Peter.

"Sorry, Em."

She buries her head in his shoulder. "Stop." She pulls back and meets his eyes. "It could have been my watch. You aren't to blame." She gives his shoulders a small shake. "So don't blame yourself, okay?" She doesn't let go until she gets a nod from him.

Then they both turn to stare at the water around them. It's so black that it sucks the light into it. There's no moon. Just the slight waves on an endless ocean, the light wind, and the two of them standing on top of a floating island of debris.

At least there's no storm. She's grateful for that.

"Where we headed, do you figure?"

Peter squints into the blackness. "Current's taking us south. Maybe to Eleuthra."

"You don't sound like that's a good thing." In the dark she can just make out the wreck of her boat.

"It's nothing." Peter shrugs. Emma stares at him for a moment, then she sighs. Whatever, she thinks. He can keep his little mystery.

"What are the odds, Peter?" She says, looking at her boat. "What are the odds that we'd collide with a floating container?"

"It happens. But I don't know how often." He squeezes her shoulder. "And hey, we didn't lose her. A bit of patching, some interior decorating ... you know...." His voice trails off.

Emma gets that he's trying to cheer her up. She tells herself she's not going to cry but she bows her head. "The *Edge* is safe. We can fix her up," she repeats until the moment passes.

"I like that you're here," Emma says after a while. "What are your favourite songs?" she says, lifting her head up.

"Songs? I'm not singing."

"Okay, I'll sing then." And she starts with a silly one about ducks on a log.

32. PIRATES

"WHERE DO YOU LIVE, PETER?" They're leaning against each other, standing side by side, propping each other up while they fight off exhaustion.

"Eleuthera."

"You live here?" Emma turns to look at him. She can just make out his face in the pale light of dawn. "You live in the Bahamas?"

"Born and raised here." He reaches out his arms and stretches.

"I don't get it," Emma puts a hand on his arm. "Our father's not from here."

"My mother is, though." He coughs to change the subject. "Not sure how much longer before we're too tired to stand."

Emma has a bunch more questions but she's tired too. She nods and rubs her hands over her face. She's starting to get hungry and thirsty too.

"I have an idea. You lie down in the water for an hour and sleep. I'll stand watch. Then we switch."

Peter looks around at the peaceful sea, considers the options. "Okay."

Emma can see that he's so tired he can hardly stand up. His quick agreement is a sure sign. He lowers himself into the water and lies on his back, letting the life jacket support him. His feet are resting on the container about two feet below the surface of the water. She grabs the end of one of the lines and lashes it to the buckle of his life jacket.

"Sleep. Okay? Or at least rest. I've got your back, Bro."

Peter's eyes drift closed before she's even finished speaking.

"Idiot," Emma mutters under her breath. "Probably didn't sleep during my watches."

The minutes tick by slowly. There's still no wind and the waves lap gently at her feet, rocking the sleeping figure gently. They can be grateful for that. She watches his sleeping face.

When the hour is up, she wakes him. His eyes pop open and he springs to his feet immediately, alert like the sailor he is. Back and forth, they spell each other until they've each got a bit of rest.

"Hey? Think we can salvage any food or drinks from the *Edge*?" Emma is starving now. She scans the horizon. No sign of land, no sign of boats. The weather is still quiet.

"Couple of dives should do it," Peter says. He's already unbuckling his lifejacket.

"Hey, I didn't mean you had to do it." She's put a hand on his arm to slow him down.

"Look," Peter laughs. "I'm Bahamian. We grow up diving. Like you Canadians grow up skiing."

"I don't ski," Emma answers snippily. "Don't make assumptions."

"You're not Canadian then, eh?" Peter snorts. "Okay, eh?" He grins broadly. "It's a joke. The 'eh' part I mean. All you Canadians say it."

"Don't be an idiot." Emma's laughing now, too. "Can you really dive? I mean are you a good diver?"

"Yes, Sis. I really am." He chucks her under her chin to get a smile out of her. And plunges off the container into the dark water. He's gone a long time, and Emma's starting to worry when he surfaces with a mesh bag full of cans of drinks and some of the bags of the freeze-dried food that once upon a time Emma swore she'd never eat. Now she's happy she didn't get rid of them.

They snap the caps on the cans and drink. They finish at the same time and grin at each other, clinking cans. Peter shows her how to fill the can with water so it sinks. Emma watches the cans disappear into the black depths of the ocean and shudders. When she thinks about the vastness around her it's overwhelming. The sun is starting to drop. She's not looking forward to another night on the open sea. Her thoughts veer toward the certainty that the wind will pick up soon and the next storms will come in as the weather changes.

Her heart starts to plunge and to stave off the beginnings of fear she starts humming a little tune, then breaks into loud singing. She even does a little dance on the top of the container to keep her body awake and moving.

Peter watches her bemused.

"No laughing, okay." She points her finger at him. "This is the way I've been getting through stuff out here on my own." She stamps her feet and belts out a made-up song, sending the words right at Peter.

Emma sailed the Edge
from Kingston to Mayaguana
All by herself. All by herself.
She learned a thing or two about
what she had to do
When the weather's rough or
some dickhead scares her silly
Out here on the sea.
Oh, hey! Yay for Emma! Emma on the Edge.

They hear the motor at the same time. Peter digs in his pocket of his jacket for the flares and sets one off. But the sun is too high in the sky. The flare is almost invisible.

"Boat hook! Boat hook!" Emma screams and pushes Peter. "Get it! It's lashed to the deck of the *Edge.*"

"I'll get on your shoulders," she explains when he doesn't get it. "And wave a T-shirt or jacket in the air as high as I can."

"No time. Just get on my shoulders now," Peter says. "Here—wave this." He strips off his jacket and gives it to her.

She climbs on his back and hitches herself over his shoulders, swinging the orange jacket back and forth, back and forth, and screaming at the top of her lungs.

Sure enough, the sound of the motor comes closer. They see it's a fishing boat.

"Man! You in a mess!" says one of the men.

"That you, Visser?" says the second.

"You know him?" Emma hisses. Peter puts his hand on her shoulder, squeezes hard.

"No salvage rights on the sailboat, 'kay Rufus?" Peter's voice is stern, business like. Emma's shocked. They're being rescued, and this is turning into a bargaining discussion?

The big man, Rufus, nods his head. "You don't want the container, man?"

"Just the sailboat."

"Done. That work for you, Eddie?" Rufus says turning to the man steering the boat. He nods. The deal is sealed.

Rufus reaches out to help Emma aboard. She stares at Peter as he climbs on board too, but he shakes his head at her, mouthing the word *later*. Emma feels her anger at being excluded rising in her chest. Then she looks at the two men. They look all business and she lets it drop.

"You want us to tow this hunk of junk to shore?" Peter and the two men chew over the problem of the amount of gas, the weight, the distance. The talk is in a fast patois that Emma can barely follow.

"Can you at least try to get us closer to shore?" Emma cuts in.

"We can try, but no guarantees, Miss," says Eddie.

"No use us getting stranded out here with you," adds Rufus. "But we see how far we get before we go for help."

They drag the *Edge* and the container behind them for about an hour before unhooking everything.

"Goin' for help, now. And more fuel." Rufus tells Emma. "You want to come with us, 'stead of staying with this ugly fish of a guy?"

"I'll stay with my boat," she answers dropping over the side of the boat onto the top of the container beside Peter.

"Your boat?" Eddie eyes her. "Well, well." Emma's not sure if it's admiration or simple curiosity. She meets his look head on.

"Will they come back?" she asks Peter as she watches the boat leave.

"Oh, you can count on it." Peter laughs. "A container like this is money in the bank." He stares at the disappearing boat and shakes his head. "They'll be back, and they'll bring friends. We'll be on the island by tonight."

He reaches over to muss her hair, but she ducks away from him. "What do you mean, money in the bank?"

"Don't you know about salvage rights?" He sweeps his hand out, gesturing the wide- open ocean. "Anything lost at sea belongs to the one who finds and claims it." He rubs his chin making a scrubbing sound as his fingers run over the stubble. "The history of the Bahamas is full of professional ship wreckers. They'd lure the boats onto the reefs with false lights and then claim the salvage. And look like heroes for helping the poor sods whose boat got smashed."

At Emma's sceptical frown he continues. "It's the law of the sea, Em. Trust me on this."

"What's to say they won't take the *Edge* too?"

"They won't."

Emma shakes her head impatiently.

"It's a kind of honour among thieves—you state your claim and shake on it." He smiles at her and lifts a shoulder as if to say, it's that simple.

Emma has a sneaky thought. "Are you a ship wrecker?" she asks Peter, studying him afresh. She realizes she doesn't know her half-brother at all.

He laughs. "We don't wreck ships anymore, no. But I've

done my share of salvaging." He raises his eyebrows at her. "A guy's got to make a living."

Emma just stares at him. He answers her stare, then looks away.

"Hey! Hear that?" They both cock their heads.

"That was fast."

"Probably ran into a buddy on the way back." Peter squints toward the sound. "Yup. Party tonight, for sure."

33. REVELATION

I T'S PAST MIDNIGHT when the tiny island of debris is finally towed into harbour and a few hours later when Emma is certain that the *Edge* is safe. Peter has to reassure her over and over that no one is going to claim her, and he gets permission for Emma to sleep in the boat house, close to where the *Edge* has been towed.

Even then, Emma has a hard time sleeping. Every small noise wakes her. She knows she's overtired and will need to let go soon, but not yet. Not till she's sure the *Edge* is safe. Not till she's spoken to whoever's going to do the work on her, so they know who she belongs to.

She finally drifts off, but it's a short, short night. At dawn she hears locals outside, voices that rise and fall with the music of the patois, and full of laughter. She wakes without being fully awake.

"It's not my fault. It's not my fault." The words spin through her head. She's filled with a rising fear that the *Edge* will be taken from her because she's been careless in some way, doesn't deserve it, isn't responsible enough to own such a beautiful boat. On and on the horrible words go till she jumps up from the cot and bursts out of the boat house, stumbling down the two small steps she's forgotten are there, right into Peter's arms.

He steadies her. "Whoa, Em. You're up?" He gives her a squeeze. "Did we wake you?"

Emma shakes her head. Must've been the remnants of her overtired mind. She realizes she'll sound crazy if she tells him her fears. "Morning," she says, forcing a smile onto her face. "Coffee? Is that coffee I smell?"

"Em, I've got something to tell you." He hands her the mug that's been passed to him. All the men are gathered around listening. Emma gulps the coffee greedily, hoping it will clear her head.

"Your GG wants to see you now. Here."

"Here? But...?" Her words are drowned out by the loud motor of a small plane passing close overhead. Everyone looks up. The men mutter amongst themselves. Emma has the feeling that they know who it is.

"Is that him?" Emma asks.

"Yup, uh huh," Peter answers, eyes narrowing as he watches the plane circle around and drop out of sight. The group of men breaks up, everyone scattering as if to start their daily work, whatever it may be.

"They know who he is." Emma says to Peter, almost accusingly. "You all know each other."

"It's a small country," he explains, as if what she needs is an explanation. He knows what she means, but still he continues. Maybe he needs her to understand something about himself, too. "People like him, everyone knows him."

Emma wants to ask what he means by "people like him," but he's already striding away. There's a jeep coming toward them. Emma has no time to prepare herself like she wanted to. She straightens her shoulders and runs her fingers through her hair. She hasn't even had time for a shower. She's wearing an old T-shirt and pair of shorts someone gave her to sleep in.

She waits while the jeep comes closer and stops. Out of the passenger side steps a tall, well-dressed dark-skinned man Emma's never seen before.

"Miss Emerald!" he says, his hand outstretched toward her, winking. "Well done! Your great grandfather is so proud."

Emma feels like she's going to be sick with nervousness. She looks at Peter. Who is this man? her eyes say. But before Peter can answer the man breaks in.

"I'm Raymond, your great grandfather's assistant. He's gone ahead to the villa and will meet us there," he smiles as if he's extending a casual greeting, as if Emma is a visiting guest just arrived for a vacation.

She closes her eyes and counts her breaths to control her impulse to walk away. When she opens her eyes again he's waiting. She folds her arms over her chest, feet planted on the ground. She's not going to make the first move. She doesn't say a word. She can be patient. She's learned that from sailing on the ocean. The moment stretches uncomfortably. Emma's aware of Peter looking from Raymond back to her.

"Won't you come to the villa for breakfast, Miss Emerald?" Raymond says, his hand gesturing toward the jeep.

"The villa." Emma's voice is cold. "How many villas does he have?"

"He has two," Raymond answers helpfully. "One on Great Abaco and another here on Eleuthera. Then, there are..."

Emma cuts him off. "My brother comes too."

"Peter?" The old man sounds surprised. "Of course."

Peter shakes his head, but Emma grabs his elbow. "I won't go without you," she whispers so only he can hear.

"Em, this is not for me." He takes her hand. "No." He shakes his head again. "You'll be okay."

Emma holds his hand tight for a minute longer. Finally, she nods and letting go of his hand turns to Raymond.

"I need a shower and some clean clothes." She looks down at the rumpled ill-fitting shorts and T-shirt.

"Of course, you do," he says, reaching out to lead her to the jeep. "You've just been pulled from the ocean."

Emma shoots a last glance over her shoulder at Peter, pausing as if to let him reconsider. But he smiles and waves her on. She climbs into the jeep as he gives her a thumbs-up.

EMMA STEPS OUT OF THE SHOWER and pulls on fresh clothes that nearly fit her. She's not the same person who tumbled off the cot full of fear and foreboding earlier in the morning. She's had time to remember who she is, what she's accomplished, what her quest is. When she comes into the room where breakfast is being served she stops and stares into the face of the man who is the father of Jess. The grandfather of her mother.

He gets to his feet, with difficulty. She's aware of his age, of his frailty. She'd never paid much attention to him before.

"Emerald," he smiles broadly. "Queen Emerald."

Emma cringes. "Don't call me that."

"But you're a queen to me," he says ignoring her protest. "Come, sit. You must be hungry."

Breakfast is a lavish affair, served by servants who bring fruit and bacon, boiled eggs, ham, toast and local jellies. Emma eats only a little.

"Emerald," her great grandfather says, after dabbing his lips with a napkin. "I have things to discuss with you." He stands up and waits for her to stand too. Emma wonders if it will be too rude if she refuses, and decides it will be, so she gets to her feet. Besides, she needs to know what he has to say. And she has things to say to him.

He leads the way into a room off the dining area. It seems to be a den, or office. He indicates a large, comfy chair to Emma and waits until she sits down. Then he makes himself comfortable in a seat near her, obviously his favourite seat, since there's a stack of books and magazines beside it, and a shawl Raymond immediately tucks around his knees, even though it's warm out.

"Emerald," the old man repeats her name as if savouring it. He beams at her and pauses, nods his head and pauses again. It's as if he doesn't know how best to proceed. Emma simply waits. She breathes and waits. She realizes that she's played this scene over in her mind many times since she found out about him, and now that she's living it, she'd rather listen than speak. At least until she's heard what he has to say.

"Your grandmother was a disappointment to me."

Emma feels the shock of those words rocket through her and she jumps to her feet, all her good intentions gone. "Don't insult Jess."

"No, wait." He puts up a hand. "Let me start again." He struggles to breathe. She notices he wheezes. "I disappointed her, too, I should say." He indicates the chair, entreats her to sit again.

Emma stares at him. She takes in the bags under his eyes, the deep wrinkles, the shortness of his breath, the white, white hair. She sits back down.

"She would have been a good person to take over the company and I refused to give her a chance." Again he pauses, as if to catch his breath. Emma waits. "Because she was a girl."

Emma blinks. Could she have heard right?

"Because she was a girl?" Emma huffs out a breath. "So what if she was a girl?"

Her great grandfather gives his head a shake. "You don't understand. No woman has ever run this company. A shipping company. A man's company in a man's world." He makes a choking sound. "It would have been so very difficult for her to be respected." He leans toward Emma. "But she would have done a good job, by god." He slaps his knee hard. "Given the chance."

Emma holds her silence and just stares at the old man sitting up so straight in his chair in front of her. A part of her still wants to hate him. She can feel it rising in her. Another part wants to be patient, to try to understand what he's telling her. The conflict confuses her.

"It was different when your mother was born." The old man pulls off his glasses and rubs a hand over his eyes. There's a knock at the door and Raymond comes in with a glass of water and some pills that her great grandfather takes without protest.

"My vitamins," he says and winks as he swallows half a dozen pills of varying sizes and colours. He hands back the glass and thanks Raymond.

"At first I thought it didn't matter that your mother was a girl—I could simply groom her to run the company." He shakes his head as if remembering. "But she was a wild one. Had all Jess's artistic talents, with none of her practical sense." He shakes his head again and gives a small sigh. "She would have done a terrible job."

Again, Emma feels the insult as if it's personal. But before she can protest he continues.

"My daughter chose her husband poorly. Your mother was very like her father." Emma was surprised by the cold dislike in the old man's voice. He closes his eyes for a minute. "And then your mother chose a terrible husband too. Much worse than your grandmother's husband." He sighs again, and lifts his eyes to Emma. "No matter," he says, making a dismissive flip of his hand. "I disowned them both, so their no-good husbands wouldn't get a penny of my fortune."

He took a deep sigh, as if of satisfaction. "Now there's you."

Emma feels her heart skip a beat. "What do you mean?"

"Well, it's you I want." The old man thumps his cane on the floor. "I want you to take over the company, Emerald."

"No!" Emma shoots to her feet. "No, I don't think so."

"Yes, by god, you're perfect, girl. Don't you see?" The old man barks out a laugh and thumps his cane again.

"I don't even know what company you're talking about."

"Of course, you do. Hargrove and Flinders Shipping." He sounds exasperated. "Well Hargrove's dead and good riddance." He gestures with his hand and turns to pick up the glass of water and sip. "British. Should never have chosen him as a partner," he continues as if talking to himself. "Better to stick to the Dutch. Like you Emerald." He smiles at her as if to confirm how right he is about his decision. "But don't you worry. I bought out his part of the company ages ago.

Kept the name. Seemed simpler. You understand?"

Emma starts backing up, away from the old man. He must be mad, she's thinking. "No. No, I think you're mistaken." She looks over her shoulder. "I'm sure I should go now, see to the repairs on the *Edge*."

"Sit down, Emerald," the old man shouts. "Sit down," he repeats more gently. "Please."

Emma's still standing. Her breathing is coming too fast now. She wants to get out of this room. "I'm only fifteen." She looks around for help, but the room is empty. He must be having some sort of senile moment. He can't be serious.

"Please," her great grandfather says again. His plea is sincere.

Emma stares and stares while she sorts through her thoughts. Why is she panicking? He's just an old man. Slowly she lowers herself back down onto the edge of the chair.

The old man continues. "I've watched you all these years, since your mother brought you to me. Well, not to me, exactly, but to your aunt and uncle's." He clucks his tongue and Emma feels a shiver shoot up her back.

"What are you talking about?"

Now the old man looks positively gleeful. "It was perfect, wasn't it? She had to bring you somewhere after the fiasco with that no-good bum she married. She was going to jail and you were in danger. So I paid for her to bring you north to the farm where I could keep a good eye on you, have you raised carefully, practically."

He's nodding his head and chuckling some more. "Not a nice woman, your Aunt Petra, but surely a sensible one. And the husband no trouble. They did their jobs well, kept you safe and out of the public eye." He meets Emma's eyes, nods again, raises his eyebrows as if he's seeking her agreement. "Yes, perfectly." He's smiling in such a strange way. With pride, Emma realizes.

"You ... you..." Emma's on her feet before she can stop herself. "You BOUGHT me from my mother!" She's shaking with fury. "You gave me to that woman to be groomed. Groomed ... like ... like a show dog!" She points her finger at him. "You selfish, horrible old man!"

She turns and runs for the door. She shoots through the house trying to find the front door. She has to get out of here. Out! He's mad. Where's the door out? There's the sound of footsteps behind her. She looks over her shoulder.

"Miss Emerald!" she hears behind her. "Miss, please."

"Let me out." She rattles the doorknob on the locked door. "Please, let me out of here."

Raymond is coming up behind her. "He doesn't mean to be like that." He makes a pleading gesture with his hand. "Won't you come back and listen to the whole story?"

Emma's shaking with fury. She can hardly get her breath.

"Don't you want to know who you are?"

"I know who I am." She lets go of the doorknob and turns slowly around to face him. "And it's nothing to do with that!" she says, pointing in the direction of the room she's just run from.

Raymond stops, then strangely he smiles. "If you know who you are, then you can hear who the world thinks you are." He nods as if he approves. "Without being afraid."

Emma becomes utterly still. "I'm not afraid," she whispers. Why's she running? What is she afraid of?

"Then...?" He extends his hand, pointing back to where her great grandfather is waiting.

She nods and the two of them walk back toward the old man. His words ring in her head. *Who the world thinks you are....* She's uneasy, but she's ready to listen.

"Emerald!" Her great grandfather raises his eyes when she comes back into the room. There's such sadness in them, she has to look away. "Listen child. Listen to me, will you?" After a minute, she nods.

"Please, sit." He indicates the chair near his again. "Raymond," he says to the man who is obviously his most valued companion. "Bring fresh lemonade for Emerald." He reaches out for Emma's hand and takes it in his. She feels the dry, papery, thin skin of an old man. "Let me begin again. And please, listen. Listen if you can, without judging."

He tells her about the company he built from nothing into a multi-national success. He explains the connection with the Bahamas.

"Lignum vitae—a hardwood, indigenous of Mayaguana." He brings out a bag of pebbles like the ones Emma had on the *Edge*. "Self-lubricating bearings." He hands one to Emma. He takes one himself, rubbing it between his thumb and forefinger. "Changed the direction of our business. Brought work to the islands." He talks about the workshops he set up, his love of the people of the Bahamas obvious, and his voice ringing with pride in bringing business to the country that hires locals and keeps young people on their islands.

"Your mother travelled with me when she was younger. She collected those lignum vitae bearings on each of her trips. They were hers. You had them with you when you came north to Canada." He places the bearing back in the bag and zips it shut.

"Your aunt took them away from you. Didn't think it was good for you to have anything to remind you of your mother." He reaches out for the one he'd given Emma, but she pulls her hand away. She wants to keep it a little bit longer.

"I asked Peter to leave them on the boat for you, while he was keeping an eye on you, hurrying you along a little bit on your way here. I wondered if you'd remember playing with them when you were a child." He looks at her, questioningly, but she shakes her head. "Well, I guess not."

Emma stares down at the small black pebble, or bearing, she's holding tight between her fingers. Does she remember? How could she not remember? Nothing of her mother. Her aunt made sure it was all wiped out of her memory. No talk about her mother or her father allowed in that house. When she lost her mother and her father, she also lost her past. Tears start to cloud her eyes. She wills herself to control them. She will not cry in front of this old man.

Raymond comes into the room and puts the glasses of fresh lemonade on the table in front of them. Emma's great grandfather lifts the glass to his lips and drinks. "Try this, Emerald. There's no place that makes better lemonade than the Bahamas."

Emma takes a sip and puts her glass down. She meets her great grandfather's eyes. She gives a small nod.

"Your mother fell in love with the Bahamas," he continues. "But I didn't believe her when she told me." He sighs. "She said she wanted to live here and be an artist." He sighs again, more deeply. "I still wanted to hand the reins of the business over to her." He pauses and waits until he sees Emma is following, is understanding what he's trying to tell her. "I didn't listen, Emerald. I didn't listen to her, and the only thing she could do was to rebel. She did that by running away with your father." He rubs his temple. "I see that now."

"Your grandmother was furious at me, furious about what Peggy had done just to escape my plan for her. Your father was no good, Emerald. And your mother paid a heavy price for it. So did your grandmother." Again he closes his eyes and rubs his temple as if he has a headache. "So did we all."

"But then there was you." He opens his eyes and his face breaks into smiles momentarily. But then his smile drops away when he tells her "I did what I thought was right, my darling little Queen Emerald."

He reaches out and squeezes her hand. "Your mother would never have been able to run the company. I see that now. But you! You're just like me! You can do anything. You've proved it!"

Emma feels her face colour. She doesn't want his compliment. But it catches her off-guard.

"Even your grandmother felt it was the right thing to do," he continues with the story. "To bring you back to the farm, I mean. You'd be accepted into the community as a Visser. And you'd have a sheltered but structured life, hidden away on the farm." When he lifts the glass to lips again, this time Emma notices his hand is shaking. The glass clinks against his teeth as he drinks.

"You must be getting tired, Mr. Flinders," she says. "We can finish another time."

The glass pauses at his lips. He says in the softest voice possible, "Won't you call me Great Grandfather, Emerald?"

Emma hesitates. She sees in front of her an elderly man she's only known in the briefest of ways during the last ten years of her life and yet, he is part of her story, a big part.

She's acutely aware of the birds outside the big French doors that open onto a vast garden and the sea beyond, of the wind blowing in the palm trees planted there, and of the elegant room around her. Isn't this also part of her story now? And her story will continue, can go forward any way she chooses. She can choose now. She knows no one can take anything from her that truly matters—her self-worth, her confidence—unless she lets them.

"Great Grandfather," she says at last.

Her great grandfather beams at her. He looks around for Raymond and beams at him, too. His face nearly splits in half with his smile.

"Peter tells me you're one hell of a sailor, Emerald." He slaps his knee again, then bends over coughing and wheezing.

Emma's alarmed. "Won't you rest now?" She looks up at Raymond questioningly. Raymond leans down to help her great grandfather get to his feet.

"Don't go, Emerald," the old man says. "Please stay. Raymond will fix you a room."

Raymond murmurs something to him. "I'll be right back, Miss Emerald."

"I NEED TO TALK TO MY MOTHER," Emma says when Raymond returns.

"Yes, Miss Emerald. We're seeing to that," he says, then

extends his hand in front of them, pointing to the door. "Your room is ready. Perhaps you'd like to freshen up, maybe rest a bit before you see your great grandfather again at lunch. I know he's counting on that."

Emma follows Raymond down the hallway of the house she realizes she's going to inherit, if her great grandfather has his way. For a moment as she's walking across the stone floors, she feels as if she's in someone else's body. But the feeling is fleeting. Inside her body there is no movement, deep inside her there's a place where the light shines so bright, that no one or nothing can extinguish it.

None of this will change who I am, she promises herself fiercely. None of this is anything more than stuff and responsibility. This walk down a corridor is just one of the many events that make a life, her life, the one she is creating and making her own.

A maid hurries past with her arms full of fresh linen. She bends slightly as she passes and smiling, saying her name. "Miss Emerald." Emma feels like she's in a movie from another era.

"Raymond, does everyone know who I am?"

"Yes, Miss Emerald," he nods. "We've been waiting months for your arrival."

Emma shivers slightly. That's just weird, she thinks.

34. MOTHER

EMMA RECOGNIZES HER MOTHER the minute she sees her sitting beside her great grandfather, holding his hand. She thinks, *there she is*. She stops just inside the doorway to the room. She can't make her legs move. She's frozen, stuck. She can hardly breathe.

"Emma," her mother says. Her voice is soft. Sweeter than it sounded over the phone.

How could she have ever known what it would feel like to see her mother for the first time after so many years? What could have prepared her for the shock, the instant terror, the joy, the sadness that swamps her when she enters the room to join her great grandfather for lunch?

Probably nothing. Her next thought is, *She's so pretty.*

Emma notices that she's wearing her hair in a long silver braid. Just like Jess. Does she know she looks just like Jess? she wonders. And then all thought stops. She's caught under another avalanche of emotions as they come crashing down over her.

Peggy Lake stands up, then. She crosses the room and stops in front of Emma. She holds her hands out, but when Emma doesn't take them, she drops them awkwardly to her side. Then clasps them in front of her.

Emma realizes that her mother is finding the moment equally difficult. The unfamiliar face of the woman standing in front of her is a kaleidoscope of expressions. Smiling, then sad, then worried, then sad again, then smiling.

"Emma," her mother says a bit breathlessly. "Won't you come in?" She turns slightly and extends her hand, inviting Emma into the room.

Emma looks then at her great grandfather who is standing now, leaning on his cane. He's frowning. Frowning and his mouth is moving, opening and closing, as if he wants to say something, but he keeps stopping himself. Emma sees Raymond take his elbow and try to nudge him into his chair, but he just shakes him off.

The silence in the room is deafening.

Emma turns on her heel and walks out.

IT'S NO USE RUNNING. Where will you go? Turn and face what's scaring you. It's the only way.

Wherever these thoughts are coming from, Emma's not listening. Her legs are carrying her farther and farther away from that room. As far as she can get. *Where can I go?* She opens a door. It's another sitting room. *This place is too big!*

She pushes open another set of doors and finds herself in a kind of garden room. She heads to the glass doors and out into the blinding sun. Her feet are carrying her toward the water she sees at the end of the lawn. It's the water she needs. The rocks. There's a bench perched on a raw, exposed promontory. There. That's what she needs.

The ocean crashes up on the rocks. The spray coats her face.

Who are these people? she thinks, when she can finally think. *Who do they think they are, to decide her fate, her life for her? Now and then?* The bitterness that wells up inside her leaves a sour taste in her mouth.

A child was taken from her mother and left with two people who had no idea what a child needs. The child was fed, clothed, and sheltered. But what of love? What of caring and nurturing? What of joy and laughter and careless playfulness?

And yet she's here. She's who she is because of all this. This disaster of a master plan of her great grandfather's.

Footsteps. She turns toward them. Watches her mother approach. Turns away again. Faces the ocean.

"Emma." Her mother hesitates, then comes closer and after another pause, moves forward to sit down. There's no entreaty in her voice. What's there is a kind of sternness. Emma likes that better than kindness.

"Talking about this is the only way I can offer you a way home."

"Home?" Emma asks. "What home?"

"Yes, home," her mother repeats. "The one you make in your heart. Home. Where you belong to yourself."

Emma lifts one shoulder and gives a toss of her head as if to say, *whatever*.

"If I could live my life over again, I wouldn't change a thing." Emma's mother spreads out her fingers wide as she swipes her hand along the rugged coastline in front of them.

Emma feels the words sink in, and anger wells up and adds a flush to Emma's cheeks.

"Life's full of compromises, challenges, choices. And they're what make us who we are. Each of us. Each and every one."

"Thanks, Mom." The sarcasm in Emma's voice hangs in the air heavily. She can't help it. In some part of her mind, she doesn't want to be this angry. She wants to be kinder. But the fury keeps welling up and spilling over.

"I'm so sorry for the pain I caused you." Her mother's words are a whisper. "I'm sorry that I couldn't and wouldn't change anything I did, even to spare you."

Emma's heart cracks open a bit, and some of the anger slides away. Her head drops forward. *These words. These words.* They seem to pulse in the air.

"You see, Emma, if I changed even one tiny thing, there wouldn't be you—just as you are, because ... you're beautiful. You're a beacon of light."

Are these the words she needed to hear? Can she believe them? Can she trust?

She turns, just a little, toward the woman sitting beside her. Just a little movement, but it's enough to see her mother's face. The silent tears that are streaming down her cheeks. The smile on her lips. Her mother's eyes, just a little like Jess's, so full of love as she gazes at Emma.

"I am so proud of you."

Emma's heart cracks open a little further.

"So proud," her mother continues, not taking her eyes off her daughter. "…Of who you've become, what you've accomplished. You came here by yourself on a sailboat, for goodness sake." She lifts her hand as if to reach out and touch Emma, but then lets it fall again. "That takes courage and so much … so much faith in yourself." Her eyes travel over Emma's face, her hair, the whole of her, as if trying to take all of her into her memory.

"You're different from me. You're different from my mother. And him." She points her finger back toward the house. "You're the best of us all, Emma, and you're also just yourself." She smiles. "It's enough to be just yourself, Emma. I hope you know that."

As she leans forward to get to her feet, a purple stone hanging on a long chain swings away from her neck. She reaches up to slip it back under her dress.

Emma's hand flies to the stone hanging around her own neck. She pulls it out. The two stones are identical. "Where did you get that stone?"

"This stone?" Emma's mother holds her stone up so it catches the light. "My mother gave it to me on my thirteenth birthday. A stone for dreaming, she called it."

This is my mother. Here. Beside me. Here. Here.

Emma's face crumples. Her shoulders begin to tremble with the sobs that she can no longer hold back. Her mother reaches out her arms and Emma burrows into them. Agony and relief pour through her. She cries and cries until she's spent, empty, quiet. All the while her mother rocks and strokes, whispering words of love. The love Emma has yearned for all these years. Unconditional. Complete and boundless. Her mother's love.

35. UNTAMED

"HIS NAME WAS GERRIT IVAN VISSER, but he never let anyone call him by his first name." The wind has come up and tendrils of Peggy's hair have come loose from her braid. She pushes them out of her face. "I didn't know Petra loved him. I didn't even know they knew each other. I'd left Kingston by the time I was fourteen."

"What?" Emma says it again. "What?'

"I went to live with my father after Grandfather forced him to leave my mother." She catches the frown on Emma's face. "There was good reason. My father was a bounder."

"What do you mean?"

"He married my mother for her money and didn't love her at all."

Emma scrunched up her shoulders. "I hate that."

"Well, your grandmother was a rebel and probably flirted like crazy with him. So don't blame it all on him." Peggy reached over and squeezed Emma's hand. "She was pretty expert in vexing your great grandfather. As was I." She sighed.

"I met your dad at my first solo show." Peggy stretched her arms out in front of her. "Imagine this: buckets of champagne, people dressed so fancy, my paintings on the wall. And they were big canvasses. So much colour. And I was twenty-four." She turned to Emma. "That's very young to have a solo show in Toronto."

"The paparazzi were out in force. I was the talk of the town."
For a moment she closes her eyes as if remembering.

Emma stares at her, fascinated, as if watching an exotic bird.

"And there he was," Peggy continued. "Tall, dark, and handsome." She laughs at the sound of the words and turns to Emma. "I was smitten."

Emma shifts in her seat. The sun is hot. They'll have to find shade soon, but just now she doesn't want to leave the bench where they've been talking for hours. She's afraid this friendly companionship, so new, so fragile, will end and she won't be able to recapture it.

"Mom," she says, and the name sounds good in her mouth. "Mom, what part of it is true? I mean about the drugs."

"Oh Emma, it's all true." Peggy sighs and brushes the hair from her face again. Her hands are long fingered and delicate, the skin paler than Emma's. "I wish I could tell you something more heroic, but the truth is the truth. He started running drugs even before I met him, and I became the perfect cover." She turns to Emma and studies her daughter's face for a moment. Then she reaches out and runs her long fingers down Emma's cheek. "You look like him, you know."

Emma smiles and turns her cheek into her mother's hand. Her family is being restored to her. Even if the truth is horrible, at least she knows it now. And it all feels unreal, like a story in a book. She knows who she really is, quite aside from stories of family and old history. Nothing can take her away from herself.

"Was my dream real, my dream about the 'monster'?" She raises her hands into the air and sketches two quotation marks in the air.

"Oh yes, sadly yes," Peggy says. "Your father gave me sleeping pills that night, slipped them into my evening tea, and I didn't hear a thing." She took a deep breath. "As far as I know, he thought that he was being asked to join a secret heist, but they were not his allies. They were sent to get rid of him." She shudders.

"Was his body ever found?" Emma asks, reaching over to give her mother's arm a reassuring squeeze.

"Yes." Peggy covers Emma's hand with her own. "Yes, they found him eventually. But first I was under suspicion for his murder." Peggy waits until Emma meets her eyes. "If Arthur hadn't helped me get to Canada, and given me his trust...." She shakes her head. "I don't know what I would have done."

"It was hard to convince your great grandfather to help. By that time, he had disowned me." Peggy frowns at the memory, lifts a hand to her forehead and rubs as if she has a headache. "When we first moved to the Bahamas, Ivan had tried to blackmail him, and he immediately cut that off, by cutting me off my inheritance."

"But when he heard about me, he realized there was still hope for the business," Emma says bitterly. There's a scowl on her face.

"Yes," Peggy says. "Maybe. It was a little bit like that, but something else too." She pauses, looking out at the ocean, as if trying to make up her mind about something. She turns back to Emma. "You see, Emma, those men who killed your father had already contacted your great grandfather and he'd dug his heels in about giving them what they asked. But then they threatened to harm you."

"Harm me?" Emma pulls back, shocked.

"And Grandfather took that very seriously." Peggy nods. "That's when we secreted you away to Aunt Petra and Uncle Derek's farm and you became their ward." She pauses again. "Your whole life has been one of greatest care, and your Aunt has had a burden of fear placed on her that was considerable."

Emma looked down at their joined hands. "It was horrible, being so completely confined at the farm." Her voice is solemn, but not accusing. There's sadness.

"I know, dearest. I know," Peggy says. "But she was your only hope of being safe, at least at that moment, and she was willing."

"But Aunt Petra.... Great Grandfather paid her to take me."

"I know, dear," Peggy cuts in. "I know." She turns her brimming eyes toward Emma unflinching. "I'm sorry. With all my heart, I wish you hadn't had that...." Her voice breaks.

Emma shifts away. "It was like she used me!" Her shoulders rise in revulsion. "I could hate you for that," she says quickly. "I could hate you all for what she did to me."

Peggy keeps her eyes trained on Emma's face, as if standing in the courtroom again, accused, and unwilling to give any more excuses. She says nothing.

"But...." Emma doesn't look away either but studies her mother's face as if she's seeking something to hold onto. "That isn't your fault, Mom."

Emma hears her mother suck in her breath.

"I saw what I saw, and your life and mine changed completely after that."

In the silence that follows, a space opens inside of Emma. It grows wider and wider and fills with light. She hears the waves washing the rocks, the gulls' cries, the wind rustling the dry leaves of the jacaranda beside the bench. And she knows in that moment what she wants next for herself. Her mother is still looking at her, and in the softness of her gaze the light inside of Emma grows even stronger. It feels like hope.

"I won't go back to the farm, Mom," Emma says.

"No," Peggy says, "You won't." She leans forward and stands up, reaching for Emma's hand again. "Come with me."

Emma stands up too but holds back. "Mom?"

"You'll live with me, Emma." She tugs Emma close and puts her arm around her shoulders. "Let's go tell your great grandfather."

"But am I safe here?"

"Yes, dear. The men who killed your father are no longer a threat. They were brought to justice in the States and your great grandfather has made sure they can't harm you ever."

"When?"

"Three years ago. I sent that newspaper clipping to your grandmother hoping she would come, hoping she would bring you. But instead, you came yourself." She squeezes Emma's shoulder warmly. "You came by boat alone to the Bahamas."

EPILOGUE

EMMA STEPS OUT OF THE BUS at Kingston Station. A small crowd of people has gathered on the platform to meet the bus. She's not expecting anyone to meet her and she turns to reach for the backpack before the bus driver tosses it onto the growing pile of luggage. It's all she's brought with her from the Bahamas. She opens the pack and takes out a sweater. It's late August and the air in Canada is already beginning to cool. She's not used to it after being away for more than two years.

She swings the backpack up onto her shoulders and turns, intending to enter the terminus and out the other side, to look for a taxi to take her downtown. She's come home to Kingston to start university and wants to settle in and meet her roommate as soon as possible.

"Emma?"

Emma spins around. Adam is smiling at her from the far side of the platform. For a moment, time stops and all she sees is him. And then she notices Uncle Derek is there with him.

"You came," she says to Adam. They've been corresponding for a full year, but seeing him in the flesh is sending her heart racing. He's changed so much since she last saw him. He's taller, slimmer, and like her he's brown from the sun and from working with her uncle on the farm.

"Of course. Why wouldn't I?"

She doesn't want to take her eyes off him, but she won't be

rude to her uncle, no matter what happened in the past.

"Emma." Uncle Derek's voice is as quiet as it always was. He stands awkwardly. His hat's in his hands and she notices he's working the brim with nervous fingers. "Your aunt went so suddenly."

Emma knows her aunt died almost a year ago. It's part of the reason she chose to return.

"But at least she didn't suffer." She reaches over to give him a kiss on his cheek and he blushes deep red.

Adam lifts the backpack off her shoulders. Emma starts to resist, then relents. "Come on," he says. "We've something to show you." He holds out his hand, and after a moment's hesitation, Emma puts her hand in his.

"Are you here to escort me to my dorm?"

"We're here to escort you to your chariot." He stops in front of a bright red Fiat 500, and lets go of her hand to dig in his pocket for the keys. He gives them to her.

Emma pulls back, stunned. She turns to look at her uncle. But he shakes his head.

"Not me," he says. "Your great grandfather."

"He didn't say anything when I left ... cagey old coot." Her voice softens and there's a surprised smile on her face as it sinks in that she has a car. "I'll have to get my Canadian licence."

"Details, details." Adam takes the keys from her hands and pops the trunk, dropping her backpack inside. "You can drive with your international driver's licence here. I checked."

Uncle Derek opens the door for her and she pauses to look at him. "I'll meet you up at the big house for dinner later. Your GG's orders," he says, using the nickname as if it's normal. "Peter's already there. Adam will join us, too. Welcome home, Emma."

Emma's heart catches at the words. They make her feel strangely exposed, but happy too. She smiles at her uncle and he walks around the little red car toward the old pickup and climbs in. He touches his finger to his hat as he drives away.

Emma climbs into the driver's side and Adam gets in beside her. She pauses before starting the car. She feels overwhelmed. There's something tugging at her belly, but she doesn't know what it is to be able to give it words.

Adam reaches over and takes her hand again. Emma feels the warmth travelling up her arm. She turns and meets his eyes, sees how they crinkle at the corners. Neither of them speaks, and in their shared silence she begins to find her balance and feels her belly settle.

She has the strong sensation that her whole life has brought her to this moment, sitting here and looking into his face. The weight of the decision she made to take over the shipping business lifts a little, feels a bit less lonely. All the boys she dated in the Bahamas were practise so she could travel the long, long way back to Adam, to this friend who helped set her free in the first place.

"Welcome home, Emma."

"Home," she repeats, savouring the word.

ACKNOWLEDGEMENTS

I began to write *On the Edge* as a way to remember a sailing trip I made from Lake Ontario to the Turks and Caicos in 2002-2003. As the book progressed, the story took on a life of its own, and my main character Emma became a composite of brave young women sailors whose stories had inspired me. Living on a small boat in a large ocean changed my way of seeing the world, and this book pays homage to the power of nature, the beauty of this planet, and to the courage of sailors, past, present, and future.

I am extremely grateful to Luciana Ricciutelli for her willingness to publish this story as part of Inanna's Young Feminist Series. The feminist values and philosophy of Inanna Publications will make this world a better place.

I'm grateful to my parents who believed a girl could do anything she set her mind to. I'm grateful to my grandmother who said, "Never let your fears stop you from doing what you really want to do." I'm over-the-moon grateful to my daughters and their families, the lads and their families, grandkids, cousins, siblings, in-laws and, in particular, my aunt Esther for loving me and helping me keep my dream of writing alive.

The loving support of friends has also been extremely important along the way. On the sailing trip south, I met Alex E. who has become a friend for life and is there to remind me that life is full of unexpected gifts. I'm especially grateful for my beloved Liz K. who has loved me throughout my many life adventures that made me a writer. Heartfelt thanks to Vicki L. for her presence and the gift of her dogs in the chapter "Sanctuary." I am so honoured that Gordon Weber created the beautiful painting that has become the cover. Thank you, Heather G. for many cups of tea and glasses of wine through the writing in the last five years. And to artist friends and lovers of art in the village of Merrickville, thank you. Your commitment to your art sustains me and reminds me to never give up.

Writer friends are so important in this solitary work. I am appreciative of my poetry writing groups, the Northern Colorado Writers Group with whom I finished the first draft, and my wonderful tough mentor, Tim Wynne-Jones, in the Humber Creative Writing Program.

Finally, I want to thank my husband Chuck for his unconditional love and support and for believing in my wildest dreams. It was he who suggested I take early retirement to devote myself to finishing this novel and, now, here it is.

Lesley Strutt is a prize-winning poet, playwright, essayist, and a blogger, with a Ph.D. in Linguistics from McGill University in Montreal. She is the descendant of William Pittman Lett, a pre-confederation poet who was known as the Bard of Bytown before Bytown was named Ottawa in 1854. In 2002-2003, she sailed a 32-foot Hunter from Lake Ontario to the Turks and Caicos, then spent the winter sailing around all the islands in the Bahamas. Her debut collection of poetry, *Window Ledge,* is forthcoming from Inanna Publications in 2020. She lives in Merrickville, Ontario.